Montecore

Montecore
The Silence of the Tiger

Jonas Hassen Khemiri

Translated from the Swedish by
Rachel Willson-Broyles

ALFRED A. KNOPF | NEW YORK | 2011

This is a Borzoi Book
Published by Alfred A. Knopf

Translation copyright © 2011
by Alfred A. Knopf, a division of Random House, Inc.

Originally published in Sweden as *Montecore: En Unik Tiger*
by Norstedts, Stockholm in 2006.
Copyright © 2006 by Jonas Hassen Khemiri.

Library of Congress Cataloging-in-Publication Data
Khemiri, Jonas Hassen, [date]
[Montecore. English]
Montecore : the silence of the tiger / by Jonas Hassen
Khemiri ; translated from the Swedish by Rachel Willson-Broyles.
—1st American ed.
p.   cm.
Originally published in Stockholm as Montecore en unik Tiger.
ISBN 978-0-307-27095-5
1. Tunisians—Sweden—Fiction.
2. Immigrants—Sweden—Fiction.   3. Sweden—Fiction.
I. Willson-Broyles, Rachel.   II. Title.
PT9877.21.H46M6613 2011
839.73'8—dc22
2010023510

Jacket illustration and design by Chris Silas Neal.

Manufactured in the United States of America
First American Edition

Thanks, Mami, Baba, Hamadi, Lotfi

They just think I'm a strange tiger who walks on two legs.

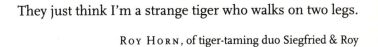

Roy Horn, of tiger-taming duo Siegfried & Roy

PROLOGUE

Hello, dear reader, standing there skimming in the book boutique! Let me explicate why time and finances should be sacrificed for this particular book!

Let us together visionate how the world's best dad, and superhero of this book, wanders white-costumed on his luxurious loft's rooftop terrace in New York. Shadows of birds soar over the reddening sky, taxi horns fade away, and in the background bubbles a gigantic Jacuzzi.

Our hero observes the swarms of Manhattan. The wind flutters his virile ponytail while his mind memorizes his life. The paltry upbringing at the orphanage in Tunisia, the relocation to Sweden, and the battle for his career. Excellent photo collections, frequent disappointments, repeated betrayals. Accompanied by the sun's sinking and the Jacuzzi bubbles' sprinkling, he smiles at the thought of his career's late success.

Then suddenly his nostalgic shimmer is broken. Who are those balloon-bearing surprise guests who, cheering, are exiting his personally installed elevator? Photographic equilibrists like Cartier-Bresson and Richard Avedon are waving. Intellectual prominences like Salman Rushdie and Naomi Klein are being welcomed. Big-hearted world consciences like Kofi Annan and Sting are arriving. Champagne corks levitate toward the sky as servers roll out a gigantic cake glazed with his name. Before the night is over, a leather-draped Bono will salute his fiftieth birthday with an acoustic version of "Even Better Than the Real Thing."

Our hero tears his eyes and thanks his friends. How was this cosmic success reached by a paltry, parent-free boy?

Invest your ticket immediately in the book's journey and you will learn!

PART ONE

Dearest greetings!

Divinate who is writing you these phrases? It is KADIR who is snapping the keys!!!! Your father's most antique friend! You memorize me, right? My hope is for your eagerly bobbing head. The year was numbered 1986 when I afflicted you in Stockholm: your smiling mother, your newly landed small brothers, your proud father with his fresh photo studio. And you who assisted your father's and my learnings in the Swedish language. Do you memorize our rules of grammar? At that time you were a corpulent, linguistically gifted boy with a well-developed appetite for ice cream and Pez candy. Now you are suddenly an erected man who shall soon publish his premiere novel! Praise my gigantic congratulations! Oh, time ticks quickly when one has humor, no?

Your house of publishing has corresponded your e-mailbox to me and I'm writing to interpellate if you have been given the gift of any news of your father. Do you know where he localized himself in all of this? Is your relation as tragically silent as it has been for the past eight years? Your father and I stood steady in friendship until a month ago, when he suddenly stopped responding my e-mails. Now my breast is heaped with an obstinate unease. Has he been kidnapped by the CIA and taken to Guantánamo Bay, draped in an orange coverall? Has he been abducted by the Mossad? Is he a prisoner of Nestlé in retaliation for his revealing photographs of their slavelike factories in Paraguay? All of these alternatives are fully potential since your father has grown to a very strong political prominence. Since his relocation from Sweden, his photographic career has been glistened to a goldish success!

In recent years he has toured the world around with his camera as a political weapon. His lodgings are localized in a luxurious loft in New York; his bookshelves are occupied by intellectual contemporary literature, and his time is passed with global world-improvers like the Dalai Lama and Bruce Geldoff. On free evenings he takes part in peace conferences or gallops the avenues in his violet Mercedes 500SL with leather upholstery and an interactive rain drier.

Write me . . . is your success equivalent to your father's? Has your bookly contract transformed you into a millionaire or a billionaire, or just secured a few years' safe economy? Are literary equilibrists like Stephen King and Dan Brown close friends, or just formally acquainted colleagues? How much muff can one stuff as a soon-to-be-published author? Are you offered perfumed panties daily in correspondence? Please respond me when time is accessible to you.

I, too, have had literary dreams. For some time I projected a biography devoted to your father. Unfortunately, my ambition was handicapped by gaps in knowledge and blasé houses of publishing. Before the writing of this message, my brain was suddenly radiated with an ingenious idea: How would you consider forming your father's magical life in your secondary book?

Let us collide our clever heads in the ambition of creating a biography worthy of your prominent father! Let us collaborate in the production of a literary master opus that attracts a global audience, numberous Nobel prizes, and possibly even an invitation to Oprah Winfrey's TV studio!

Correspond me very soon your positive response. You will NOT condole yourself!

Your newly found friend,
Kadir

PS: In order to moisten your interest in my proposition I am attaching two Word documents. One is adequate as a prologue to our

Once upon a time there was a village in western Tunisia that was named Saqiyat Sidi Yusuf. Here my birth was localized in the fall of 1949. Here I lived in familyesque idyll until 1958, when a tragic accident terminated my father's, my mother's, and my four younger siblings' lives. Unfortunately-located bombs from the colonial powers' Frenchmen in Algeria chanced themselves down onto our village on their hunt for FLN sympathizers. Sixty-eight people died and as a consequence I became family-free. A friend of the family transported me to the city of Jendouba and the house where the generous Cherifa and amiable Faizal accepted my entrance into their unofficial orphanage for anticolonial martyrs.

Has your father exposed you the skeleton that remains of this house? It is localized in Jendouba's eastern district, not far from the sculpture park and the now-defunct cinema. There were two dormitories with turquoise shutters and decorative black bars. There was a kitchen and a dining hall, a schoolroom with uneven double benches and a worn chalkboard, as well as complete colonies of nightly ticking cockroaches.

Already at this historical time, Cherifa's heart was as big as her backside was wide. Her gigantic belief in potentials could compete only with her burning hate for the Frenchmen's task as spreaders of civilization. Faizal, Cherifa's husband, was a timid village teacher who, as compensation for his inability to sexually reproduce, had authorized his wife's care of solitary martyr children. My lodging was partaken with the large muscley brothers Dhib and Sofiane, whose parents had been murdered by the method of attack against FLN terrorists that the Frenchmen comically dubbed *"des raton-nades"* (rat hunts). Lodged in the room beside mine were Zmorda and her sister, Olfa, whose parents had been found dead with sabotaged fingernails and flambéed skin from electric shocks. Also there were the hearing-impaired Amine; Nader, who had one leg shorter than the other; and Omar, with a high-strung belly which gave nightly discharges of gas. All of their parents and siblings had been erased as a consequence of the French troops' effective hunt for suspicious terrorists. [N.B.: Do not place a tragic weight on the children's stories in the book. Focus on your father's mysterious arrival rather than the million dead in the wake of France's spreading of civilization. (Certain eggs must be decapitated for a delicious omelet.)]

My premiere rendezvous with your father was installed in the end of 1962. In many ways the morning was ordinary. I lay, wakened early, on my mattress as Sofiane mooed his snores and Omar released flatulence. I heard Cherifa's morning body as it shuffled its steps toward the garden to gush the water pump. And then suddenly . . . in between two hoarse-throated rooster melodies . . . a knock at the door. First faint and fluttery. Then stronger.

Cherifa went toward the door, mumbling; I levitated myself and followed her steps. The door was turned out toward the sunlight of the dawn and on the outside stood . . .

Your father.

Here his age was that of a small twelve-year-old, his arms twiggily thin and his black hair a burred outgrowth. His shirt bore reddish traces of vomit and his body vibrated in the sunlight. Cherifa interpellated him his errand. Your father separated his dry lips and gesticulated his arms like a desperate bird. He hacked his throat and rattled up hoarse sounds. But no words were pronounced. I remember how he himself looked very disbeliefed at his muteness.

The limit for Cherifa's sympathy was more than reached. The house was topped and she had guaranteed Faizal that NO more martyr children would be saved at his expense. But how could she act? Should she return this poor mute being to the street? While she contemplated her decision your father presented her a well-folded envelope. She gaped its contents and quickly aired her lungs as when the water in the shower suddenly becomes ice-cold. She immediately conducted your father into the cool shadow of the hall. What did your father delegate to Cherifa? My guess is an explaining letter. Or a generous sum of finances.

While Cherifa looked to the envelope's contents as though to guarantee that she had not misestimated the substance, your father's eyes mirrored mine. I erected my safe hand against his spongy one, and calmed his nervous eyes with a sparkling white welcome smile.

"My name is Kadir," I auctioned. "Welcome to your new home!"

". . . ," responded your father.

"Um . . . what?"

" . . ."

Your father regarded me with questioning eyes. It was as though black magic had blocked his speech. In reality, it was a natural shock consequence of a nightly explosion, a mother's death, a confused flee, and the emotion of being the absolute solitariest in the world. I patted your father's shoulder and whispered:

"Don't worry, you are at home here."

In the book, this scene must be filled with great dramatic gunpowder and symphonic bass tubas.

Write:

"So here they are. My father and Kadir. The hero and his escort. Kadir, who will follow my father's fate forever, kind of like how Robin follows Batman or the Negro in *Lethal Weapon* follows Mel Gibson. They are two newly found best friends who will never break each other's promises."

[Maybe you can then form two soaring birds out in the dawning sky who meet and smile their beaks at each other and then sail away toward Kroumirie Mountain. (That would be like a symbol of our initiated friendship.)]

Your father and I quickly knotted our band of friendship into a beautiful, wordless rosette. Already on the first day we parked our bodies on the same double bench when Faizal performed lessons. At lunch I showed how one hid one's sweets under one's shirt so as not to attract the older boys' jealousy. During siesta I uttered many questions about his origin, which he tried to answer, but . . . his tongue still did not work. He waved his arms. He exposed me to a black-and-white photo depicting a suited man being suppered with two Europeans. He let me hold a gnarled chestnut. But not one word was pronounced by his lips. For that reason he was soon nicknamed ironically with the Arabic equivalent of "the one who talks as much as one who has swallowed a radio."

Your father's muteness grew Cherifa's sympathy. He became her new favorite and he assisted her often with domestic assignments. She tried to cure his muteness by constantly conversing him. She discussed heaven and earth, weather and wind, village rumors and relations, scandalous pepper prices, and erotic neighbor visits.

Jealous of the active attention that your father got from Cherifa, Faizal began to plow his palms with hard, punishing blows of the cane. He anticipated moans from your father, but all that happened was that your father's palms reddened, bled, and were scarred into stable scabs. Your father's muteness was intact. (Incidentally, isn't it bizarre that your father's speech problem was later inheritaged by you? For you must remember what problems you had expressing simple letters like *r* and *s* in your childhood?)

Let the date now leave the spring for the fall before the next winter. Let the frost enshroud the yard, let the crickets become silent. Your father and I played wordless games, partook sunflower seeds, spied on the water-fetching girls of the district. We developed an advanced sign language that only we understood.

Your father's nights were still perspiring wakes, memories of a mother's screams, sparks and fiery roars and nightly crossed borders. Frequently the tears welled his eyes with mental pictures that always bore the character of indistinctness. I tried to comfort his tears but only certain sorrows are comfortable. Others are not. This is the tragic fact of life.

Here I propose that you inject some of your own memories from your yearly vacations in Tunisia. If you fear needing to compete with my metaphoric magnificence you can vary your font. Do you memorize anything from Jendouba?

Sure you remember Jendouba . . .

The city in western Tunisia where Dads grew up. The city where wrinkly, straw-hatted farmers sit crookedly on horseback and red trailers rattle iron bars. You remember the hectic souk, hajjis who bite together their white veils with their teeth, the movie theater where they showed Chinese kung fu films with German subtitles.

You remember the pounding at the hamam, the eternal rubbing out of sweat dirt, Dads's hairy bodies, and then go home on the truck bed with cactuses whizzing by and stacked mountains of garlic.

But your strongest memory is Grandma Cherifa, who was so fat she always went sideways through the doors. Cherifa, who welcomed you with a pat and called you *felouse* and always pinched your spare tire to check your subcutaneous fat and always scolded Dads because you were practically starved to death from all the strange Swedish food. And you remember Grandpa Faizal, the retired village teacher with a doctor's bag who always defended Jendouba and maintained that the city actually has a lot in common with New York. Both cities are quite near rivers, for example. Both cities are run by idiots. Both cities have yellow taxis. Both cities have big garbage problems. And both cities are hard to get lost in—New York has its grid system and we have our brilliant alphabet system—and then Faizal smiles so his white mustache becomes an extra smile on top, because he certainly doesn't need to explain whose cousin it was that thought up Jendouba's street system . . .

And both cities have also earned a long list of nicknames. New York has "the Big Apple," "the Melting Pot," "the World's Capital," "the City That Never Sleeps." Jendouba has "the Asshole," "the Armpit," "the Sauna," "the Colon," "the Donkey's Ass," "the Grill," "the Fireplace," "the Oven," or maybe Dads's ironic "the Freezer." And it's only when Dads want to be a little extra academic that he says that you will be spending the summer in "Anus Rectum."

And you remember all of Dads's friends. The journeys home from the airport in Omar's 1960s Mercedes with taped hubcaps, the welcome-home couscous with Olfa's family, Amine's roaring greetings, Zmorda's warm lap. Everyone's sighs when Nader starts to brag, as usual, about that tailor who believe it or not sews pants with legs of different lengths at no extra cost. And you remember so incredibly much more, the tattoos on Sofiane's gigantic biceps, Dhib's left arm that's always extra brown from all the sunny hours in the taxi, the nights sleeping on the roof, and the smell of just-washed sheets, hookahs with apple flavoring, and just-baked cookies from Emir's factory. Twilight on the medians of the downtown streets, where you sit with Grandma and break off pieces of watermelon with a splitting sound, spitting seeds at passing cars, waving at Dhib's taxi, enticing him with the pulp while the light pink watermelon juice runs slowly down your forearm. But the question is, does any of this belong in the book about your father? Presumably not. Presumably it's better to let Kadir steer in the beginning . . . because of course you remember Kadir, too. Dads's best friend. The woman-hungry compliment sprinkler in a violet suit who visited your family in Sweden in the middle of the eighties and left in a fury for reasons you don't remember. What was it that really happened?

In the next scene it's the winter of 1964. The peaks of Kroumirie Mountain glitter snow and your father has lived at Cherifa's house for two years. Two years of total muteness. Two years without the tiniest whisper.

On that wintry day everyone sat shivering in the dining hall; we intook our food and blew warm air in our hands. I remember how your father suddenly levitated and marched toward Cherifa's kitchen, even though this was very illegal. I saw from a distance how he hacked his fourteen-year-old throat, unstuck his tongue, and . . . spoke!

"Um . . . may I have seconds, please? I am not full."

His voice was perfectly normal, with the exception of a very wide hoarseness. Cherifa's mouth circled itself and flapped up and down like a disbeliefed fish.

"Excuse me. May I have a little more food?" your father repeated, with his voice's volume turned up even more.

"If you do not give me seconds I might relate certain rumors . . . No one hears more stories than the one people think are mute, if you understand what I mean. You probably do not want Faizal to find out about . . ."

At this point your father's voice was reduced to an inaudible whisper. Cherifa's confusion was so great that she actually (for the first time in the history of the world) granted a foodwise refill. After that day, your father was even more favored by Cherifa (and even more despised by Faizal).

Why did your father's tonguely effectiveness suddenly return? No idea. Sometimes life persists in not following those patterns that are bookishly adequate. In the book we will do our best to formulate an obvious motive for your father's cured tongue in order to avoid confusing the reader. What do you say we have your father march into a forest, pass under a chestnut tree, take a chestnut to the head, and then cry, "ow!" Then you can have him say: "Oh, a chestnut, how symbolic that this should cure my muteness." Or you could have him be afflicted by a magical dream sequence in which his future is depicted in a modern Joyce-esque stream of consciousness: "Ow-ow-there-I-am-going-to-have-to-court-a-Swedish-stewardess-and-there-I-am-going-to-dine-with-Jürgen-Habermas-and-there-I-will-give-an-acceptance-speech-for-a-photography-prize-at-the-Canadian-embassy-in-Egypt! I-should-probably-force-my-tongue-to-be-cured!" Choose the direction of the path yourself.

With the gift of speech, your father's and my friendship grew to an unshakeable foundation. I never asked about his motive for muteness; instead I wanted to know everything about his parents and his history. And your father shaped it for me with a voice that was his and words that suddenly came flooding out like the blood from the elevator in *The Shining*. He spoke about his father, Moussa, and described him as a wealthy Algerian who lived his life in international airspace and wore sumptuous silk pajamas at night.

"My father, oh, my father!" he cried, until he had attracted everyone's attention (except for half-deaf Amine's). With our ears listening eagerly, he told about his father's career as a chemical water purifier. Soon your grandfather's picture was mirrored throughout the whole world and he had sufficient finances to invest in frequent candy factories and jukebox stores.

"Then he met my mother at a symphonic concert in Monaco. She is one of the world's most beautiful models, born with Algerian parents in Miami Beach in America. Now she's an actress and good friends with Grace Kelly and Humphrey Bogart. By the way, have you seen this?"

With his pride shining, your father presented the worn photograph he always carried with him. He said that the man who sat, black-suited, at the table in fine European company was his father, Moussa. On his right side sat the celebrated film star Paul Newman, and on his left was the water-waved rock singer Elvis.

"And by the way . . . ," he added after having examined the photo in detail. "Do not be upset by the nose-investigating bodyguard in the background."

We were all very impressed by your father's stories. Our eyes shone in stereo when we cried, "Tell more! More!"

The consequence was an expanded stimulus of the buzzing dragon we call imagination. Your father continued:

"My father, Moussa, also has frequent golds in the world weight-lifting championships and has worked as a tamer of tigers. He has four Pontiac V8s; two black, the rest red. Now he lives in a luxurious district of Paris where the lawn mowers look like small cars and weekends are spent on golf or at the racetrack. All colors of women swim his swimming pool topless and oil their shoulders with costly coconut-smelling cream. Why was I relocated here? After my mother's unlucky death in a car accident, my father's intention to teach me the hard school of poverty grew. But soon . . . anytime, maybe tomorrow or next week, his body will arrive to fetch me to the abundance of freedom in France. In the harmony of commonality we will afflict cinemas and meet film stars and practice windsurfing and test his large collection of luxury cruisers. If you want you can come along . . ."

I observed your father and asked (with a certain newly wakened suspiciousness):

"And how has he arrived at this success?"

Your father folded the picture carefully, returned it to his pocket, and said:

"My father is a triplicate of talent: water purifier, Casanova, and cosmopolitan!"

Why did his tongue cultivate such a great many glissades of truth? I don't know. However, we can see two interesting tendencies:

1. Everything in your father's life that had political blackness was filtered out. Politics were, for him, a swamp that had already drowned too many in his vicinity. Not until late in life would your father change his relationship with politics. Perhaps too late.

2. Certainly we all realized that your father's words were not totally correct. But still we were hypnotized and stimulated. Is it not bizarre how the words of imagination can rumble forth a certain comfort? And is that not reality's reason for the existence of superfluousities like horoscopes, psychologists, and authors?

Before I terminate this collection of data about your father's childhood, I want to detail something important: If you are still hesitating about the geniality of this project, I want to emphasize that NO economy is vital for my assistance. Do not let your Swedish stinginess limit our book's future! All I ask in exchange for corresponding you my collected data about your father is that our book's honesty should be maximally spiced. This guarantee is vital to me, because false rumors swarm your father's life. THE TRUTH and nothing but THE TRUTH must be our lighthouse in the shaping of a liter-ary master opus. Can this promise be cast me in steel? In that case I promise to correspond you the reality of truth about your father's background. It will shock and horrify, not to mention stimulate and erect, both you and our future readers.

Dearest greetings!

Thank your effectively delivered answer! To read your positive response to my bookly idea warmed my humor (despite your sloppy grammar and the lack of capital letters after periods). Is "wzup dawg" a frequently used greeting in today's Sweden? In any case, I am extremely happy about our found relationship. To be messaged by you feels almost like being messaged by your father, and this anesthetizes the anxiety that constantly pounds my soul. You still have not obtained any sign of life from him? Last night I dreamed that he had been put to death by a stray machete in a Brazilian smack town. I awoke bathing in perspiration and I devoutly hope that the dream was only a dream . . .

I present great understanding that you "can't guarantee any-thing" and that at the moment you are "sooooo not pumped" (sic!) about thinking about the writing of book number two. That is exactly why it is fortunate that I can assist you. More difficult to understand is your volcanic hate toward your publishing house. Why so angry that Norstedts presented your novel as "the first novel written in authentic Rinkeby Swedish?" Isn't that probably just their method for increasing interest before reviews? Terminate immediately your naming of them as "Whorestedts." And no, "bourgeois Swedelow idiots" is not an adequate name, either. Return your youthful rage to the deposit box that we call self-control! Is this the avalanchesque wrath that your poor father was subjected to during your adolescence? It cannot have been mild to be your father.

To read now, eight years later, how you describe him as a "damn unforgiveable betrayer" makes me more than sorrowful. Fathers and sons must share their time, not separate it! I have great under-standing for the magnitude of your conflict. But will your relation-ship never be renovated? Your father is still your father; he may have constructed occasional mistakes in life. But who hasn't? Unfortu-nately, I recognize the character of your father's pride—it makes certain things impossible (and to contact a son with an apology is one of those things).

You wonder suspiciously what I will get out of helping you ("like what's in it for you"). Let me respond by describing my usual day: I authorize a small hotel in Tabarka. I am fifty-four years old. I have a saved economy that will securitize my pension. I have no family. I do, on the other hand, have a passport that is not welcomed without a visa in particularly many tempting countries. Thus my workday follows the patterns of tradition: I awake, I place my body at the reception desk, I take keys, I direct some tourists to viewpoints, I point the cleaning lady to newly left rooms. But mostly I sit still and surf the global world net. I download humorous Japanese commercials, read about J-Lo and Paris Hilton in American sensation journals, watch *The Worst of Jerry Springer*, localize gratuitous facts. (Incidentally, do you know the global record in banana eating? Only twenty-three.) So I have great quantities of superfluous time, which I will gladly sacrify in order to reafflict the sphere of Swedish and correspond you your father's history. I owe him that. At least.

Your directive about the book's need for "a super-obvious dramatic curve" has influenced me in the preparation of the attached document. I propose that the chestnut theme can be the common thread with which the episodes in your father's life are woven together. I also agree that certain people's need for anonymity could be damaged if we employ their real names. So let us call the book "fiction" and modify certain names. What shall we name your father? In order to prophesy his future relocation to Sweden, I propose the symbolic name "Abbas." Then we can write: "Thus my father's name bore similarity to the Swedish pop group that would heap the dance floors of the seventies with hits like 'Dancing Queen' and 'Bang-a-Boomerang.' Was this a coincidence, or a sign of fate? We'll tend toward that later . . ." We could also call him Hammah. Or Bilal. Or maybe Robert, after his idols Robert Frank and Robert Capa?

Attached you will find the truth about your father. Do not be shocked by the surprise.

Your stable friend,
Kadir

PS: I radiate you positive thoughts and intersect my fingers in antici-pation of the coming day of publication. Good luck!
PS2: I assume that we will continuize our relationship in Swedish? Your naïvely crooked Arabic is probably not serviceable to us in the forming of a book . . . ?

During the spring of 1965, your father's nightly wakings continued. The difference was that he could now scream both himself and the rest of us to awakeness. Some nights I spied on his body where it lay wet from perspiration with wide-open eyes. When dawn approached, he located himself by the window and gazed out over the yard. One night I padded my steps toward your father where he sat curled up in the window with his shoulders vibrating up and down. His crying sounds had a low volume and in his hand he cradled his beloved chestnut.

"How is your health feeling, honestly?" I whispered with a brother's caring. Abbas quickly dried his tears and tried to return to normalcy.

"Very well. Thank you for asking."

"But then why are you pursued by such repeated nightmares?"

Your father looked down at his chestnut and said:

"Can you guard a secret that you may not describe to anyone?"

"I promise."

"On all your existing honor for all time?"

"I promise."

"I have not been entirely honest about my history . . ."

"How so?" (And I must admit that here I felt that type of pleasure that can be stirred when suspicions are verified.) "Isn't it your father in that photograph?"

"Yes, it's him. And he is Algerian. But . . . he doesn't share his company with Elvis and Paul Newman. Do you know who is sitting beside him?"

"No."

"It is Maurice Challe and Paul Delouvrier."

"Wow!"

"Do you know who they are?"

"Uh . . . no. Who are they?"

Your father explained that Challe and Delouvrier were the two French governors who were responsible for the Algerian colony before the liberation.

"Do you want to know why my father is sitting in their company? Because he was a *harki*. A *béni-oui-oui*. A collaborator. Imagine what Cherifa would do if she knew . . . Or Sofiane . . ."

During the following hours, your father whispered his entire true story for my ears. He said that he had been born in an Algerian mountain village near the Tunisian border. His mother's name (your real grandmother!) bore the name Haifa. She was a powerfully strong woman who grappled with her context like the wrestler and actor Hulk Hogan. Haifa's ideal was never that of tradition or religion. Haifa had Western habits and spiced her exclamations with French phrases, and this increased the village's irritation. But Haifa did not let herself be quieted.

One day she proclaimed proudly for Abbas that the name of the man who had signed her pregnancy was Moussa. They had rencountered by chance when she visitized Alger. Moussa had promised her a mutual future with matrimony and a sumptuous life. After their erotic rendezvous, Haifa returned to her home village with rainbow-colored dreams of the future. Unfortunately, it turned out that Moussa's words were promises of that special character we call lies. Haifa was isolated by her family, and the only person in the village who did not refuse her company was a young, povertous neighbor farmer by the name of Rachid.

Simultaneously, Moussa's exterior began to be recognized as the Algerian who preferred the politics of the Frenchmen. Moussa eagerly defended France's civilization task and denied its label as a torture-cultivating occupying power. He rented his tongue to the Frenchmen and in this way padded his wallet.

I interrupted Abbas's story:

"Have you ever met your father?"

"Yes. One time he afflicted our village. But my age was reduced and I do not remember much of that day. I believe we ate at a restaurant. I remember that he had a substantial gray beard on his chest. I remember that two lifeguards escorted his steps.

And I remember that he delegated me this chestnut. That's about it."

"Why a chestnut?"

"Because . . . no idea. I wish my memory presented a greater clarity."

It was mostly your grandmother's stories about Moussa that influenced your father's soul. The insight that he had a father with an international reputation lifted him to a rocketesque pride (rather than shame). Your father was heaped with a cosmopolitan euphoria, which maximized his emotion of not being like everyone else. Many in the village skirmished and demonstrated, they formed their tongues into discussions about the horridness of the Frenchmen and voiced demands for freedom from colonialism. But your father visualized everything political as a virus. He promised himself as a child that he would NEVER anoint his wings in the spilled oil of politics. Instead he fantasized dreams of the international world.

(A whisper from the parentheses: Can you relate to the emotion of never partaking in the generality of your surroundings? In that case, cultivate this emotion in your writing! To form something that is totally separate from your experience is an impracticable task, a little like not laughing when you observe Kramer's alert hairstyle in *Seinfeld*.)

Your father continued his story with the turbulent years that terminated the fifties in Algeria. It was political chaos; demonstrations bled the streets and terror shook people's daily lives. In your father's village, people's irritation was reflected against the Frenchmen until it involved your father and grandmother. But Haifa refused to conform; she continued to salute the Frenchmen, she sprinkled her language with French phrases and proudly auctioned that her genetics were certainly more global than Algerian and more cosmopolitan than Arabic.

In 1962, when your father's age was that of a twelve-year-old, the Évian agreements were terminated. The Frenchmen promised to leave power. The liberation was a fact of Algeria. The consequence was a chaos that we can call typically Arabic. The blood of the power struggle. More protests. More terror. Fifteen thousand dead in FLN attacks in the summer of '62. Up until Ben Bella took power, initiated his one-party state, and unlawfulized all parties except the FLN. (Write me . . . without becoming unnerved and without retarding us to the disrupting discussions you had with your father: What people is more creaky at democracy than Arabs? That you don't concur with your father about this is to me a mystery.)

Many French collaborators, or *béni-oui-ouis,* were forgiven and forgotten to the success of continued bureaucratic careers. Only a few were painted in the colors of shame by the magazines. One of them was your grandfather Moussa. His body had apparently fled the country and now he was depicted in articles and caricatures as a France-controlled dog. The consequence of this campaign? In typical Arab manner, the people let themselves be led like dumb sheep. They began to protest outside your grandmother's house. They insulted your grandmother; nightly cries echoed the district's street. Once, her door was colored with malodorous substances which do not deserve descriptions.

Simultaneously, Haifa began to worry about your father's mental stability. He carried out expeditions in his sleep, he fantasized forth shadow friends, which he conversed. Once he even clad himself with your grandmother's veils and tried to mask himself as a woman. The only person who afflicted Haifa with support during this problematic period was Rachid, the povertous neighbor farmer.

Unfortunately, Rachid was absent the night that someone invisible smuggled himself into Haifa's kitchen, punctured the gas pipe, and lit a cigarette in anticipation of the sedating mass of the hissing. The invisible one transported the cigarette into the house and disappeared without a trace in the shadows of the night, accompanied by the petals of the roar-proliferating fire. The one who, at the last minute, saved your father from the explosion fires was the newly wakened neighbor . . . Rachid.

"And it was Rachid who transported you here to Jendouba?"

"Yes, I think so. But I actually do not remember," whispered your father with that sort of dry tone that one gets at dawn when one has been speaking solitarily for several hours. "I remember that I vomited. And I remember that you welcomed me out there in the hall. In between, most of it is blurry and vague. All I have from my home is this photograph and this chestnut . . ."

The roosters hacked their singing voices in the neighboring yards and my eyes had begun to itch and be sanded by tiredness. Still I didn't want to sleep. Not yet. I said:

"Strangely enough, our respective histories have certain things in common. My family, too, was erased in an explosive fire as consequence of the colonial time . . ."

"Mm . . ."

"Hey, are you listening?"

"Mm."

But in reality your father sat as though bewitched by the photograph. I wanted neither to distract him nor to leave him. So I waited. What woke his stupor in the end was a pompous passing of gas from Omar's mattress. We smiled our lips at each other and I said:

"Hey . . . let us try to catch some sleep before the dawn becomes day."

I remember the details of the photograph very well. It was granulated and mottled gray, waveringly cut out from an Algerian magazine. The tooth of time had crimped its edges, yellowed its color, and crumbled its corners. Moussa sat, white-smiled and black-suited with visible finger rings, with a thin-mustached Challe on one side and a stiffly water-waved Delouvrier on the other. The photo was actually rather ordinary. Except for the detail that I found comical but that frustrated your father: the background contours of the anonymous lifeguard who was carefully taking inventory of the interior of his nose. His entire index finger was hidden in the black hole, and this, according to your father, threatened the excellence of the picture. "How can such a small defect have such a large consequence?" he would often interpellate, without anticipating a response. Has your father exposed this photo for you? Perhaps we can localize it and inject it into the book? Or else you can inject your memories of the photo below, in a varied font.

And you remember Dads, who many years later change the name of the armoire and start to call it the *mémoire*. Behind the padlocked door there are Otis Redding albums on cassette tapes, small perfume bottles with scuffed-off labels, and thousands and thousands of photo negatives. Because Dads have explained that a real pro never throws out a negative. And there's also the old photograph from an Arabic newspaper that shows three smiling men at a restaurant. The paper is so worn that the text is almost transparent. Who's in the picture? Dads just clear his throat, put the photograph back in the envelope, and hold up his chestnut. A little decrepit chestnut that's not even very smooth, and you ask Dads: Why did you save a chestnut which looks a little rotten and wrinkled besides? Dads explain: This is no ordinary chestnut, this is a magic lucky chestnut. I have had it in my pocket my entire life, and once I used it to win my first marble on the streets of Jendouba, and in the military I used it as ammunition for a slingshot when I was attacking a general who was trying to rape a woman, and when I met your mother for the first time I threw it at her to get her attention. And you don't know

if Dads are joking or not but he's laughing so you laugh
and he throws the chestnut straight up in the air and
has just enough time to clap three times before it lands
safely in his hands.

What explication has your father delegated you for his growing up
in Cherifa's home? Perhaps he has not even told you that he was
actually born in Algeria? Perhaps you are just now reading these
words in a shocked emotion that Cherifa is not your real grandmother? If this is the case I want to remind you of something vital:
Whatever version your father has selected, I am the one who forms
the reality of truth for you. Memorize that your father always had
the truth as an ideal. But sometimes the complications of truth
have forced him into lies. Okey-dokey?

Dearest greetings!

Praise the publication of your debut novel! Hail my fourfold congratulations! How does your emotion taste? Like Nutella crêpes of
crispiness in a sunny park? Like a kiss of surprise on the nape of
one's neck in the summery smell of lilacs? Like wind in hair when
one cycles hands-free down bridges with the laying of the sun in
silhouette?

I am still awaiting your reactions to my presiding document.
While waiting I have read the reviews on the world net and noticed
a certain . . . ambivalence. Despite your protests you are celebrated
because you have written a book in "authentic Rinkeby Swedish."
Apparently you have brought "the immigrant's story" to life in a
language that sounds as though one has "dropped a microphone"
into an immigrant area of one's choice. Did you not write that your
book was about a Swedish-born man who breaks his language with
intention? What happened to your asserted exploration of "the
authenticity theme"?

On Norstedts's net page I found an extract of your novel. My
appraisal is . . . hmm . . . let me be honest and hum the eighties hit
by Yazz: "The only way is up," yes? Your novel seems to me perfo-
rated with inconsistencies and besmirched by precisely those foul
words that your father denounced. "Bitches"? "Fucking"? Why does
the book use precisely that language which your father hated the
most? No wonder that people "misunderstand."

Another question involves your interviews. Why this expanded
multitude? Did you not write that you would never allow yourself
to be interviewed by any "goddamn fucking bourgeois philis-
tine newspaper"? Shouldn't anonymous transparency à la your
idol Thomas Pynchon be your ideal? And now your beardless
figure is being exposed in revolutionary magazines like *Woman's
World*. Have your principles already been abandoned? Admit that
it went more quickly than prophetized. Who is "the betrayer"

now? Is it still your father? Or are you actually cut from the same crap?

Respond me soon.

Your disquieted friend,
Kadir

ps: A terminating question. What is your principal character actually called? Halim or Hamil? Hamid or Harim? The Swedish journalists seem to be concerningly disagreed.

In the next scene we soar the reader forward to the year 1969. After his military service your father has decided to leave Jendouba.

Write:

"In Jendouba there were imams and figs, mustachioed women and spiny palms, tired oxen and cyclical desert storms. But there was nothing that my father likened as a home . . ."

With astonishing generosity, Cherifa had promised him finances for studying legal courses in the metropolis of Tunis. We said our farewells but promised a soon reunion.

I sought work at Emir's cookie factory. With the security of the handshake and my smile wide in both senses, I informed Emir that an expertish cookie sorter stood ready for employment and the smick was sufficient for a salary. Ten minutes later I stood parked at the conveyor belt with a dirty white coat and a paper hat for the premiere of my work. The heat in the factory was hellish; the smoke billowed from the metal discs of the oven, which twisted and thundered and tumbled down new cookies of sporadic sorts approximately every ten seconds. All day long I picked cookies for the cartons, four of each, no more, no less. All while Emir circulated nearby and verified the piled cookies of multitudes. My fingertips were soon burned to hardness, like the fingertips of famous players of electric guitars.

It was at the cookie factory where, during the summer of 1970, I reestablished my relation to your father. Still today I memorize how he sullenly invaded the factory, took upon himself a paper hat, and was awarded the position on my right side.

"Abbas!" I cried. "Praise my congratulations for your return to Jendouba! What happened with your legal studies?"

"Who are you?"

Your father's tongue had now darkened with a certain overacted metropolitan accent.

"It's me, of course! Kadir, your antique best friend!"

"Yes, of course, now I memorize you."

"Why so melancholy?"

"Excuse me. But my mood is far from sunshine. Political turbulence has strained Cherifa's economy. The finances ran out and therefore I have been forced to pause my studies to stand here as an idiotic cookie picker. Trapped in this damned, miserable, assholey, depressed, hot-as-an-anus, abominable hell city." (Here your father continued with even more insultations than I remember.)

"But . . . there's one pleasure in any case. Right?"

"What is that?"

"That we have rediscovered our friendship?"

"Sure," mumbled your father (but I suspect that his happiness didn't really compare to mine).

Write me . . . do you carry any photographic evidence of your father's exterior as a twenty-year-old? His outfitting was . . . how shall I write it . . . bravissimo in its excellence. All the other farmer boys at the cookie factory bore a solidarity in short-cropped hairstyles and bath slippers. Your father, home from Tunis, was different. He was the first man in Jendouba who presented a style of such long hair. His black locks curled effeminately, and (never inform him of this) when I saw him again a suspicion germinated in me that he had become infected with homosex. (Isn't it interesting how his taste for long hair has been inheritaged by you? And that the photos he exposed of you in your pimply teenage years filled me with exactly the same suspicion?)

Your father's cheeks had two smiling hollows, which he only demonstrated for women who sold *casse-croûtes* on breaks. His legs bore blue jeans of supermodern European bell-bottomed style and his favorises bore an increasing size that referred to early John Travolta or late Marvin Gaye. His tongue exposed a sudden knowledge of numerous European authors, artists, and poets. Many were impressed by your father's newfound person. (Even me.)

. . .

Write:

"Let us present my father's youthful exterior. Home from Tunis, his eyelashes were arches of blackness, his eyelids curtains over brown velvet wells, his corporeality that of a growing Greek god. His mentality was a cosmopolitan artist's and his face referred at the least to a young Antonio Banderas."

(Your father's modesty would of course redden his cheeks and not at all agree with me about this description.)

Our shared words, however, were few in number until the autumnal day when the photographer Papanastasopoulou Chrysovalanti afflicted Jendouba. Do you know this photographer's work? One thing is my secure certainty—his name MUST be simplified in the book.

The rumor about Papanastasopoulou's arrival was whispered on streets and squares; his form wandered about the souk and the cultivation fields with his camera like a friendly weapon. The rumor whispered that at night one could see his photographic lightning flash the sky (like lightning) in an attempt to capture Kroumirie Mountain's moonlit silhouette. The street boys followed his path and played charades in the hope that the clicking sound would immortalize their forms into the exhibition that he had been commissioned by the Institute of Greek Culture to implement. Certain tradition-loving tongues mumbled "Haram" and described how the Greek had tried to photograph hajjis outside the mosque, even though they had tried to hide their faces.

The next scene is a regular workday; the metal trays are turned and they tumble down packable cookies; the sweat runs our faces and the clock ticks slowly; Emir swears in the office and your father is wearing his self-boasting, ever more worn-out gigolo jeans. After lunch he turns to me:

"Do you know whose body has been invited to the Greek photographer's studio in order to be immortalized for the future?"

I denied and your father beamed:

"Mine!"

I praised my congratulations to your father's fortunate happiness and inquired about the possibility of escorting your father as company to the Greek's photo session. Your father conferenced his thoughts before he submitted his positive response.

After the termination of work we companied to the terracelike apartment that the photographer had rented for two weeks from a local clothes tailor for an astronomical price. The door was opened by an oiled Greek man with the age of a forty-year-old, a tight shirt with a flower motif, and sharp cornery teeth which glittered his large smile (and then disappeared quickly when he understood that we were two boys who had arrived for a visit).

My memory smiles when I think of the curious eyes that your father and I exposed in contact with our first photo session. All those things that your father would get to know in detail later were there, but right now they seemed most like spaceshiply equipment: the flash cables, the tripods, inside-out umbrellas, strongly aimed spotlight shine. I counted the number of cameras to be three of varied style and model. In focus for the tripod stood a half sofa on a patterned rug, and as photographic props the Greek had invested fezzes, fake mustaches, gold platters, tea services, djellabas, veils, decorative hookahs, and eight or nine pairs of leather slippers.

The Greek indicated how your father should place his body on the half sofa and convinced him to decorate his head with a very humorous turban. Your father did not find the humor so humorous. While Abbas was flashed by cameras I felt the bodily emotion that most closely resembles cold back winds. Without knowing why, my arm skin was bowled up to small bumps, as though I could feel that this glimpse would have great consequences for the future. All the while the flashes blinded and the Greek pronounced "Fabulous!" and "Magnificent!" and "Perfect!"

The work-related time was expanded and the amount of photo clicks only continued and continued. Sometimes breaks were taken for communication between your father and the Greek, but because my tongue at that time only controlled Arabic and a little French, their English meaning was not understood.

The Greek wanted approximately "Relax" and "Yes yes" and your father wanted "No no." This was repeated approximately every five minutes while I glided my fingers through black mini-photo squares, negative cards, piled fashion magazines, and glossy photo books. My surprise became great when the Greek suddenly left his camera to show your father how his ultramodern gigolo jeans ought to be unbuttoned and abducted for the sake of the picture. Your father responded with an exploding aggression and the result was the blood gush of a Greek nose; your father's foot visited the Greek's stomach and your father's mouth added a glob of spit on the Greek's neck where he lay coughing on the ground. The tumult of turbulence, Greek hands wanted to catch your father, who, with the effectiveness of Van Damme, ducked and hopped aside, served new strikes and kicks combined with a cascade of insultations which noted the Greek's mother's resemblance to a prostitute and the Greek's own resemblance to a stray dog.

A second later your father and I rushed our legs toward the stairs; the Greek did not manage to collect his body and we did not reduce our running tempo until we were on the street, three blocks away. Then I noted that my hands held one of the Greek's photo books. Observe: This was not my intention. Write:

"Dear reader. Kadir is neither thief nor raven; in the confusion of the tumult his hands had acted solitarily and the consequence was the collection of a book by the photographer Philippe Halsman. This book was delivered by Kadir to my father as proof of his desire to share his future friendship."

In coming scenes your father and I begin to restore our amicable duo. Together we became the only people in Jendouba's early seventies who presented a rebellious discrepancy against the ideal of tradition. Our nights were passed on the roof of the student housing where we shared our lodging. With stars as our audience we smoked hashish and drank Celtia and listened to your father's audiotapes from Tunis. In the quiet of the evening we echoed soul at the sky with Otis Redding's stomp and James Brown's rasp and Etta James's blues. For the melodramatic final, the authentic French song was vocalized by not-particularly-authentic Frenchmen like Charles Aznavour, Léo Ferré, or Edith Piaf.

As musical illustration there were Halsman's magical photos. We let ourselves be shined by eternity in his photographic excellence. There were celebrated actors; a stripe-shirted Brando, a melancholy Bogart, a smoking Hitchcock with a little dickey bird at the end of his cigar. There were assorted Negroes: a yawning Muhammad Ali, a perspiring Louis Armstrong, and a sad Sammy Davis Jr. peeking forth from behind a house corner. There were the levitating hopping photos that were Halsman's specialty: Marc Chagall and Jackie Gleason, Dean Martin and Jerry Lewis, Richard Nixon and Robert Oppenheimer. Everyone's names, which to us were unknown, and everyone's feet frozen in the freedom of the air.

But mostly we observed the women, of course. Oh, the women, so differentiated from the Jendoubian women's exteriors! Judy Garland sitting backward on a chair with her gaze turned away . . . Brigitte Bardot with the bumblebee's waist, the billowing of her breasts and baring of her shoulders . . . Audrey Hepburn with arms stretched up in the apple tree and her plaid skirt pleated . . . there was a smiling Ingrid Bergman and a street-crossing, hat-wearing Zsa Zsa Gabor with dog-filled purse. There was Dorothy Dandridge in the whiteness of underwear and the polish of fingernails presented on a sofa. There were Lucille Ball's wide open eroticism eyes, Grace Kelly's mirrored double form, Gina Lollobrigida in that sort of taut dress that most closely resembled a bath tricot. Our nightly dreams were hunted by Sophia Loren as a breezing farmer woman or Elizabeth Taylor with a horizon look, a necklace, and pearlish ear ornaments.

Only periodically was your father's mood clouded with that sort of cyclical darkness that would disturb his later life. I noted how his eyes began to look inward instead of outward. He rediscovered the silence of his childhood and shared the company of hours with Halsman's photographs. He studied them with centimetric distance, browsed the pages discreetly, and refused to respond me or share his thoughts. These periods usually continued for several days.

Then your father's presence returned; he woke from his thoughts and saluted Halsman's photographic talent. One day he auctioned:

"I have discovered my life's mission, Kadir: To hell with law! I am going to become Tunisia's first world-celebrated photographer. With the camera I will modify the future of photography. From now on all of my life shall be sacrified this ambition. We must leave this rat hole of a city as soon as possible! Do you want to follow in my footsteps?"

I bobbed my head and served him a classic thumbs-up. With Halsman's photos and modern soul music we projected future plans of how we would soon meet the tourist town Tabarka on the Mediterranean coast.

Write:

"In the soft fog of intoxication, the friends visualized their futures. My father's ambition was to become an international photographer. Kadir's ambition was to become a tourist guide or a professor of samba dancing or a billiard instructor or why not a future master of hotels. My father's way was Art's; Kadir's way was Economy's. The duo's goals had been pronounced and the starting shot had . . ."

(How does one write correctly here? Been discharged? Banged? Shod? Inject correctly, please!)

What do you say about the drama in this section? Not so limited, certainly? Have some of these anecdotes been depicted by your father? Do you know why not? Me neither. I wish I knew . . .

Dearest greetings!

Thank your extensive message! Delightedly I read about your new-found daily life as an author.

What an atmospheric honor it must be to pass time at book fairs in Gothenburg and be invited to literary festivals for rendezvouses with intellectual giants like Unni Drougge, Katarina Mazetti, and Björn Ranelid! Because you're being ironic when you describe yourself as a "mass-media whore," right?

No excuses are vital to you for your served silence. I bear great understanding for the ticking unease that one can experience in the rendezvous with one's memories. The same emotion can sometimes infect me. But we must not let the fear of memory handicap our book! Let us instead seek the response to the mysterious riddle that you identify as "like, the book's theme." I, too, have long heaped my soul with the question of how a father can leave his children.

My fictive hat is put off to bend and bow for your flattering words about my data. My cheeks are pleased to redness when you hail my texts as "vivid," "fanciful," and "extremely over-romantic."

Here follow my responses to your questions:

1. Yes.
2. This is no surprise. Your father has undergone frequent reformations on the way to his late career's success. He has wandered from a mute boy to a jeans-draped smile-dimpler to an amorous metro driver to a stressed studio owner to a world-celebrated photographer heroically fighting for the weak. That you do not continually recognize your father in my text is therefore to be expected. That you did not even recognize the background of his photographic interest is to me a tragic surprise.
3. No, definitely not!

4. Certainly you are correct that your father was also nick-named by some in Jendouba as "the one with the elephant ears" and "the cookie lover." I forgot to inform this. Has he said this himself, or was it one of his gabbing friends during your vacations in Tunisia? Was it Amine? If I had not been bound to serious work I could have been present with your family and nuanced their flapping tongues. And you—let us not exaggerate your father's ear size or excess weight in the book. Soon the hairdresser hid his ears and the fatness was transformed with the years into supple biceps and a squared washboard.

5. Yes, certain things perhaps indicated the wordy interest that your father would inherit you. He had, for example, already when young, a tendency to inventory his own names for things. To his gray T-shirt he gave the name "the Silver Arrow." His student room became "the Burrow." His future touristic mademoiselles he called "Vanilla" (if they bore whiteness of skin) or "Chocochoc" (if they bore brownness of skin). The wit of words has, as you know, always attracted his boisterous humor. Presumably it is this specialty that has infected you with the ambition of an author.

6. No, neither "social services" nor "student aid" existed to support your father's legal studies. But you are a very funny Swede who asks. However, we had much assistance from our friends from the orphanage. Not financial help but muscley. With their soon-scarred faces and broad muscles, Sofiane and Dhib protected us to safety—even if your father happened to swipe some dates or I happened to be accused of cheaterly card games.

7. He had many favorites; here are some examples:

· The Fafafafafa song by Otis Redding
· "Sittin' on the Dock of the Bay" by Otis Redding

- "Super Bad" by James Brown
- "Love Man" by Otis Redding

8. Yes, your father has always had an expanded difficulty with people's whispering tongues. The rumors of his love affair with Emir's daughter gave broad frustration. "People's curiosity is entirely too expanded" was a citation that he often pronounced. A recipe certain to cloud his mood was to say something of the character "My ear perceived that you were at the souk on Wednesday and invested this and this from him and him . . ." Then your father always denied and said, "Who has related this?" The emotion of being observed has always borne a great complication for your father. (According to your father this seems to have infected you too? Or what do you respond yourself, Monsieur Paranoid with Permanent Blinds? Señor Brown Velvet Curtain in the Room in Stockholm? [These words bear the tone of the humorist; do not let yourself be unnerved!])

9. Audrey Hepburn in front of the birdhouse. Or perhaps the photo of Ingrid Bergman. I'm not entirely sure.

10. "Smick" is of course the word that denotes our Tunisian minimum wage, didn't you know that? And do you really not know the word "favorises"? In English it is given the name "sideburners." It consists of the protruding beard that is localized in front of the ear, below the hair, extra common in disco dancers, motorcycle chauffeurs, and wolves. Do I have your understanding? An enlarged vocabulary is vital for your future career as an author.

11. Yes, your father's pride has ALWAYS borne a prestige that we can hardly name adequately. One disappointment against your father, and its forgiveness is far away for years to come. This is your father's character and he would gladly modify himself. But how difficult is it not to teach an antique dog new techniques?

Affixed you will find the describing of our rendezvous with Tabarka (and your father's rendezvous with his first working camera).

Your refound friend,
Kadir

PS: Your suggestion to start our book in Sweden is interesting. But not correct. Recall your father citing the Baudelaire photographer Félix Nadar: "The best portrait is made by the person one knows best." This rule also applies to authors. How can you (and the reader) know your father's contours and understand his later actions without the forming of his historical history? Hopefully you recognize certain patterns in your father's life as reflections of your own. Furthermore: To form what you call "prehistory" in Proustish flashbacks requires an author of monstrous talent. Do you really bear this? You who barely manage to formulate a single e-mail free from English words or spelling errors? No, to guard chronology is my directive.

The year was 1972 when your father and I dismissed our bodies from Jendouba's cookie factory, packed our cardboard-like suit-cases, and entered a collective louage with Tabarka as its des-tination. Our collection of finances had borne that particular industriousness that refers to the Japanese. With the economy's status secured for a few weeks, we were on our way toward our new lives!!!

In the next scene we have stabilized our mutual lodging in a white *paillote,* a minimal one-room house with a straw roof, which at that time was localized on the beaches of Tabarka and hired out for scanty economy. At nighttime, small lizards zoomed over the interior of the roof without ever falling down. Perhaps you can con-sult these lizards as symbols for our existence? ("Like lizards our duo zoomed through life under the roof without ever felling their backs against that ruin which we call the floor.")

Your father sought a position at Tabarka's photographic labora-tory while I obtained work as a dishwasher in the kitchen at Hôtel Majestique. While I rinsed silverware and glistened glasses, your father learned the foundations of film development. The friendly (but extremely cross-eyed) master, Achraf, received Abbas as an assistant and taught him how one temperature-verifies and agi-tates, stops and fixes, rinses and dries. How the development is followed by the printing, the stop bath by the fix bath, and how vital it is to carefully rinse away the fixer remains so that the photos will not yellow prematurely. The utensils that were found in Achraf's laboratory were very simple: Achraf had painted the backdrops himself and named them titles like "Modern Love," "Classic Love," "Love in Venice," as well as the comic "Asterix and Obelix." The fix bath, which professional photographers usually only employ one time, was used by Achraf until the liquid was transformed into thick porridge. Instead of light meters, Achraf relied on his ticking intuition, and instead of gloves there were hands to dip the nega-tives in the developing bath.

The true creation in the process was initiated when Abbas had produced the negative and Achraf presented his paint box. Here was a pointed pencil with which he darkened the negative until the portrait's face colors became exactly light enough that the customers looked like their ideals. Here were the Japanese paper colors that Achraf cultivated in order to carefully colorize the customers' clothes to a perfect shade. Your father drank in all this knowledge with the thirst of a dry sponge.

Your father's time was mostly occupied by passport portraits, but sometimes touristic customers, whose negatives always mirrored one another, arrived too. The same red-scorched, smiling tourist bodies in airy linens in front of the artist district of Sidi Bou Saïd, in the souk in Tunis, outside of the ruins of Carthage. In this historical time, tourism in Tabarka was growing weakly. Only two big hotels had opened their doors and the amount of European tourists was still limited. All of today's deluxe options like parasailing, riding banana boats, or European daily journals lay far forward in time. No boutiques yet sold stuffed camels or humoristic T-shirts with texts like "I Love Tunisia" or "My Parents Went to Tunisia and All I Got Was This Lousy T-shirt."

Still, Tabarka's daily life was night and day in Jendouba's comparison. Instead of cookie packeting, our first summer in youthful freedom was a rosy time of beach parties, hashish, disco dancing, and repeated nightly visits in unfamiliar hotel rooms. Mark my words—the touristettes hung about like grape bunches with longing for our one-eyes.

Here you can inject an erotic scene where your father and I limbo oiled Belgian girls, disco-dance horny Brits, afflict French girls' backsides, and encounter German twins in hot tubs. You can expose well-filled Portuguese girls on their knees on hotelesque balconies, perfumy mouths wide open, sucking the friends' ecstasy while the duo toasts coconut drinks.

Does this erotic diversity sound bizarre? Perhaps you interpel-

late how we could attract the touristettes' interest? Let me explain—
this epoch was widely differentiated from now. At this time "Arab"
was not a denotation that was used as provocation or virus. Rather
the opposite. At this time, Arabicness attracted sexual frequency!
The nationality of Arab was at least as positive as . . . a crank organ.
(Do you understand the metaphor?) Frequent were the touristettes
who invited me to their nightly hotel rooms after I had praised
their golden skins. Numberous were the touristettes who sighed
erotic moans when your father wrote their first names with Arabic
letters in the beach sand or hailed them with made-up Arabic
poetry translated into French. (He usually employed Arabic non-
sense phrases like "gravel is good" or "take your towel" or "your
nose is very ugly" and then with a serious mouth transformed the
words to amorous French translations.)

Still, our courting routines were rather separated. Where your
father did his "quiet wounded striving poet who glances his sad eyes
to the starry sky" with habit, I did my "enthusiastic compliment-
sharing dishwasher with a great interest in poker and a wide portion of humor."

The youthful intoxication of luxury lent its character to this fantastic time. When I remember all the erotic nights now, all the
shadows of limbs, all the melting moans, and all the head-banging
remorse-awakings in strange hotel rooms, I am filled with that particular joy that we can call nostalgia (or sorrow).

In the fall came the day when your father's collected economy
bought its first functioning camera: a shining black Kodak Insta-
matic with the form compact, the material metal, and the loading
system extra-modern. How much technical information does our
book require? Do you think the reader is interested in photographic
data like shutter speed and aperture and genre of lens? Perhaps we
should just write:

"My father invested a camera and initiated documentation of
the Tabarka of the past. The *picture* rather than the *technique* was

his focus. He was in the habit of formulating himself poetically like this: What is the *picture* other than the bath plug of truth in the sandy sieving that we call the hourglass of life?"

Or we can write:

"My father's camera bore, of course, the deluxe brand that still today is associated with the grandiosest quality: [x]."

(Here you can inject the name of the camera producer who will furnish you the biggest economic advancement.)

Suddenly your father bore the camera in his constant nearness. He began to form his fingers to the negative of fantasy, made thumbs and index fingers into a box, pretend-flashed scenes, and mumbled, *"Parfait, parfait,"* to himself. He began to present himself as *"photographe artistique"* and invested a beret in French black style. In the small hours of intoxication he testified with a front of suffering about how the craft of photography had modified his soul:

"I mean . . . the reality of life is, like, too . . . I mean since I discovered photography much more has . . . how should I put it . . . life has, like, a new shine . . . I mean . . . (hic) every sight gets like a

a

a

(hic)

sort of dimension of eternity . . . you know, Kadir? Hey . . . are you listening, or are you letting yourself be hypnotized by that Dutch cow's breasts?" (I must confess—the breasts had me hypnotized.)

I remember that your father returned to this subject in 2001 in an e-mail he wrote me from a Palestinian family in the Ramallah of occupation. He wrote: "Oh, Kadir. What modifies life more than the magical insight about the potential freezing of everything?" This is a very beautiful phrase, which should be injected later in the book. (But exclude your father's continuation: "Wait, there is one thing . . . fifty-three years of permanent oppression by a blood-thirsty occupying power! Fuck the potential freezing of everything!") Do you understand your father's words, or are they on the side of fuzziness? Perhaps this emotion refers to your discovery of writing? If so, inject a section where you write, "As usual, the genial Kadir is entirely correct . . ."

And Kadir actually has a point, and when you read his letters you remember that day when you had just learned to read, and it has to be the year before Kadir comes to visit. You take the commuter train south with Dads to help with cleaning the stockroom in Grandpa's sign store. The stairs up from the platform, pass the place where the shopping center is being built, cross the ghostlike empty square, and open the door to the sign store, where Grandpa is sitting hidden behind the gigantic huge cash register with stand-up buttons and listening to PI. You greet Grandpa and Grandpa clears his throat back and scratches his stump arm and you go right into the stockroom, where you pick up rags and start to polish the old metal signs with a special liquid that stings your nose. You wander around in Grandpa's crammed stockroom, where one corner is taken up by old yellowed refrigerators with round corners and bags filled with bottle caps from the time of Gustav Vasa. You finger a few signs and pretend to polish but you're really mostly just imitating Dads's motions. And then suddenly your eyes land on a sign and you finally understand that Grandpa's collection isn't just a weird old man hobby but an ultimate time-travel portal for messages from the past. Because not just one but every single one of the old signs are full of letters that look just like the ones you practiced before school started. Slowly you start to spell your way forward. Th-th-thaamaaa- . . . weeen . . . k-ke-ee-pth your body lean! Thun-light Thoap, Thtomatol, Philipth wadio, known fow ith good thound. At first you do it mostly to show off, to show Dads that you're really quite a pro at read-ing. But Dads don't seem to care, no matter how loudly you read. Dwink Champith. Fithkeby papew thold hew. Mathetti'th Ögon Cacao, deliciouth, thtwong, healthy. The only thing that's hard is the *s* and *r* sounds. But you continue because the signs are chock-full of secret mes-sages, codes that only you understand about mysterious historical things like Okthan Wood or natuwally alka-line Wamlötha minewal watew. And your strongest memory is the sign with the pipe-smoking man who's standing in a brown floppy hat in front of a watery hori-zon, and you have always thought of him a little like an old ancestor because his skin is brown like yours and his crossed hands are almost hairier than Dads'. But now, on this day, you realize that he is actually an ad man for something called Tiedemann'th Tobacco and you're just about to brag to Dads about your unpar-alleled reading abilities when Grandpa's voice roars from the register: Tiedemann's, for God's sake. "S!" Not Tiedemann'th! When are you going to learn to talk properly? And Dads asks: What did he say? And you say: That I have a great talent for reading. And Grandpa yells: What did he say? And you say: That your sign col-lection is very impressive.

Do you want to know what your father's camera registered? Every-thing. Absolutely everything. The beauty in his photographic rolls prophetizes his future success. There are smiling restaurant own-ers, winners of fishing contests, cliff-diving young boys. There are hundreds of photos of birds' silhouettes in the laying of the sun. There are British tourists numbed in the hashish intoxication of the beach. There I am, your father's best friend. With the mouth-gap cigarette, squinting eyes against the light, beige army shirt, in the company of two sauce-red, big-smiling Germans. Or with my newfound poker partners who shared my company when your father photoed. And there is, of course, his self-produced personal portrait, in black-and-white blurriness with the grown-out curls, the meticulous, melancholy Otis look, his outfit the shabby European standard—V-shaped pants, tight white T-shirt, and softly smooth leather sandals.

Sometimes your father made solitary nocturnal expeditions up to Kroumirie Mountain to document the splash of mountain rivers, the water fetching of farm wives, the morning dawn of mosque minarets, and the waving arms of wheat fields. He came home to the *paillote* in the dawning light with lips grinning gladly and newly invested bread under his arm.

Here it is proposed that we inject some photo taken with your father's first camera. What do you think about the scanned picture that is corresponded you here? It visualizes your father and me in a hotel room belonging to a very overweight Belgian touristette. The sharpness quality is not ideal but certainly the nostalgia value is adequate for publication?

Daily life continues with fluctuating seasons and years; Bourguiba is electered for permanent lifetime to be president, Tabarka's tourist industry grows steadily in similarity to your father's photo collection. The whole time he has the ambition of saving his economy and crossing Tunisia's borders for an international photographic career.

A doubting reader might shout: "Then why doesn't he go abroad? Why does he remain in Tabarka if his enticement to the outside world is so well formed?"

This will be the book's response:

"Dear reader. You must NOT believe that my father was of the sort that the Germans dub '*Hähnchen*' or the Brits call 'chicken boy' or the Swedes put to sound as 'hare.' To define these years as lost or unproductive would be a lie that is not true. Certainly my father's words about the future may have overstepped the number of ready-to-print photos. Certainly he invested broad economy in umbrella drinks and presents to miscellaneous touristettes. Certainly he consumed frequent daily beers in Kadir's company and sometimes slouched his evenings in the vapors of hashish. But I auction with stately tongue: Who did not do thus in his days of youth? I must also call attention to my father's planning talent! With the single-mindedness of the German and the taste for organization of the Swede, my father initiated mental preparations which would realize his international photographer career.

"Most important was language; Abbas was his own professor and his impressive dressage of the world's tongues was . . . impressive. Still today he makes a habit of spreading the citation 'What is language if not the picklocks' locks to the keys of doors where the souls of different people live (or rest)?'

"While some fellow countrymen confused themselves further in the muddle that we can call political fundamentalism, Abbas anointed many a dinar and hour to touristic phrase-book compositions invested from Tabarka's bookstore. With guidebooks for different countries his tongue perfectioned vital photo phrases in English, German, Spanish, Italian, and Russian. With the cowboy's confident hat lift he practiced, 'Hey, nice beautiful girl, how are you, do you want to please be a supermodel?' With the Spaniard's bullfighting smile he lisped, '*¿Dónde está el museo de arte?*' With the Italian's straight-backed stiff tongue he expressed, '*Aspetti! Può parlare piu lentamente, per favore?*' And in front of the mirror he bounced his hand against the tennis racket of his imagination and asked himself, '*Tennis willst Du spielen?*' The perfection of French was of course already my father's private property.

"With control of the languages Abbas also expanded his broadness to investments in French fashion magazines. It was here where, in 1976, he was blinded by a photograph of a very attractive Brazilian. Her name was spelled Silvia and the article summarized how she had recently advertised her alliance of love with the king of Sweden. Did this influence Abbas's future? Perhaps. But probably not. More vital was probably the biography dedicated to his idol Robert Capa, which Abbas read again and again. Capa, the master photographer with the velvet gaze, who documented everything from the Spanish Civil War to D-Day, who enjoyed Hemingway's close friendship and Ingrid Bergman's close love . . ."

Let me present:

My father!

"A symbol for the globally modern meeting place where East crosses West, where Jesus crosses Muhammad, where redemption is a rendezvous in symbolic manly form, a little like the Lionel Richie of race and music!"

Hmm . . . I hope you do not perceive this section as on the quarrely side? With consideration for what happens later it is vital that the reader understand those dreams that burned your father's breast when he was young.

The next scene welcomes the reader to the end of the summer of 1976. It is the year that the whole world suns itself in KC and the Sunshine Band, the year that terrorist groups like the PFLP, the Carlos group, and the Baader-Meinhof group fear-fill the world with hijackings, kidnappings, and bombings. The year that both your father and I have begun to grow our youthfully squared bodies to a certain bartender corpulence. But our mentalities are still constant. Neither religion, politics, nor tradition stops us from celebrating nights in the bonfire shine of beaches with soft touristettes in bikinis. Waves wash, someone's guitar clinks "Lay, Lady, Lay," a pipe is passed around, and discussions of harmony consider life's shortness, the West's stress, and the Orient's beneficial mystique. This was a repeated subject that the tourists wanted to round up, and we chorused along with them. Even if your father had begun to grow his irritation about everyone's constant focus on the vital difference between our world and theirs.

Suddenly I see your father, orangely fire-lit on the other side of the bonfire with the star frame of the night. His eyes, which normally usually seek the touristette with the night's largest bosom, have suddenly relinquished their looking-around quality. Instead he is sitting with his back stretched like a hyena and his eyes magnetized to a group of women at the outer edge of the group. I remember distinctly his moistened lips and his swallowing throat. Then he advances his body, step by step, nearer and nearer the women, whose voices speak a language that to me sounds like singing in the tones *dutty-dutty-dutty-dutt.*

The special thing about this episode is that it is suddenly as though your father's courting quality is kidnapped. When he is about to act his "poetically wounded Casanova with horizon gaze" he happens to break a wineglass and almost gets shards in his foot. In the stumble of the sidestep he places his hand on a burning fire log, and when his body finally achieves balance and advances toward the giggling women, they all turn down a swig from his wine bottle. And your father?

The quality courter just stands there, with soft jeans rolled up and the wind softly blowing his curls. His hands seem to be two too many, his foot digs in the sand, his teeth bite his upper lip and . . .

Then she FINALLY turns up her eyes. The one who until just now has dealt with your father as transparence. Her . . . the Swede who kidnapped your father's eyes.

Let time freeze and waves cease. Let the long shadows be immobilized and the crackle of the fire stiffen. Their gazes meet. Let everything rest in total silence and then . . .

Then?

Then BANG she presents her hand. Your father stands lost like a missing mitten when she takes the initiative and her hand is soft like white sand but strong like harrisa and her eyes don't yield and she says her last name and she doesn't smile at all and he reflects that she must be the first of all of them who doesn't mirror my courting smile. And he holds her hand and he smells her lavender odor and it SWOOSHES itself into his brain and the ground begins to vibrate under him, his brain is hazed, the clouds gather, the night sky is crackled with lightning and suddenly a hundred meteors fall from the sky and suddenly the horizon's fish boats shoot artificial distress lights and sunken choirs of angels sing SYMPHONIC SONGS and organs play at BOOMING VOLUME and STRAY DOGS HOWL and THE AIR LOSES OXYGEN and VOLCANOES ERUPT and UMBRELLA DRINKS CRASH FROM BARS and ACHRAF'S PENCIL BREAKS AGAINST A NEGATIVE and SOME-WHERE IN AN UNDERGROUND RESEARCH ROOM THERE IS A RICHTER SCALE MEASURER THAT RISES AND RISES AND RISES UNTIL THE MERCURY EXPLODES ITS CHAMBER AND SPRAYS ITSELF OUT LIKE OIL AND BLACKENS THE RESEARCHERS' WHITE COATS, THE HISTORICAL FAX MACHINES, AND THE ANTIQUE GREEN-TEXTED COMPUTER MONITORS!!!

(N.B.: None of this happens in reality! This is metaphorical symbolism for your father's strong emotions during the rendezvous with your mother.)

How is their discussion begun? Who remembers? Who cares? Perhaps your father unluckily tries to compliment her similarity to Queen Silvia? Perhaps he says something comical about Sweden's cold climate? Something about polar bears, penguins, Björn Borg, or ABBA?

I have no knowledge. All I know is that it takes some fifteen minutes before she releases her skepticism. Slowly her responding words grow to more than one at a time. Slowly your future mother begins to smile her first smiles. Slowly your father recovers his courting routine. He pronounces his humoristic stories. He presents his finger-cracking trick. He blows his burn injury covertly.

The whole time my brain is entertaining with the thought: This is special, this is the first time that Abbas seems to be lightninged with the incomparable infection that we call true love!

I was correct. Late at night your father crashed into the *paillote* with the brownness of his eyes burning with desire.

"Her name is Bergman! Her name is Pernilla BERGMAN!"

Again and again his tongue mantraed this bizarre name: "Bergman . . . Pernilla Bergman! She is a stewardess from Sweden! Bergman! Like Ingrid! Have your ears ever heard a more delicious name?"

As though he had been waiting his entire life for this very Swedish stewardess with this strange name. As though the memory of all the other European women who had betrayed his heart upon returning home had been forgotten forever.

I praised my congratulations and added:

"Is she related to Ingrid?"

"No, of course not. I asked the same thing. Bergman is a very frequent name in Sweden. Would you like to hear about the symbolism of the name? Do you know what Bergman means in Swedish?"

"You are welcome to explain."

"The man from the mountain!"

"Really?"

"Compare it with my name . . . Khemiri!!! It is almost the same! The man from Kroumirie!"

Confronted with your father's naïve euphoria, I was filled with something that, bizarrely enough, can be likened to jalousie. Instead of congratulating him or correcting his invented symbolism, I said:

"So you were hungry for a little vanilla tonight?"

Your father quieted sharply and focused me with pointed eye-blackness.

"Excuse me?" he cried. "What did you pronounce? Did you

besmirch my newfound relationship with Pernilla with an expression like 'vanilla'? Repeat if you dare!"

"Sorry, sorry! Excuse my excuse!"

Your father lowered his right arm, paused it by his waist, and then erected it to an amicable handshake.

"Forgive me, Kadir. I don't know . . . it's just that . . . this is something special . . . I have never experienced something like this before."

Before we fell asleep your father whispered:

"Kadir . . . by the way . . . do you know which country manufactures the notorious Hasselblad cameras?"

"Let me guess . . ."

"Precisely . . . Sweden. It was she who informed me of this when I told of my photographic dream."

Several minutes of silence followed.

"Psst . . . Kadir . . . are you sleeping?"

"Not yet."

"Did you see her sandals?"

"No . . ."

"They were enormously excellent. Of a light blue color."

"Mm . . ."

Silence. Wave whoosh. Cricket song. On the way to sleep. Until:

"Hey . . . do you know what she said?"

"That she was tired and needed her sleep before the coming workday?"

"Ha ha, very funny. No . . . she said that in Swedish one expresses the surprising power of passion with a photographic phrase."

Silence.

"Don't you want to know which?"

"What?"

"Don't you want to know which phrase illustrates the flash of love in Swedish?"

"Of course."

"One says, 'It just clicked.' She told me. In Swedish it sounded something like this: *De saya bahra klik.* Isn't it beautiful? What a sign from fate, right?"

He continued like this all night. While my wakefulness alternated between dozing and sleep, I heard your father rave sporadic words about Pernilla's comic encounter with some actor on the approach to Tunisia. There were words about her planned nursing education and homages to her political solidarity. He talked about her satirical humor, downy earlobes, the odor of her sun skin, the odor of her lavender soap. Her throat softly patterned by translucent blue veins, her light blue sandals, her jumpy Swedish French pronouncing, her compromise-free fury when he had happened to attract the eye of another woman . . .

And . . . of course . . . his eternally parroted . . .

"Honestly speaking. Have you ever seen a woman's smile that can compare to hers? Honestly? Pernilla will be my Ingrid and I will be her Capa."

I did not response. I had a little trouble understanding how your father could be so fascinated by this twiggy, elongated woman with unglamorous makeup, nonexistent bosom, and obvious snub nose.

That night, then, was their premier rendezvous and the events of the following days I do not know for certain. I worked with overcast spirits at the hotel while the newfound pair of lovers passed all waking hours in company. Sometimes I saw them in some hotel bar, your mother's agitated voice discussing some political injustice while your father sat as though magnetized by the shine of her eyes. Sometimes I saw their amorous silhouettes wander beach edges at a distance, your father as straight-backed as a major in an attempt as desperate as it was pointless to measure up to your mother's one hundred and eighty centimeters. At the beach parties they bore each other's constant nearness; their hands were never separated. And one night I happened to hear how your father named his parents as Faizal and Cherifa, living in Jendouba. I commented on nothing.

Night after night for three weeks your father invaded the *paillote* with the same imbecilic dawn cry:

"Her name is Bergman! Pernilla Bergman!"

How far they went sexually is unknown to my knowledge. But before their farewell they exchanged addresses and promised the promises of a future relationship.

Thus it is here that everything begins. Which will end with plane trips and moves and love and matrimony and conflicts and three confused mix sons and perpetual misunderstandings and terminal tragic silence between a son and a father.

During the coming period, Abbas placed all his wakefulness on two things: the occupation of a lab worker and the letter correspondence with Pernilla. He declared self-composed love poems to the sea instead of to German touristettes. He was TOTALLY sexually solitary (which of course supplied an increased sexual plurality for me). While I rose in the gradation of the kitchen from washer of plates to washer of glasses to preparateur of simple bar menus, your father began to serve his pictures to local papers. Soon his name was spread; he was hired to document weddings and invited to photograph before-and-after photos in a hairdresser's salon. Abbas climbed his first steps on the steep staircase that would become his photographic career. It was as though his love for your mother motivated him to finally find a focus. Simultaneously I spent more and more time with my poker partners and planned for the upcoming establishment of my own hotel.

While waiting for new letters from Sweden, Abbas developed magical double-exposed photos in which your mother's silhouette encountered groves or cork oaks or dramatic mountaintops. He sat sighing toward these photos for hours. Then he corresponded them in envelopes to Sweden with specially written love poems or applied them to the wall in the *paillote*.

Then in September 1977, your mother's longed letter of invitation arrived. Abbas was free to journey. What happened? Did he telephone her and travel directly—euphoric from the chance? Did he immediately bid farewell to the photo lab and whiz up over the Mediterranean? No, instead something happened which I cannot explicate.

Your father made himself transparent.

First he passed a week with a quiet, overcast mood. Then he was just gone. A notation in the *paillote* expressed a simple wish: "Bear no worry. I will return soon."

I trusted your father and waited calm. Hours became days. No one heard from him. Achraf from the laboratory afflicted us in a rage and I could only shrug my shoulders and questioningly tell the truth: that I knew nothing about Abbas's disappearance.

Then one morning your father was back. He invaded the *paillote* at dawn with his camera around his neck, a stale stink from his tight polyester shirt, and a multitude of twigs in his black hair.

"Kadir! Now I am going. I have found my insight. It is time."

"Where have you been?"

"On a photographic and spiritual expedition!" responded your father with his smile shining.

Still today I am unstable about where and why he localized his body during these eight days. Your father can be so curious. Perhaps one must just observe and accept.

I admit that I tried to convince him to stay in Tabarka. I described my plans to open my own hotel and cautioned him humoristically about Sweden, that northerly country of chilly blonds, Eskimos, and fully frozen winters. I pointed out the risk of colds and the threat from hungry polar bears. But your father only laughed and promised his cyclical letter correspondence. "A friend's loss is a loss. But a life without one's beloved Pernilla is no life."

This he repeated again and again. Only to later pronounce an interpellation that would be fatal:

"I must, however, ask you for a favor of gargantuan value. The tongues of the village whisper about your latest period's gigantic prosperity at the poker table. Can you delegate me a loan to enable my move abroad? I have invested my last finances in the obtaining of a falsified Tunisian passport to enable my exit. If you accept this inquiry I promise you a repayment with well-formed interest. What do you say?"

This was not an ideal position. I had packed abundant amounts of cookies and glistened monstrously many glasses and invested everything on exactly the right poker card in order to save my finances. And now they were to be delegated to your father? He observed me breathlessly:

"My future is in your dependence. Do not deny me. You will get interest. I promise. As soon as my photographic success has been achieved in Sweden. Please. Do not be a doorsill on that wide motorway we call love!"

It was truly impossible for me to deny your father this service. I generously delegated him my saved capital and detailed in a document how the interest would grow exponentially during the coming years. I postponed the opening of my hotel and wished your father's happy journey.

If there is anything that is vital in this chapter it is this: Many consider me to be a man of risk, with a great portion of courage. In reality I have wandered carefully through life as though in a newly colorized corridor. I have invested all of my risks in the secure context of the poker game. Considerably larger balls are required by the man who invests his risks in life itself. Your father staked EVERY-THING on relocating his address to Sweden. All for his love for your mother. Never forget that, Jonas. Never. No matter what the future has in its muff.

PART TWO

Dearest greetings!

Thank your continued description of daily life as a Swedish debut author. Are you serious when you write that you trained all the way to Sundsvall to "chat books for three coffee-slurping ladies and a snuffling bulldog?" HA HA, this aroused much humor in me! Are you entirely honest when you write that you are enjoying every second? Is there no glamour missing?

Also thank your diligent questions. Who is it that has radiated you this information? Of course I am grateful that you are collecting data in other directions as well, but . . . Do not play on the high side of ambition! Too many cooks can transform our delicious broth to soup in the alphabetic sense.

When you write that "certain sources" characterized your father in Tabarka as "the stallion from Jendouba" or "the Tunisian Stud" or "the eternally unfaithful," I am filled with unease. These sources must be contaminated! Is it your father's flapping friends who reported these nicknames to you during your vacations in Tunisia? Was it the semideaf Amine or the semidwarf Nader? Do not rely on people's flapping mouths! Certainly your father had a reputation as a Casanova, but this is NOT the same thing as if he were to share a plurality of women's relationship in permanence. In any case not after his rendezvous with your mother! And that he would have courted your mother AFTER having "been totally dissed" by her red-haired, large-bosomed flying colleague is also the type of lie that we can call untruth!

There are many women but only one Pernilla. There are many rumors but only one truth. It is the truth that will be presented in the book. Nothing else. Do I have your full understanding?

One question has pondered me lately: What do you define as the biggest risk against the quality of our book? In my opinion it is the dullness of the reader. Entirely too many books exist where the dryness of the phrases monotonizes the reader to sanded eyes. I presume that your book view is compatible with mine? Your father has detailed how in your teen years you made a repetition of racing swearing out of heavy-aired literary readings and feeding the garbage chute with newly published novels. (By the way, is it true that you and Melinda splintered Norstedts' show window in the early nineties in rage over the book *Colored Conspiracy*, where Tom Hjelte and Dr. Alban interviewed "coloreds" like Mauro Scocco, Jan Guillou, and Izabella Scorupco? Have you admitted this to your editor, Stephen? HA HA, you were comically confused in your youth . . . [But I realize why your father did not share this humor.])

In order to feed the reader's successive will to read I propose the following: Let us cyclically transform our book into new literary molds! Let us now initialize the secondary section of the book, where we will first serve the reader your father's authentic letter texts and thereafter invite you to present your first memories of your father. How is this idea appraised? I am snugly securitized about its ingenuity. Let your father be the pilot of the section; I will reduce myself to footnote level. (And you will be . . . the map holder? The stewardess? HA HA! I am just tickling.)

Affixed you will find your father's corresponded letters translated into melodious Swedish. I have maximally forced myself and my hope is your appreciating appraisal.

Your ceaseless friend,
Kadir

Stockholm, February 2, 1978
Greetings, Kadir!

Many salutations are presented you in capitals from the wintry European corner that we can call Sweden. I am sitting in Pernilla's minimal kitchen and formulating you these phrases. The frost is whistling the exterior of the house but today the cold is still somewhat humanized. Compared with before. Even by a Swedish standard this year's winter has been brutal; the cold record has been demolished, and one night the temperature crashed to thirty below. But with triple clothing layers and a newly invested tricolored scarf I have passed the winter's cold before the radioactively strong fire that we poets call love.

Let me first describe my arrival: The journey passed pain-free. Pernilla's letter invited me to cross the border to my new homeland. Pernilla's lodging is localized in a very modern neighborhood in Stockholm's vicinity. Her house is one in a row of eight identical boxes. They are all well formed, with modern angular lines, brown color, mirror-clad elevators, and floor buttons that glow when you push them.

The bolt of nervousness filled me when I elevated my body toward her seventh floor. I alarmed her bell and waited in silence. Nothing happened. I alarmed her bell again. Nothing happened. I alarmed her bell again and again and again and again. Then I heard pattering whispers from her neighbors. I alternated my strategy. On a scrap of paper I noted the following phrase:

"Je t'attends à Centralen . . . /Ton Chat Unique"[1]

---

1. Translate this in the book: "My body awaits you at Central Station . . . /Your unique cat." (It was your father's tradition to always nickname himself with different titles in the company of different women. With Pernilla he was "the unique cat" or, short and delicious, "Capa.")

I dropped the paper in the mailbox and then I returned my body to Central Station. Sitting in a multitude of hours at a café, drinking coffee with added cognac, I was piled with the questions of doubt. Perhaps I should have forewarned Pernilla of my arrival? Perhaps the ingenious idea of offering her the surprise of my presence was not an ingenious idea? Perhaps she is on vacation? Perhaps she is full of wrath about my method of silencing my correspondence? All these questions grew me in tempo with the time of hours. Lunch became afternoon became evening. The disappointment about my fiasco, the inconvenienced hmmings of the waitresses, the mountain of splintered toothpicks and consumed sugar packets. She must have forgotten me, everything is lost, what have I done? The level of the alcohol added my tragedy and my remorse grew.

Then . . . in the midst of the twilight of disappointment I heard a call from the entry of the café: "ABBAs!"

And there she stands in the mistiness of the backlight. Pernilla. Her long body with the firish gaze and the goddessish nose. And then she sprouts the smile. The smile that avalanches forth through the dark-as-night twilight room and shines the café's colors to new levels and is reflected in the pastry glass and dazzles punks and interrailers and tired conductors . . .

She studies my gaze and she shakes her head and we meet our smiles. She reaches my table, she notes my alcoholic odor, she studies my shabby status, and expresses in a whisper:

"Couldn't you have called first?"

And I find no response. No words are nearby to me. All that exists is she. She! I sobered myself quickly, transported the bottle to my inside pocket, and followed her to the metro.

Since this day we have lived in fantastic symbiosis in her little two-piecer where Bob Marley sits as a poster on the wall and odor of the incense is to me homey. Pernilla flies domestically so it is seldom that I am forced to pass longer times in isolation.

When she is working I associate with my notebook where I collectionize observations and poetic phrases. Like for example this: "Sweden . . . oh, Sweden. A land of quiet metro cars, delicious women, and possibilities of the plurality. Sweden is airy cleanness, watery celestiality, and breathtaking views from centrally located bridges. Everything in Sweden is odorless and colorless, properly squared, white and pink and soft in resemblance to the forearm skin that is Pernilla's. Oh, Pernilla's skin. Only one of numberous motives for why I chose to leave my best friend and newly started photographer career."

The celebrating of Christmas was lived through by me without great difficulty. Before the festival Pernilla said:

"Just so you know—Swedes' Christmas traditions are a very internal affair and it takes many years before one reaches the status of being invited as an external guest."

Consequently I passed my Christmas holidays waiting solitarily in Pernilla's apartment. The silence of the neighborhood was tombish. Nowhere was there the tiniest indication that this was a festival of rejoicing. I portioned my company with the television, I forced myself to understand sporadic Swedish words and mixed my *julmust* with alcoholic reinforcement. I played my newly invested Stevie Wonder record. I smoked frequent cigarettes on the snow-filled balcony. The time without Pernilla was experienced by me as bizarrely protracted. I do not understand what she has done with me. Is it really this that is called love, Kadir? To experience oneself in solitary status as so split that each breath becomes an effort?

Pernilla returned from her parents two days after the eve of Christmas and I noted the modified shine of her eyes.

"What has taken place?" I interpellated.

"Nothing."

"Come on, tell me."

"No . . . I do not want to summarize it."

"My dear Pernilla, let us not carry secrets between us. Now portion me your emotion."

Pernilla sighed her lungs and vibrated her lower lip.

"It is just that . . . Do you know how it feels to be crestfallen by the prejudices of the people you are closest to?"

"Well, that emotion is actually not particularly known to me."

"Then you do not know how I feel. My mother is scared to the death over our initiated relationship. Ever since I told her about you she has warned me cyclically about the aggressive temperaments of Muslims. She has presented me numberous articles about Muslim terror; she persists in calling you 'the gold digger.'"

"Hmm . . ."

"And now she refused to invite you to our Christmas celebration."

"But . . . you said that the celebrating of Christmas was familially internal . . ."

"I lied. My older brother's goddamn tennis partner and his girlfriend from the U.S. were invited. The whole neighborhood gathered on Christmas Day. Neighbors, cousins, the cousins' kids' goddamn dogs. But not you, who share both my love and my lodging. Sometimes I really hate them. HATE."

Here her tears burst and I held her shaking shoulders and hugged her warmth. I thought: "Even her crying presents its own character. Pernilla's crying is so far from the generality of other women. Never can it be referred to resignation or weakness. Instead it is vibrations with volcanic internal hate. She dries all the tears with her hand as quick as the windshield wipers of a car. Every tear that she does not succeed in holding in seems to corrode her pride. We comforted each other's sorrows all night and at the moment of slumber my lips whispered:

"My dearest Pernilla. I love you above everything. We will survive this, together we will show them, we will never be conquered. NEVER!!!! We will dazzle your damned family, we will break their images, we will delight their forgiveness. They commit me as a political fundamentalist and you as a duped daughter. These are my whispering words; I think them now and let them be tattooed on my forehead as punishment if I fail: After my success your family will, crying, lap the sweat out of our sumptuously invested shoes. My mentality will be more Swedish than their imaginable ideal. My photographic success will be more illuminated than their goddamn Christmas trees. The assets of our economy will grow higher than their goddamn Kaknäs Tower. Let us start the countdown to the day when Khemiri creates a familyesque Swedish superclan with the influence of Bonniers and the finances of Rockefeller."

Pernilla woke and whispered with diamondish eyelashes:

"But . . . We can't forget the people's fight."

No one has been more lovable to me than that bizarre woman, Kadir. I solemnly auction that we are going to share our common futures for all of the future!

Our New Year celebration was sparkled with all of Pernilla's friends in a big house in the Skarpnäck neighborhood. There were woodish parquet floors and monstrous multitudes of alcohol. Pernilla's friends were warmly inviting to me, they smiled me kindly, requested my view on politics, and praised their repeated tributes about the book *The Prophet* by Khalil Gibran. At the countdown of the strike of twelve, Pernilla dragged me aside, she whispered me words that I can't write you, and we shared heavenly kisses accompanied by the heavenly explosions of artificial fires.[2]

---

2. Here your father is probably using metaphorical imagery language. Rather than the sky it was probably his imagination that flashed with explosions. Or what do you think? Write me, Jonas—have you ever been seriously in love? Have you ever experienced the kind of love that wakes you to the sweaty panic of the night with the dream that the life of your beloved has been terminated by the rendezvous with a cancerous disease or a toaster unluckily placed near her bathtub? Have you then calmed your heart bolt, rubbed your eyes, cleared your brain, and sighed your lungs? Have you then discovered

In the dawning of the new year, Pernilla and I promenaded Stockholm's hundreds of parks, lakes, and bridges. The snow softened itself down from the sky, the air smoked our mouths, and the chill was so cold that the interior hairs of one's nose adhered themselves together when one breathed (an unusual but not uncomfortable emotion). The snow crunched our shoes, the sun was squintingly beautiful, and the water lay deeply iced. One day we observed the majority of children who threw their backs into the snow and kicked and twisted their bodies in wild spasms. Pernilla pointed the pattern of the snow and informed that they were making so-called angels. Then we mirrored each other's eyes and without saying anything we said something—if you understand what I mean?

I am terminating here with hope for your soon response.

Abbas[3]

---

her sleeping shadow there beside you in the dark? Have you heard her light snores? Have you returned your head to the pillow, buried your nose in the vicinity of her napely hair ends, nosed her lovely sleep skin, and realized in your mind that nothing, NOTHING in life, can measure up to this emotion? If this is not in your experience, you have truly not lived. Ask me, I know. It is this hurricanic love that your father lives in this historic time. Therefore, excuse him his romantic wishy-washing.

3.   Your father is probably referring as follows: Angels as a symbol for heaven = heaven as a symbol for snow = snow as a symbol for the generality of weather = "We could achieve angels!" = Our love could modify everything, including the weather.
     As you observe, your father's letters are deliciously formulated, perfectly adequate for bookly injection. But I wonder one thing: Why does your father not relate the motive for Pernilla's late arrival at Central Station? Do you know the circumstance that gives the story its truly mythological value? She was actually on the way north for a ski vacation with her parents the same day that your father arrived in Sweden. She planned to stay away for two weeks, but a conflict with your grandmother irritated her to tears. (Your grandmother persisted in saying, "What did I tell you?" because your mother mourned your father's letterly silence.) Near Uppsala your mother noticed great flaming rashes on her forearms and legs. She used these rashes as a motive for leaving her parents' car

Stockholm, April 15, 1978
Greetings, Kadir!

Thank your finely formulated letter and your particular specification of how my interest on the loan has expanded this first half year. My Swedish life has now found its everyday. Pernilla and I share our permanent company, a little like you and me in Tabarka. Together we manifest for the expanded power of women and choir our critique of nuclear power, capitalism, apartheid, and fur industry. Together we pass evenings at cinemas and wander toward the metro enjoying the smells of wakened spring: carefully sprouting leaves, the food odors of the hot dog men, my beloved's lavender soap. Do you remember how I named Sweden as "the land of odor- and colorlessness?" This is no longer adequate. Spring in Sweden smells and lives, people are dormanting from their hibernation, they smile on the metro, and sometimes (but seldom) the neighbors return one's greetings in the elevator. The warmth of spring modifies everything.

Parallel with Pernilla's and my love progression I have devoted time to my photographic career. The premiere step was to localize an assistant job. I wandered my steps from studio to studio; I presented my portfolio from Tabarka and offered myself at a reduced or almost free cost. My success was not particularly abrupt. Frequent were the photographers who detailed that they unfortunately could not assist an assistant who does not cultivate the Swedish

---

and returning to Stockholm. There she found your father's scrap of paper and with bolting breast she took a taxi toward Central Station and localized his alcohol-filled body at the café. Where did her rash come from? Your mother suspects that, despite her allergy, she happened to intake hazelnuts via a pastry. In the book we could introduce another more adequate nut allergy . . . Perhaps your mother was allergic to . . . chestnut jam? (Remember: Everything in life can be woven together; life is a coded pattern, and it is our task to crystallize in bookly form those small details that the people of the plurality let pass unnoticed.)

language. My arguments that the world of images does not automatically require linguistic exactness were ignored.

Luckily enough, one of Pernilla's colleagues has introduced me to a Swedish-Finnish photographer by the name Raino. Raino is specialized in the delicate art that we call food photography. His eyelashes shine like white mammals above his reddened nose. His mustache is of yellowed walrus model and his drinking habits are unmoderate. The studio is very modern in comparison with Achraf's primitive utensils, however. It is localized in the luxurious neighborhood of Flemingsberg, near Stockholm. I pass circa twenty hours per week in service to Raino, developing potatoes au gratin, warmly steaming Falukorv, and delicious pâtés. I am learning many special tricks. For example, do you know how one photographs the most delicate portrait of a cup of coffee? One fills the cup with soy sauce mixed with a few foaming drops of dish soap. Consequently one escapes the uglifying surface coating! Methods like these reinflate my fascination with the magic of photography. Which other expression has such a privileged relation to reality that it can grow one's appetite for coffee at the sight of a cup of soy sauce?

When the customers of photo tasks are limited, I assist Raino with other services.[4]

---

4. Do you want to know what your father did? Let me show you . . . Look, who is that? Do you see him? It is your father sneaking his steps out from Raino's lab, crossing the street, and invading the stairs where Raino localizes his lodging.

Your father elevates himself toward Raino's floor, alarms the bell, and is welcomed by Raino's beer-smelling body in slippers and an undershirt. Your father is delegated the leash and is presented to Raino's dog, a corpulent figure of the race Golden Fetcher. The dog is nicknamed alternately by Raino as "Dumbo," "the Whore," "the Dick," "the Dumb Fuck," "Carina," or "the Cunt" (all names christened after Raino's ex-wife, who left Raino for a statistician from the tax board). Before your father goes, Raino presents him a knotted plastic bag.

"Here, take this."

"Sure. But why?"

The position with Raino strengthens my routine, but the economy offered me is nonexistent. The weight of the worth lies in the chance to be able to polish my own projects. Let me take the opportunity here to repeat my thankfulness for your generously dele-

---

"You have to have it with you."

"Okay. But why?"

"If Dumbo presents a poop it must be picked up and transported away in a bag."

"Hahaha, you are a funny Finnish man with a humor as well formed as your mustache. Bye."

"I'm not joking."

"Hahaha!"

"Hey . . . I am serious."

"HAHAHA!"

"Silence your laughter! You must pick up the poop."

"Hmm . . . Is this humorous joke not a joke?"

"No . . . bye."

Raino conducted the dog out into the stairway with a well-aimed kick. And there they are standing now, whining golden-haired dog and your masterful father. They sink themselves down toward the spring-frosted ground; they do a quick circle promenade in the park. The dog galumphs around and smells posts; your father observes him suspiciously, with nervous clampings of the bag knot in his pocket. The dog pees sandbox and noses flower bed. Your father hacks his throat. The dog bends his back legs like a Buddha and performs a light brown, very liquidy poop. Your father sighs, looks at his surroundings, bends his back, and with the façade of distaste he scrapes up the poop, which lies gooed onto the asphalt. Then, just as he is standing bent forward like a shoe tyer and feeling the warmth of the excrement, he promises himself a promise:

"THIS MUST NOT BE IN VAIN!!! Can one sink any lower? To stand in a foreign country with bent back in order to collect a diarrheic poop prepared by a dog with a name taken from a betraying ex-wife?"

Your father battle-raises his hand with the poop bag over his head and lets his voice echo over the park:

"NO MORE GAMES! NOW IT IS SERIOUS!!!"

At that second the sky of grayness is separated into a shining blue hole. The shining promises of the sun peer down at your father. He sees the sky, lowers his arm, and presents the poop bag to the specially marked dog garbage can. His fingers' emotion of having picked up warm poop after an animal remains long after your father has returned the dog to Raino. It increases his ambition of never giving up his dream.

gated economy. Thanks to your loan my arrival in Sweden has not been honorless; I have not had to profit from Pernilla's finances, and in addition I have invested myself a new system camera.

The multitude of motifs in this country is monstrously many to me. In every neighborhood, at every metro station, through every window it seems to me motifs lie brooding, awaiting their documentation. Sometimes it experiences me as inspiring, sometimes as stressful.[5]

Today the spring was invited to Stockholm. The sun shone in the typical Swedish way; it dazzled one's eyes without offering more than the superficial warmth of the skin. Pernilla was at work, Raino had liberated me early, and I wandered my solitary steps through central Stockholm. Soon I parked my body on a bench in a park that in Swedish is given the name Humlans Gård. On the opposite side of the street was localized a sunshined corner; birds chirped, and everything was maximized harmony. Then I suddenly noticed a man who was swinging his briefcase, flapping his skinny tie, stressing his clomping steps, and glancing his wrist . . .

"A typical office drone," I thought. "Run farther, you poor slave, while we artists delight sunshine on parkish benches."

Then something bizarre occurred. When he turned around the corner of the neighborhood and collided with the sunlight, he was hypnotized into stillness. He stopped his steps in slow motion, localized his body to the vicinity of the wall, stretched his neck like an odor-searching dog, closed his eyes, and then . . . he just stood there. Like a statue. And enjoyed with a heavenly expression, which

---

5. Here we can inject a separate scene where your father walks the streets of Stockholm with his constantly clicking camera. He captures smoking *raggare* gangs in Kungsträdgården, smiling mounted police, chess-playing pensioners, waving dog owners, spit-shouting Save-the-Trees demonstrators. He documents lost tourists, gleaming king statues, broken telephone booths, symbolic bridges. And of course your father's favorite motif, collected in your wardrobe by the hundreds: all the snow-covered, pedal-frozen bicycles, which delight your father's photographic eye with their inherent conflict.

of course I documented with my camera. The interesting thing was that he was not solitary in his behavior. ALL of Stockholm was filled with compatible patterns this first spring day; in EVERY sun-shined neighborhood, at every bus stop, on every square they stood, suddenly placed out, all the neatly dressed office Swedes with the same backward-tilting head, delighting mouth, and closed eyes. Hundreds of people who sought the first blessing of light like thirsting plants. Often accompanied by a noise trickling from their lips that is best described like this: Mmmm. My camera docu-mented this bizarre behavior and my plan is to name my premier collection *Stockholm: Sunnish Corners and Wintry Bicycles*. It will probably be ready in the summer.[6]

I have also followed the latest episodes in Tunisia's tragic fate from a distance. Did you participate in the general strike also? My eyes have read the letters of the journals, but my brain refuses to realize the magnitude. Fifty to two hundred dead? Thousands arrested? Do not let yourself be lost in the cul-de-sac of politics!

Certainly Pernilla's political engagement has found a certain mirroring in me. But sometimes I stare at her coat-wearing friends as they stand, filled with red wine and swaying and babbling their mantra about the repulsiveness of the American imperialism and the threatfulness of capitalism, while at the same time they frizz their beards and persist in constantly asking me about my perspec-tive on the Middle East and my view of Sadat and . . . My eyes are

---

6. Excuse me, but I just noticed an unparalleled phenomenon on the Eniro Web site: Do you know where Raino's studio lay localized? Near Regulator Street in Flemings-berg. If you accompany this street to the west it changes its name to Health Street. If you then twist yourself to the right on Katrinebergs Street and continue forward to Mellan-bergs Street, and then give way to the right and traverse Nibble Hill . . . Guess where you're standing? Chestnut Street! A coincidence, or a sign of fate? Who can separate them? (By the way, do you know how many Chestnut Streets there are in Sweden? Fifty-six! All of these patterns are almost beginning to scare me. To where will this journey be terminated?)

filled with contempt. Accompanied by thoughts like: What do these sumptuously bred, monotonous politicizers know about life? Why do they think they have the patent of truth? Why do they regard me with disappointment when I express my disinclination to name Sadat as an abandoner, just because he is seeking the path of compromise? And why do they persist in constantly, constantly pointing out to me the heavenliness of baklava and the deepness of *The bloody goddamn Prophet*? I am truly starting to be filled up to here with that book. Why doesn't anyone want to discuss anything but the Middle East or baklava? Why doesn't anyone want to discuss Otis Redding? Why can we not, just for tonight, release the chains of politics, ignore the starving children of Africa, and invest our collected economy in sumptuously bubbling punch bowls? And perhaps discuss Otis's motive for singing "sitting on" in the first verse and then in the last verse "sitting AT the dock of the bay"? Why can't we humans ever satisfy ourselves with the littles of life?

Excuse all of my characters, Kadir. But I have no other friends to share my words with. And to be able to return to the familiar sphere of Arabic is divinely liberating. So far my Swedish knowledge is very limited.

Abbas[7]

---

7. Before we wander further I want to repeat you something vital: ALL potential information about Tunisia's contemporary political situation MUST, for reasons you are surely aware of, be excluded from the book. This is a piece of advice that must become your law, Jonas. It is vital, central, and concentrated that we do not in ANY way, under ANY circumstances, happen to smuggle political views of today's Tunisia into the book. I presume that I have your understanding about why? You are not solitary in having a Tunisian passport that can cause complications . . .

Stockholm, July 22, 1978
Greetings, Kadir!

Summer is here! Birds are chirping, lilacs are smelling, and Pernilla has become my official wife! In her cautiously growing stomach she bears my future child! Our collective future is securitized!

We promised each other our eternal promises in a simple ceremony in the courthouse; Pernilla's two beard-brothers witnessed our joy, but her parents had unfortunately enough been struck by double influenza. This did not dim anyone's celebration (particularly not mine). Pernilla's friends cheered our alliance and presented us multitudes of presents: handmade rag rugs, incense burners, Indian shawls, and a darbouka drum. After the ceremony we marched home to the apartment and delighted a quiet evening with salmon pasta and wine.

Pernilla and I are very, very happy and our happy joy is spread to the maximized joy of the general public.[8] After our promised alliance, Pernilla and I were invited to the Swedish authorities to be interviewed about our marriage. We were conducted to different rooms, I with an interpreter, Pernilla without.

We were served coffee by smiling suit wearers and interpellated about our respective habits. What does Pernilla intake for breakfast? How often does she brush her teeth? What time does she usually yield her body to sleep? What color does her potential room robe bear? How was she draped when you met for the first time? Their ambition, of course, was to guarantee that our alliance was not motivated by my hunger for a Swedish residency permit.

When we came out of our rooms, Pernilla's cheeks bore a lobsterish red color. She called their questions insulting and yelled, *"Eins, zwei, drei, Nazipolizei,"* to the confused receptionist.

---

8. Here your father atrocities a certain wordly repetition, but I am letting his mistakes be translated for you word-faithfully.

Of course the interviews grew an unpleasant emotion in me as well. But on the metro's way home I reminded her that Sweden happens to be a country that bears a peculiar organizational ambition. And to guarantee itself that marriages are honestly meant is probably not automatically incorrect. Or? Am I wrong? Pernilla did not respond me.

Another thing has been perceived me since my alliance with Pernilla and my first rendezvous with her reluctant parents: An economy is vital in order to receive the respect of the Swedes and leave the pigeonhole of the immigrant. The winner takes it all, as ABBA sings. The winner really does take it all, and the winner will be me, Kadir. This is my secure certainty, and my desire for success is fed by my beautiful-mother's *manière* of speaking to me like an imbecile and refusing to understand my English. Certainly it is a bit twisted, but NOT worse than hers.

My beautiful-mother's name is Ruth. Her makeup is in deep quantity; she often repeats me that she comes from a noblish history in Denmark with strong Christian values and that she certainly doesn't oppose immigrants in Sweden just as long as they conduct themselves properly and learn Swedish and do not cement their traditions. Then her cigarette-wrinkly mouth gaps smile and inform me that the evening's dinner unfortunately contains pork and will that be a problem for "our guests from far away"?

Of course I answer "No," and Pernilla looks strongly ashamed. My relationship with my beautiful-father, Gösta, is simpler. He is an aged road worker with a beard and a crooked body who has passed a great deal of his life constructing roads and bridges. After a handicapturing accident, he has pensioned his body ahead of time and now runs a store south of Stockholm where he offers a broad quantity of antique signs for sale.

At times I have assisted him with the renovation of his store-room and our cooperation always takes place in exceptional silence; from his welcoming "Good day" to his farewelling "Good-bye" we most often share nothing more than gestures and pointings. But it is a silence that is of goodwill and understanding rather than the pressing silence that characterizes Swedish elevators.

In order to secure my future family's finances, I am also working as a dishwasher at a restaurant on Rådmansgatan. That position is exceedingly short-term, however, because my Swedish premier collection will soon be prepared. It is now called *The Topographic Proof of Stockholm* (as a reference to Atget's *Les épreuves topographiques de Paris*). I affix to you some photographic samples. Hasn't my talent flourished since my departure? Which motif is your favorite? Mine is probably the crying girl with the petal in her hair.

During the coming fall I will present my collection to galleries and let them battle for my artistic representation. I only hope that those who are denied my talent do not become too disappointed.

I hope your life portions my life's fortunate development!

Abbas[9]

---

9.   Here follows a six-month letterish pause between me and your father. By the way: That your father's English was "twisted" is an excess that we can call exaggeration. It is, of course, yet another example of your father's notorious modesty. His English was and is excellent, just like his French and Spanish. "Few men share this man's tonguely talent for languages!" auctioned Qaddafi in a speech of praise to your father when he was delegated Libya's official photo prize recently.

Stockholm, January 20, 1979
Greetings, Kadir!

Visualize the photos of my newborn son!!! I have become a father!!!
His name is Jonas in the Swedish version and Younes in the Arabic. His nationality will be doubly Swedish and Tunisian. His mentality will be diagonally opposite of the man who died the same day he was born. Is it not symbolic that Houari Boumediène died on December 27, 1978? Exactly the same day that my son was born! This day will truly be preserved in the calendar of history: a radical's death and a future cosmopolitan's birth!

Forgive me if this letter is confused. My happiness is indescribable. My position as a dishwasher will soon be paused in order to be a house dad! Pernilla will initiate her education to be a nurse and I will pass all free time with my firstborn son. I will mash own-made purées and delight the exclusive Swedish parental leave. I will proudly push my stroller through bird-tweeting parks. And furthermore, I have smoked my absolute last cigarette! It was a piece of cake to terminate that unnecessarily expensive habit.

My happiness is indescribable. My wife is as dear to me as usual. The only conflict we have is about finances. Since my son's birth, she has with subtle indications pointed out the importance that I begin to perfection my Swedish. She has presented me with multitudes of forms from the teaching institute and repeated the mantra that Swedish in Sweden is a very vital knowledge. She has pointed out that I have now passed a long time here and only achieved a position as a part-timely dishwasher and working-for-free studio assistant.

We have decided the following: If my next photographic collection does not result in more interest, my tongue will dedicate night and day to perfectioning Swedish. Swedish is a complicated language, but extremely delicious with a hoppy tone that resembles the melodic song of small birds. My happiness is indescribable, by the way!

Abbas

PS: Do not feel unease about your finances; the loan will soon be returned. You do not need to correspond me more reminders about the development of the interest.[10]

———————————

10.   Your father actually repeated "my happiness is indescribable" triangularly in the same letter. Do you realize, then, what an indescribable happiness your birth gave him? He lived in a divine bubble the evening he returned from the hospital after your birth. He has described how, the entire first night, he parked his body at your kitchen window, stared at the desolation of the yard, toasted himself to tears, and chorused along with Stevie Wonder's "Isn't She Lovely?" (He just replaced "she" with "he.") That for you he focused more on the disappointment you brought him is something that he presumably regrets. Here follows yet another pause in my correspondence with your father. During this time Tabarka's tourist industry grows. I polish my career from kitchen-responsible to pool-responsible to planner of dance competitions. In parallel Swedish time, your father maximizes his attempts to sparkle his photographic career. While your mother recovers her strength after your delivery, your father passes his time at the restaurant on Rådmansgatan. He cleans the greenness of the carpets of gum, he glitters the toilet's shine forth from vomit, he searches under the coatroom's counter in pursuit of forgotten one-crown coins. In the afternoons he assists Raino's developed entrecôtes and adjusts the light and contrast of fish soups and desserts. On the weekends he combs his curly coiffure, puts on his beret, and wanders his steps from gallery to gallery both in Gamla Stan and on Hornsgatan. His two prepared photographic collections lie ready in his portfolio. His fingers sink door handles, bells jingle; black-polo-shirted gallery owners with big plastic lunettes receive him, smiling nervously, browse his portfolio, hmm their approval, and accept his homemade business card. They praise his talent. They promise potential cooperation. But . . .just before he goes, they ask, of course, the oh-so-vital-for-Swedes question of national background. And your father's tongue auctions with more and more tired voice that his roots are unimportant for his photographic ambition. The gallery owners excuse themselves and promise their effective telephone calling. Relieved, your father goes home to his wife and auctions: Soon my career will find its gallop!

Is it not bizarre that your father, who would later expose suspicion toward everything and everyone, actually seems to believe the gallery owners' words? Perhaps the desire to believe was so well formed that no alternatives were provided to him? Because do you know how many gallery owners picked up the phone and called your father?

Not a single one.

The years pass.

In 1982 your father transforms himself from dishwasher to metro driver for Stockholm Public Transit, SL. He receives his position after having passed a Swedish test by actively reflecting his glance toward his neighbor's paper . . .

Here I suggest that you inject your three earliest memories of your father. Do you feel ready? Good luck!

The first memory is from day care, and you're lying hidden in the pillow room after having fought with someone, probably that jerk Gabriel. You have shuddery breathing from crying and you're waiting for Dads and plugging in your invisibility shield and thinking about the difference between various parents. Normal parents are like Gabriel's, dim gray shadows with brown coats and creaky voices who tiredly pick up their children and disappear out into the fog. But Dads eclipse the sun in a bright Djurgård scarf; Dads, who will soon come roaring with laughter into the pillow room with a beret on, who will start a tickle attack and pretend to take pictures of you with fingers and thumbs made into a rectangle. Dads charm pretend-angry day care ladies and use their shoulders to carry you all the way home. And normal parents have reading glasses, and they yawn and watch Eurovision and Tipsextra soccer matches on TV. While Dads subscribe to *Current Photography,* where the classic photos are so beautiful that Dads sometimes stop short in the middle of their homage speeches and tear their eyes. And normal parents work normal jobs and fantasize about normal charter vacations and normal Volvos. But Dads dream about changing ART forever, and every time they say "art" they say it in French and pronounce it with an a that's elongated times four. *L'aaaaaaart.* Dads always talk about new plans for how they will follow in the great photographers' footsteps. Dads have namely switched homelands in order to spread their photographic talent in foreign lands, just like the Roberts Capa and Frank and Philippe Halsman and Yousuf Karsh. ALL great photographers work in exile, shout Dads and give more example names than you can remember. Because normal parents have normal heroes like soccer players or politicians or the comedians in Monty Python. But the idols that Dads have have changed the history of photography. And not just photography, Dads shout. Because photography is art and art is seeing and seeing is the world! And not just history, because history is the future and the future is history, and you remember what Cartier-Bresson said about our relation to history, right? We erase the past but it returns as burps. You remember, right? And of course you remember and you nod proudly because normal parents don't know any photographer quotes and when they go to the city they melt into the masses and when they crack their knuckles it sounds like quieter than when you break tiny toothpicks in airless Star Wars space. But when Dads go to the city people turn their heads out of joint and when Dads crack their fingers the noise is the ultimate hugest cracking sound, like if you break dry twigs or drive a monster truck into a mountain bunker and then close the door like on a safety deposit box and then slowly start to pull the hand brake. CLICK CLICK CLICK so that it thunders in your ears. And just then you hear Dads' voice out in the hall and you know who it is because the voice shouts: Hello, you damn fools! And right after that it always gets a little quiet because the day care ladies never know how to answer.

The second memory comes from the time when Dads had just started driving subways and sitting at the gates and waking up sleeping drunk men at last stops. It's the time when Dads stamp tickets and guide German tourists out of the labyrinthine platform at Kung-

strädgården. It's Dads who find left-behind evening
papers and rattle their gigantic bunches of keys where
the solution to everything is found, where the ʟ key
opens the door to the driver's compartment between
the cars when the train is too full and the square key
opens the door on the escalator when hooligans have
pushed the emergency stop. Dads unlock, make the
escalator go, and return the grateful smiles of baby-
carriage parents.

It's the time when Dads let you skip day care even
though of course they understand that you're faking
being sick to avoid hanging out with Gabriel and the
others. As soon as Moms have disappeared running to
the bus with their marmalade toast half eaten and the
kisses on their cheeks half pecked, you fly up out of
your bed and give a thumbs-up to Dads in the kitchen.
Then you go to work together and Dads introduce you
proudly to the others in the lunchroom: *Voici mon fils*
and partner. Stefan with the horse-racing coupons and
Jeffrey who drinks coffee from a plastic bottle are there,
and Aziz, who is half Dads' size and has a big Afro and
always wants to talk pop artists you haven't heard of.
Then you go down to the trains and you hold Dads'
rough hands and Dads say that everyone else at SL is
a complete loser, they'll never get out of here, they're
content to just drive trains back and forth, they are the
"generality of commonness," Dads say and look proud
about having mixed a little proper Swedish into the
French-Arabic.

Dads let you open the side door to the cockpit with
the ʟ key, and soon you're riding at the very front
through endless tunnels, and sometimes, only sometimes, you get to call the name of the station over the

loudspeaker system. And Dads always choose stations with both *r* and *s* in the name because then the effect is extra funny for both of you. "Next thtation Wopthten! All pathengew exit the twain, pleathe!" And Dads just have time to release the microphone button before you fall together in a laugh attack and you remember the dark and the shadows and the quiet swishing of the lights, and no matter how much you laugh, Dads never lose control of the double-connected hand accelerator.

It's Dads in the blue polyester suit and the cap with the silver SL logo on the front. Dads who carefully save tip money. Dads who have stopped marketing their collections for fake-smiling gallery owners. Dads say: "As long as one goes via the establishment one is never free; one must stand solitary in order to be able to transform one's future. That is why I am going to start my own studio. I am tired of being dependent on others and now it is up to your father to realize his dream and . . . oops, now we're getting close, are you ready?"

And you let yourself be lifted up onto the stool by the shadow-silhouetty bending microphone with segmented metal stripes like a steel worm, and when Dads give the sign you call out, "Next thtation Öthtewmalmthtowy."

Dads laugh until their eyes tear up while the train hisses on, rushes itself though the tunnel with white laser-light lamps, and suddenly you leave the solar system; you and Dads are lone cosmonauts in outer galaxies and Dads are Shoobacka and you are Varth Dader, and together you're going to get fuel on a supersecret planet that's light-years from here, and it's almost an photography is a true art because photography can lie. And Dads tell about August Sander's photographic catalog of the German people and Atget's gray Paris photos and Abbott, who captured all the nuances of New York. And in particular you remember how Dads' eyes shine when they tell about Capa, Robert Capa with the velvet gaze, the world's greatest war photographer, who was born in Budapest and who, in exile, developed his own way to speak, which his friends called Capanese. And here you always interrupt and say: But Dad, you have your own language, too! And Dads answer with a smile because what is more welcome than similarities to heroes? Besides, it's true, because normal parents either speak Swedish or Not Swedish, but only Dads have their own language, only Dads speak Khemirish. A language that is all languages combined, a language that is extra everything with changes in meaning and strangewords put together, special rules and daily exceptions. A language that is Arabic swearwords, Spanish question words, French declarations of love, English photography quotations, and Swedish puns. A language where g and h rumble way down in your stomach, where you always "walk" abroad instead of traveling, where toys must always be picked up from the "ground." A language where *"daccurdo"* means "okay" and "herb salt" is synonymous with "really good" (just because Moms love herb salt on popcorn). Treatment of illnesses is called "Vicks friction" and to rub in cream is to "Pond-ize" and to eat muesli with jam is to eat "TSO" (or "the same old"). Something soft is "Pernillish" and something sad is "extra blue" and something that is super great is "excellent!" When you greet someone you roar, "Hello, you throw in the developer and start to agitate and tell the story of how one time in Tabarka he accidentally started with the fixer and the customer was a rich German tourist and Dads laugh and shake the spiral box while you let your gaze wander between all the cutout photos from *Current Photography*'s classics series that are nailed up on the wall. There's that sailor who left his super-flexible nurse wife and then regretted it and now he's back in the city and they're kissing each other for the first time and the girl bends her back backward like a bridge and people in the neighborhood are so impressed that they throw small bits of paper and yell hooray and have started a big carnival on the street. And there's that poor blurry soldier who's being forced to walk in a gray sea up to his waist as punishment for stealing a medal from his general and you can see how angry the soldier is because in the background there are metal islands, boats, and a regular beach. And there's the poor white-haired, bearded old man with laced fingers and leathery hands whom Dads call Einstein. He's waiting for his grandchildren, who never want to come visit because they're tired of how he always slurps his soup and needs help both putting on his slippers and trimming his mustache. Hello, are you listening? ask Dads and of course you nod while the instructions continue, pour the fixer back, rinse carefully for twenty minutes, open, dry, wash the equipment, prepare for copying. The developer fluid in the red, stop in the blue, fixer in the white, never mix together and never use tools in more than one chemical and remember to be careful because they're flammable chemicals and one little mistake can destroy a future masterpiece and . . . The air begins to get humid.

The mirror steams up. The chemicals stink. But still there's nowhere you'd rather be.

Dads are kneeling in front of the chemical basins with their butt cracks showing. Dads swear. And you are back with the old man Einstein; he twists his mustache and winks at you and says that you look brave sitting there in your long underwear, huddled on the flushing box of the toilet. The light is going to be turned off again soon, but you don't need to be afraid, okay? It's not dangerous, you know, dark is exactly like light, only it's, hmm, a little less light? And he smiles his toothless hobo smile and the sailor, who's done kissing, gives you a thumbs-up with one hand and pinches the nurse's behind with the other and the soldier in the water waves to you and . . . Who are you talking to? Listen instead! Dads continue swearing about the bad copy machine, adjusting the aperture, dodging themselves sweaty. And finally on the fourth try the contours of the perfect copy emerge. Yet another snowed-over bicycle has been documented. Excellent! yell Dads.

Khemirish is Dads' language and the family's language; it's a language that is only yours, that no one else owns, and that you will never show anyone (until now?).

Dearest greetings!

Thank the correspondence of your three earliest memories. Hmm . . . I presume that we will class this text as preliminary and in need of a great deal of polishing? Why have you decided to describe yourself as "you" instead of "I"? Why do you write "Dads" instead of "Dad"? Is this carelessness, or intention? The quality of the text can be substantially stimulated, with my opinion, with a more classic form, à la "Oh, my father, let me now form my first memories of my great hero . . ."

Did this take you three weeks to formulate? Now I am starting to realize what you mean about being "sooooo not pumped" to write your secondary book. It must be so much easier to accuse one's dear author colleague of insufficient honesty and competence . . . Is it not tempting to mask one's own inability by aggressively attacking others'? Because is that not what you are doing? In the next message you are welcome to disambiguate your ambiguity. First you hail your father's poetic letters. You write that my translation is reminiscent of the professionalism of BabelFish and you write that their injection into the book would be like "gilding the lily." What is more beautiful than a gilded lily? Then your tone suddenly becomes harsh and sharp. You write that now it is your turn to participate more in the book and you suddenly accuse your father's letterish writing style of being "suspiciously like" mine? Let me response like this:

1. Your father wrote me in Arabic. I have translated the letters to Swedish. That my linguistic tone could not be modified from its foundations in order to PRECISELY capture your father's phrases is a surprise that we should call entirely expected. I write with those knowledges of the Swedish language which I have at my disposal. My effective time in Sweden was limited and I am aware that I cause certain grammatical glides.

It would not raise my eyebrows if you were to find three defects in each document! But it would detach my eyebrows if these defects were to grow your doubt about my honest ambition.

2. But . . . With the ideal of honesty I must simultaneously admit that you are correct when you write that your father's letters are not ENTIRELY objective from my influence. Certainly I have SOMETIMES let a little Kadir be injected. For example, I embroidered the text with certain life-giving metaphors (see: your mother's crying hand likened "as a car's wind-shield wipers"). I also amplified the visuality (see: your mother's shined smile at Central Station). But I have not modified ANYTHING that your father would oppose, I know this with voluminous certainty. That is how well I know his soul. He often talked about how your mother's smiling lines could placate everyone from social-service ladies to metro inspectors to police to camera sellers. And incidentally this is what he wrote in an e-mail in 2002, just home from a photo session with the Dalai Lama: "But his [the Dalai Lama's] smiling power could still not measure up to Pernil-la's. Certain smiles shine like suns; others like stars. But only one smile presents its rays with radioactive volume." If I have amplified your father's letters in order to truly reflect his opinion, then a streak of fantasy cannot really be called dis-honesty. Right?

3. Of course it is now your turn to take over the baton of the narrative. Prior to the triangular section of the book it is dele-gated wholeheartedly to you, which is perfect because the rela-tionship between your father and me is frozen to stillness during the coming years, a little like a paused DVD.

.   .   .

Feel free to correspond me your developing text, and I will promise you prominent, not to say exalted, commentary. As inspiration for your continued work I affix to you a text that forms your father's dramatic return to Tunisia in 1984.

Your charming friend,
Kadir

After a lengthy illness, old Faizal farewelled this earth in the spring of 1984. Abbas returned to Jendouba to participate in the funeral. I myself could not take time off from the Hôtel Majestique because of the tragic poker misfortunes of my latest period. The cards had tortured more than stimulated me, and I was forced to work very harshly in order to be able to pay back my latest losses. Patiently I awaited your father in Tabarka, in the hope that he would convey my loaned economy.

One cold February twilight, a taxi retired outside the entrance to Hôtel Majestique, and out journeyed your father's silhouette, clad in dark brown Ray-Bans, grown-out hair, and a light blue T-shirt from the magazine *Current Photography* on which the letters spelled forth: "Photographers make it a memory for life."

"Abbas!" I cried happily, and our arms hugged each other, accompanied by repeated confirmations of each other's health. Then we released each other and your father observed me. He was just about to formulate something; his lips circled themselves, but no sound came. In the next second his legs swerved sideways. His body timber-fell toward the sidewalk, and his near fainting was my fact. I supported him into the foyer on shaking legs and parked him in the leather sofa that was actually reserved for guests. His cheeks bore a pale color and it seemed to hurt to separate his adhered lips.

"What has happened to you?" I asked, again and again. "Is it the funeral of Faizal that has ached you so much? Or is it the return visit of Jendouba? Calm my unease, my dear best friend."

Your father collected his nerves, cooled his throat with a few gulps of water, and began his story. I remember his words like this:

"Excuse me, Kadir. I am very glad to see you again, do not believe otherwise. But to see Jendouba again was a very suffocating process. I really understand why you do not return. To participate in Faizal's funeral awoke an inexplicably strong emotion in my breast. The tears welled my eyes in rivers, and my leg muscles betrayed me cyclically just like here. That he was not my real father could not comfort me. I do not know why the consequence was so great."

Your father was interrupted by some drunk Dutchmen who bellowed their happiness from the bar over a soccer goal. He continued with a steadier voice:

"After the funeral I did not find any peace. Of course, I portioned my sorrow with everyone else; of course, it was happiness to see Cherifa again. But every day our sorrow was disturbed by afflicting neighbors and poor families with hopeful expectations that my saved Swedish finances had been maximized to that of a millionaire. They knocked the door and interpellated me about investment aid for taxis, finances for cheese factories or travels abroad, bribes for visas or for supporting their cousin's children's study diplomas. Even our old friends from the orphanage days were looking forward to sumptuous presents as a matter of routine. Dhib and Sofiane, Amine and Omar, not one understood that I have my own family and that my finances might not measure up to JR's in the TV series *Ewings*. Do you know that TV series, by the way?"

(Your father really did say *Ewings* but was referring to the series *Dallas,* of course. I did not want to correct him right then.)

"Anyway, it is a big success in Sweden; Pernilla and I observe it every Saturday evening when Jonas has gone to sleep. It is about JR and Bobby and an alcoholic woman by the name Sue Ellen. The music sounds about like this: daa-da-daaa-dadadadadaaa . . . ?"

"Abbas . . . weren't you going to relate the background of your mental imbalance?"

Your father quieted his song.

"You are right, Kadir. Excuse me. You are truly the only person in the world who sees through my attempts at dodging. Let me instead tell you about the true background of my confusion. It happened this morning . . . It was the souk in Jendouba. As usual, the city was full of agricultural families who auctioned peppers and figs, apples and pears, wagonloads of golden melons. Salesmen's throats roared sweetness of peaches, durability of lightbulbs, softness of rugs. Bananas and green cubes of washing soap, veils and spice buckets and extra-fresh goats at the price of the sale . . ."

(Yet again your father tried to evade in a drawn-out description of the souk. You have, of course, visited Jendouba during the souk? Feel free to inject your own memories of the market—just remember that this is 1984. Subtract consequently all commerce of neon yellow cell phone covers, batteries, Eminem T-shirts, and fake Nike shoes.) Finally I interrupted your father:

"Abbas . . . get to the point."

"Yes. Sorry. Here it comes. Anyway, this morning I wandered my steps toward the *louage* station, happy that I could leave the city. My camera was escorted as usual on my chest. Suddenly I noticed a dispute between a street boy and a potbellied seller of saucepans. Here is photographic potential, I thought, levitating my camera and assuming a perfect angle."

"Well?"

Your father took his bracing in order to be able to terminate the story.

"I adjusted the focus and discharged the camera at the exact second that a face wandered right in and blocked my motif. His head bore a twisted, worn keffiyeh; his bagging blue jacket was combined with thin drawstring pants. In his hand he transported a foot-borne turkey which gesticulated its arms. I lowered the camera with an insultation ready on my tongue. Our eyes were reflected in each other. A few seconds' searching, and then my insight struck with the power of a waterfall. 'RACHID!' roared my tongue so that the potbellied man shortstopped himself in his kicking series against the shorts-clad rear of the street urchin. 'RACHID!!!'"

"Your antique neighbor from Algeria?"

"Yes! First he seemed to mistake himself for someone else. He accelerated his steps to running speed and refused to give hearing to his name. But I caught up with him and captured his shoulder: 'Hello! It is me! Abbas! Haifa's son. Whom you saved from a sure death!' Rachid stopped, out of breath, focused me from toe to top, and cracked up his smile.

" 'My dear boy, you have been transformed to a man! And you are not angry with me?'

" 'Angry? How could I be angry?' For a long time we hugged each other, teared our eyes, and returned our greetings. All while the turkey cawed confusion and wobbled its throat."

"Did he look as you remembered him?"

"Well, the tooth of time had munched a festive breakfast on his exterior; the sun wrinkles hung heavy over his furrowed eye corners, his black beard shone gray, and his shoulders had thinned to the boy size."

"Then when happened?"

"We accompanied our steps to a café, where we shared our résumés. Rachid was very impressed by my life. 'Who could believe this when we farewelled each other in Cherifa's yard?' he said. 'That you would live in Sweden, have a stately stature and a photographic career?'

" 'And that you would bear your exterior with the same youth as always,' I responded.

" 'Thank you very much, you well-mannered liar.' We laughed in stereo and the atmosphere was excellent."

"It sounds like a perfect rendezvous. Right?"

Your father extincted his smile.

"It was a perfect rendezvous. Until I happened to ask Rachid whether he was acquainted with anything about my real father's news. I interpellated whether my father's life was ended like Ali Boumendjel's, or whether he is perhaps living in luxury somewhere in the world. Rachid fixed his eyes on the horizon and let his lungs produce a deep sigh.

" 'Your father . . . dear Moussa. Is your separation not tragic?'

" 'Please, Rachid, tragicness exists to be overcome. This is my life philosophy. But are you acquainted with any information about his present existence?' Rachid's face looked ashamed.

" 'I promised your father, you know . . . to assist you if anything happened . . . He had given me the pay of advance . . . But I didn't have any chance myself to . . . Well . . . Of course I couldn't take care of you alone . . . After all the rumors that Haifa had spread. And the economy he left behind was barely enough for . . . My hope is for your broad and eternal understanding?'

" 'Of course, of course . . . My understanding is wide as a soccer field,' I noted impatiently. 'But my father . . . Moussa . . . do you know if he survived his journey abroad?'

"Rachid observed the angles of both of his shoulders and then gave a close-leaned whisper.

" 'I believe that your father is alive . . . but under a modified identity in a secret place . . . '

"My nervousness throbbed when I asked:

" 'And do you know which name is his name now?'

" 'According to the rumors, he names himself . . . What was it now . . . Ron Arm Stuntech. I think.'

"With the beating of my heart and my tongue sticky, I wrote the name on a scrap. Rachid leaned back and looked like someone who had settled the payment of a long debt. Before we . . ."

"Speaking of debt and payment . . . ," I interrupted your father.

"SHUT UP!" your father cried. "Do not interrupt me now! Before we separated our paths, I asked Rachid if he knew why my father had delegated me a chestnut that time we saw each other so many years ago. Rachid observed me with a sorrowful face.

" 'When you saw each other?'

" 'Yes, my father gave me a chestnut when he afflicted us in my childhood . . .'

" 'But . . . Your father never afflicted you. You have never spent time at any restaurant. He did not have any lifeguards. You must be remembering wrong. You must have fantasized that . . . Just like Haifa, you have perhaps been infected with that infection which has always characterized your family—the one where the forms of fantasy are given life in excess and in dangerous cases collide with reality.'

" 'But . . . then how do you explain this chestnut?' I roared in desperation, and tore the chestnut from my pocket.

" 'Hmm . . . perhaps you found it yourself in your yard?'

"These words lurched my entire existence. Suddenly all the details of my life seemed to be suspiciously slipping and uncertain. What else could I have fantasized? What else can be untrue that is reality in my thoughts? In a last effort to find assurance I quieted my questions, localized Rachid's body near mine, and eternalized us with a sequence of photos. After this we said our good-byes. Rachid wandered his steps back up toward the souk, waving a humoristic farewell with one of the turkey's wings. Then he was gone. And I was alone with my confusion."

"But not totally alone!" I placated.

"Actually, yes, Kadir. Totally alone."

"But you have your family. And me!"

"Yes, but . . . who knows . . . Perhaps you are not real, either?"

We reflected each other's pupils and then broke the silence with a tension-breaking laugh attack.

"HA HA! That was a humor that we can call extremely comical."

Your father stuffed the paper scrap with his father's alias in his wallet.

"What are you going to do now?"

"I don't know," your father said tiredly. "But if this is Moussa's new name I should try to localize him. Sometime. In the future. A son and a father must never separate their relationship, no matter what the magnitude of conflict."

Abbas and I passed four days' nostalgia in Tabarka. We afflicted restaurants, summarized memories, joke-uttered our antique pickup routines. Your father did not sexualize any touristettes. Even if frequent invitations were given. Then your father informed me that he still lacked the capacity to repay me my economy. Then he said:

"But feel no doubt, Kadir. Success is waiting 'around the corner,' as one expresses in Swedish."

Then we said our farewells.

You can conclude metaphorically:

"Without his family, Abbas felt holey in symbolic form. A little like the cheese that the Swiss eat on mountaintops in the company of yodely watch sellers and professional chocolate designers. Kadir noted a parallel emotion from never recovering his finances."

As a farewell gift, your father delegated me a sagging envelope with photographs. In it were numberous photos of your steadily growing body, your cramped apartment, your mother with those gigantic seventies eyeglasses and her hippie shawl, your father's growing record collection, your Swedish relatives' country cottage. As well as a portrait where your father shared his company with his colleagues at the metro company SL. He was standing straight-backedly positioned in a coldly shining coffee room in his metro getup with a blue suit and pointed hat with the silver logo. The last photo made me a bit sorrowful. Your father's mouth showed the sort of smile that most resembles a grimace.

Now it is up to you. Do you feel prepared? My hope is for your emphatically positive YES! So that you do not stray yourself in side-tracks, I propose to you to structure your memories as follows: Begin with your father's homecoming and the information about your mother's pregnancy. Then possibly something about "the dynamic duo." What was this phenomenon, exactly? Your father mentioned it, but I never understood its exact meaning. Terminate the triangular section with the description of your brothers' delivery and your grandfather's tragic death.

PART THREE

So now you're sitting there, just back from a reading in Södertälje, with a paper-wrapped bouquet and a book about rune stones by a local author. You read Kadir's commentary and feel an aching sinking feeling in your stomach, the kind of sinking that says that this will never work, that you're not ready, that instead you should concentrate on working more on one of the other projects. The ones where you devote time to thinking up plots, where the characters are just inventions, and a moderate amount of peripety can be injected in just the right place. And you have just finished writing the sentence when you realize that "inject" is Kadir's word and not yours, that it's his language that has started to influence you, and then your doubt gets even stronger. Because how good an idea is actually a collaboratively written book?[11] You read his latest mail again and decide to give it yet another try. You take a deep breath and make use of his instructions . . .

Dads' homecomings. There are so many. But this one must be when they came home in the spring of 1984. Moms have taken time off from their jobs as stewardesses even though of course they're really "airborne people's representatives of the overexploited service sector." On the same day that Dads are supposed to

---

11.   BRILLIANT!!!

come home you borrow Grandpa's car and have a winter picnic by the lake Trekanten. You slide around on the ice together and play Bambi and drink hot chocolate way too fast from the thermos and so you get that special rough tongue that in Khemirish is called "picnic tongue." Even though it's wintery cold, Moms have green sunglasses, which are as big and round as boat windows, and over their hair are the thin shawls, which you can borrow and put over your eyes so the smell is Moms' and your nose is coldly rough and the world is light blue with gold stripes. You can still see Moms' contours where they're standing farther away against the light, the world's most beautiful Moms, who are taller than regular Dads and who have purses as big as hockey bags and always have to have their seats in the car as far back as they go to have room for their legs.

After refueling and candy buying you go back to nervously waiting Grandpa; you sit in front and are on police lookout while Bob Marley clunks himself out of the speakers and careless drivers roar-brake and taxis honk and bus drivers blink their headlights. Because Moms persist in driving at speeds that make the Toyota's glove box open and sometimes Moms happen to signal left turns by turning on the windshield driers instead of the blinkers, and all the road signs are mostly like recommendations, and sometimes you drive one way for several blocks and sometimes you back out onto major roads and Moms just smile at shaking fists and honk back with a little melody. Then Moms continue to tell you about the order of power in the world. Everything in life is politics and nothing is a coincidence and that is why we will never fill up at Shell because they support apartheid in South Africa. To choose a party is politics and to choose gas is politics and to choose friends is politics and . . . Candy? you ask. Yes, even choosing candy is politics. Here, give me the bag and I'll show you . . . You reluctantly hand over the bag of candy. If all this is the Western world's money, then this raspberry boat is the poor world's money. Do you understand? Injustice is everywhere; everything is power structures and nothing that we see in this corrupt society is real. Everything is imperialism's damned attempts to keep us quiet. TV is opium for the people and your father is a bit of a dreamer, but you can never let yourself be fooled. And you quickly take back the bag of candy and say: But what about *Dallath*? Because you watch that series together every Saturday. And Moms explain that *Dallas* is like a terrible warning about how the system of capitalism distorts people's brains. And besides, that Bobby is a real hunk, Moms add, and laugh their bubbly laughs while you skid up onto the E4 highway.

Soon the police car rumbles up in the rearview mirror and it shines its sirens and Moms swear behind smiling lips because they have just played the zigzag game between the centerline dashes or considered doing a U-turn on the highway. And as usual you do the routine where you play sick and whimper while Moms slow down, roll down the window, and: Excuse me, Officer, my son doesn't feel well and of course you may see my driver's license. Moms look through their entire gigantic handbag a second time and it rustles and jingles, but too bad. I must have forgotten my billfold at home. Again. And then the smile that melts all policemen in all parts of the world, and the policeman clears his throat and looks toward his colleague in the car and says: All right, but try to keep on the correct side of the centerline in the future.

And Moms promise and wish him a good afternoon and dump the handbag back over onto you. And you remember how weird it seems that the police always fall for the trick because even before Moms have rolled up the window they shout SUCKER! and gas away from the scene of the crime in second gear. Also, Moms' handbags are a little like Noah's ark because there are at least two copies of everything in there: billfolds of soft Indian leather, Band-Aid packages, loose change and old SL tickets, house keys and fliers from demonstrations, nail scissors and nail clippers, packets of tissues and rolled-up extra socks, old Läkerol lozenges, and a few bags of green tea in a plastic bag. But the only thing that isn't there is a driver's license, because it was confiscated by that class-traitor policeman two summers ago.

Then you're back at Grandma and Grandpa's and Grandpa is swearing because the antenna is bent and the choke has been pulled out all day and Moms are swearing about Grandpa having the energy to care about something so worldly and then you take the commuter train home to the apartment to wait for Dads.

It's Sunday evening and Moms are freshly showered and have gone from robe to clothes instead of to the nightgown with Chinese embroidery. The apartment is newly cleaned, with newly smoothed newspapers as a shoe mat and newly lit fancy incense on the special dish in the kitchen and a filled fruit basket, and Moms with evening perfume. At eight o'clock it's *Cosby* and you ask Moms: Is this capitalist propaganda too? And Moms smile and say: Not too much. So you keep watching while the clock ticks in the kitchen. You're waiting for

Dads, who have been home in Tunisia to bury Grandpa. But Dads are late and while Moms start to call Arlanda to check the delays, you crawl down on the floor and growl the noise of superstrong jet engines. It's the old apartment from below; the scratched coffee-table legs and the parquet squares on the floor which are the perfect pattern for car races in angular figure eights with garage spots in the secret underground tunnels of the rag rug. It's one gummy Ferrari against another and they are different colors and they're sitting ready at the starting line and belching their motors. It's the red Ferrari against the black one, and of course the black one is theirs, the bad guys', U.S.A.–sponsored and capitalistic and full of Shell gas. And the red one is yours, the good guys', righteously communistic, *halal* from the headlights to the trunk, full of Arabian gas and Arabian horsepower. Fatima's hand is hanging from the rearview mirror and a keffiyeh is flapping from the radio antenna. Tires that vroom, mirrored visors that are flipped down, leather gloves grip the wheel and you're sitting ready in the red Ferrari and looking at the girl who's waving her long-nailed manicure hands from the cage where she's sitting locked up over the crocodile pool. Now everything is up to you, either you win the race or we colonize new territory and she becomes crocodile food, laughs the bad guys' boss, who is called Ray Gun, where he's sitting high up on a throne with a spiked hand that's petting a black red-eyed cat and she's waving and crying and blowing you kisses and you are just about to imitate Dads' thumbs-up sign when the starting flag is waved and it starts, the audience crowd roars, gas pedals floored, and the bad guy takes the lead! Max speed through the first curve, the wheels roar on,

Marlboro ads quaver in gas fumes, the draft blows off audience toupees, curves are taken on two wheels and you ease up, the speedometer that laps itself, spinning around and around like a propeller, the red car nears the black car and on the third lap you're neck and neck and you're leading, no he is, no you, no him, and the audience screams itself hoarse and choruses your name and then you push the extra-turbo-booster and swish by him and you see him in the rearview mirror, the size of an ant, waving angrily, and it's you alone on the last lap and there's the finish and there's the referee and there's the checkered flag waving, and do you make it? Of course you do, first to the finish and then victory lap and wave to the crowd's cheers, let the girl out of the cage, foam her in champagne, be introduced to her equally beautiful twin sister, and then into the car with them to glide on to new adventures.

Uppuppupp, yell Moms when you try to put the Ferraris back into the candy bowl. Not a chance, you eat those up now. You look down at the worn-out Ferraris, dusty after the race around the parquet floor, with crooked grills and scratched hoods and strands of hair around the wheels, not at all as good as the other candy, which lies shiny and ready to go in the candy bowl. You're just about to protest and explain that your cars are used and in the next round you have to be able to upgrade when you hear the elevator noise and Moms give a start. A shadow passes the balcony walkway. But no Dads.

Moms wring their hands and look anxiously at the clock. Moms get up from the chair, make a round of the kitchen, and come back with an apple, which no one eats. Dads have disappeared.

Then, just as you're trying to smuggle the Ferraris to the flowerpot, you hear the creak of the elevator doors and the walkway door clunks and Moms meet your gaze the second before Dads stomp in through the double doors with snow crisps on their boots and their berets at an angle. HELLO, YOU DAMN FOOLS! Dads' faces are browner than usual; their teeth are shining white and their mustaches are back and they prickle you during the hug while Moms stand blurry in the background. Dads are home! Dads smell like newly tested airport perfumes and tax-free drinks, a little like wet wipes and a lot like travel sweat. As usual, Dads have gotten stuck at customs but as usual everything made it through, the new leather ottoman and the refill of olive oil and the new brik ingredients. And a candy refill for your Mickey Mouse Pez, of course. Dads say hi from Grandma and say that the funeral "went bravissimo." Then Dads look down on you where you're Velcroing yourself to their legs. With slightly anxious eyes Dads ask: And how is my Mowgli? You answer, "Jutht fine," and Dads tousle your home-trimmed bowl cut and say that you have done well, having responsibility for the family all by yourself.

Then Moms clear their throats and say something that is not "welcome home" at all. And their French voices are unusually strong and sharp and there's a word that you don't really recognize. *Enceinte*? Twins? Dads freeze their movements in the hall dimness, stop in the middle of their duffel coat removal, and let their mouths make the sound like when you create suction with the hose to clean Grandpa's aquarium. Dads stand with their berets on, snow on their duffel shoulders, and the new newspaper has gravelly shoe prints.

What are Moms saying? You don't care. Because Dads are home and you press your face harder against the duffel pocket and smell the prickly wool smell and you think that no matter what Moms say it doesn't matter because Dads are home and that's all that means anything because Dads are the world's biggest heroes and Dads are everything and Dads will never be like other dads.[12]

And you remember the coming weeks that spring, when kitchen doors are often closed and you hear French voices mostly as vibrations and it's Moms' light ones and Dads' deep ones and then silence and then Moms' light ones and then silence again. It's dinners when Dads have no appetite and sit in their workrooms instead of eating. Dads who lift a stool and move the copy machine, rolling out drawings of possible studio locations and writing in numbers on the calculator. Dads who wrinkle their foreheads and hmm their voices. While Moms remain sitting at the dinner table with their hands on their stomachs and don't answer when you ask if you may leave the table. You can tell something is going on, but you don't know what. Soon you run back and forth between the lab and the kitchen with your Mickey Mouse Pez sticking up out of your pocket. Dethewt? Want dethewt? Dads mumble numbers and Moms sigh and no one answers. You and Mickey go into the living room instead and Mickey asks: Dessert? And you answer: Yes, please, with pronuncia-

---

12. The finale is very delicious! More like this! One reminder: Memorize that it is your father who is the principal character, and not your mother. Certainly your mother is magnificent in all ways, but her magnificence can be formed another time. Perhaps in your triangular book?

tion exactly as good as regular people's, bend Mickey's head back, and feed out a raspberry-flavored rectangle candy. Mickey smiles and says: By the way, fuck all the day care idiots, just fuck their teasing and laughing because you have a special way of talking! Fuck everyone who laughed when you said that your mom was going to start her education to be a wedge-turd nurse soon. And most of all, fuck that speech therapist! And Mickey shouts his swearwords with the exact same girl voice as on the Disney hour and it sounds so funny that you laugh out loud and you push his head back again and feed out a new rectangle candy. Because this is the same spring that you visit the speech therapist for the first time, Dads, Moms, and you. The speech therapist sits there behind her tall desk and folds her hands like a priest and says with concern that your delayed speech development is presumably due to a linguistically confused home environment and Moms and Dads hold each other's hands and look quickly at each other; no one says anything. Except for your newly filled Mickey Mouse Pez, who hops angrily out of your jeans pocket, pogos himself onto the shiny speech therapist desk, bends himself backward, and starts to pepper the speech therapist with rectangle candies. The sound is machine-gunny and the projectiles bounce and the speech therapist tries to take cover behind her briefcase but it's useless because pieces of candy block her eyes and explode her ears and when she's lying there dead in the corner with running blood from her nose Mickey Mouse laughs scornfully and you say: Well done, Mickey! And you do repeated give-me-fives until you look up and discover three pairs of concerned grown-up eyes looking at you. And the speech therapist asks if Moms and Dads have noticed anything else . . . special? You and Mickey don't care because it's you against the world, you against the day care idiots, you against speech therapists and dark rooms and closet phantoms and the lady who whispered nigger lover to Moms that day at Skansen when Dads were photographing his first Swedish National Day. Besides, Dads have explained that the speech therapist was a typical Swede. A real racist.[13]

It's your family against the world, that's what you think as you're sitting on the living room floor. Then you're interrupted by parents' magic timing, because you hear Dads, who are opening the lab door, and Moms, who at the same time are leaving the undishwashed kitchen, and their steps are hurrying themselves to each other and then they meet in the middle of the hall floor and they kiss each other the way they only do when they think you're can't see and they promise each other's forgiveness and Dads stand on tiptoe in order to be tall enough and you turn red and don't want to see but you peek anyway. Then they come into the living room and their bodies stretch all the way to the ceiling and their eyes shine like satellites when they tell you that, sure enough, you're going to be a big brother soon and not just any old big brother but the big brother of two future twins! And you become almost entirely honestly happy and Mickey whispers congratulations from your jeans pocket and you celebrate with

---

13.   Well, I do not think your dad said that. We must be distinct about that; your father did EVERYTHING in order to rake your cosmopolitan future. That of course he never fed any outsiderness into your brain. Perhaps you heard incorrectly? Perhaps your father said: "She is a typical Swede. A real careerist." (Or tourist [or circus artist]?)

yet another rectangular raspberry candy and hope that not too much is going to change.

The Dynamic Duo. Three words that fill you with so many memories that you can barely write them down.

Of course it's Dads who come up with the idea. Moms' stomachs are growing and spring is getting closer to summer and *Current Photography* is presenting a new competition. Last year it was "the Summer Picture" and a few years before that "the Thousand-Crown Picture," but this year we invite you, our dear readers, professionals as well as amateurs, to take part in "the Sweden Picture." Dads explain that no theme could be more suited for him. I will do what Robert Frank succeeded at in the fifties, come in from the outside and capture a country in photos! Frank's book became the classic *The Americans,* and my collection will be called *The Swedes.* Or maybe . . . *Svenskarna,* say Dads, and put the just-polished camera into the special case.

This is the spring when you become an adult, the spring when Dads explain that now the time for games and fantasies is over. For both of us. Leave the Mickey Mouse Pez at home. Now we're going to start the Dynamic Duo! Okay? Like Batman and that guy, what is that little guy in the tights called? Robin, right, Robin. I'm Superman and you're Superboy. I'm Obi Ken Wanobi and you're that guy Luke. Understood?

Your salute is so eager that your temple is sore, but Dads don't notice. Dads are too busy planning motifs for his future collection. Everything that is Swedish will be documented, and Dads write long lists and mutter:

Now we have to work really hard to save money for our very own family studio. Is that understood, soldier?

And you answer: Aye aye, Captain! and do a more controlled salute and Dads look down at you and smile. If we just help each other, we'll win at least first, second, and third prize, I can feel it. That money will go a long way.

The Dynamic Duo is launched and you take your place as redeemable-bottle hunter, film-canister opener, tripod placer. And idea spouter for motifs, of course. The whole spring it's being woken up on early weekend mornings, Moms who are still sleeping when Dads come into your room and whisper: Up, my son, the Dynamic Duo calls! And dad waking is always a hundred times easier than day care waking because now it's family duty calling and not elephant songs or childish plastic mosaics or fights with Gabriel. Now it's early weekend mornings of quick breakfast without waking Moms and then choose plastic bags from under the sink and break sticks of the right stiffness for poking from the rowanberry tree in the yard.

On the way to Tanto park, Dads plan motifs. How does one capture the soul of the Swedish people in the best way? What is *suédi en maximum*? While you're looking for redeemable bottles in the first garbage can down by the day care, Dads polish the camera lens with the special soft towel and crack their knuckles, one by one. Dads are getting ready. And before you get down to business you always say: Now it's time . . . and with one voice you switch to Swedish and yell: . . . to get with the picture! Because that's one of Dads' favorite expressions because it is both a pun and has such symbolic photographic content.

Then Dads position themselves right next to flagless flagpoles, shoot right up into cloudy gray skies, and shout: What is more Swedish than that?

Then Dads point the camera at lost gloves arranged on wooden stair railings and say: What is more Swedish than that?

Then Dads shoot two community garden plots with tarpaulin-covered ground and padlocked gates and say: What is more Swedish than that?

Then Dads shoot the stump of road where there are three one-way signs in forty meters and say: What is more Swedish than that?

Then Dads get down on his knees in front of some red-and-green lumpy wino puke, click the camera, and cry: What is more Swedish than that?

While Dads document motifs, you fill the bags with so many bottles that the handles get totally sticky and you leave a trail of drops of brown liquid behind you.

On the way home you discuss which other motifs would be suitable for the photo collection. And you suggest midsummer celebrations and Disney on Christmas Eve and Lucia processions, and Dads say: Too typical. And you suggest blue-and-yellow flags and snuff and those ugly Graninge boots, and Dads say: Too typical. And you say Skansen, travel trailers, and Fjällräven backpacks and Dads say: Too typical! It has to be subtle and obvious simultaneously. No damn Dala horses . . . like for example . . . Dads think. Levels! Levels are the most Swedish instrument in the world. Everything in Sweden must be just right, not too much and not too little! And if you deviate the tiniest bit the air bubble slides away and everything gets crooked. Levels, I'm going to photograph

levels en masse! say Dads and put the camera back in
its case.

While waiting for the elevator, Dads mumble with a
voice that is barely a throat clearing: Thanks for the
help. And you grow to a height of about four or five
meters and have to bend over triple to fit in the elevator
and you promise yourself to almost never again eat
childish Pez candies.

The Dynamic Duo is done with its first task, and the
bottle money is saved in that special cabinet with a padlock that Moms call the armoire and Dads call the
mémoire.

Moms' stomachs grow until the skin gets split marks
and soon Dads stop taking double shifts at SL and start
being home in the evenings, taking a break from the
photography, and helping make dinner. Every evening
it's recipes from *Anna's Food* and you help with the
translation as well as you can. Cumin, who is cumin?
And you make things up sometimes and say the right
thing when you can and most of the time the food tastes
a little strange and it never looks like the pictures; it
ends up being meat casserole with raisins and oatmeal
pancakes roasted in the toaster and the family specialty,
which is saffron cod. And Dads joke and blame the
cookbook and say that Anna is a real marketing ploy
and presumably a racist Swede and Moms pretend not
to hear and just answer that it must be time soon
because otherwise we will starve to death.

And you remember that night when the suitcases

smash some plate that has a valuable special mark. Grandma, who bakes gingersnaps and pancakes that make regular baked goods collapse in shame. Grandma, who has devoted her entire life to helping others, first as a swimming instructor in her former home country, Denmark, then as a missionary's assistant in Africa, and then as a social-services lady in Stockholm. Then she met Grandpa and became a family raiser and then Grandpa's accident happened and she was there for support and said her constant One should be thankful that it wasn't the right hand. Grandma, who collects things for charity in black garbage bags and sends them to orphanages in Eastern Europe. Grandma, who is your great hero the night that little brothers are born because Grandma calms you down and sits beside you hour after hour and she strokes your eyelids and hums songs which don't have words while Moms lie in hospital rooms and push and snort and toss her head back and forth. It's More morphine! shouted with a disaster voice and it's nurses who are watching nervously and sweaty doctors with backward coats and mouth papers and beeping noises from heart monitors and the whole time Dads who stand pale at the head end and sponge with a little towel and try to soothe. It's screams and blood pails and nurses who are changing shifts and red-drenched white coats that whisper about the poor Turk dad with the crazy Swedish wife in number four. It's doctors who say we might lose her, and doctors who say it might be too late. And of course it's Moms who regret it, Moms who swear that this is the absolute last time, Moms who say Swedish swearwords that Dads have never heard before. It's the green heart monitor which changes waves and beep beep beep toward a long line and beeeeeeeeeeeeeeeeeeeeeeep. And it's emergency runners who take out the iron and rub it into a current and shout stand clear! And bzzzzzt and waiting and rubbing and clear! and bzzzzzt until Moms come to life again, keep on pushing, keep on swearing. And then finally Moms exert herself until she throws up and then, with a plopping sound, two screaming little brothers hop out into nurse arms and they smile and laugh and it's a river of blood and you made it! and Dads who choose the exact wrong time to say: There, that wasn't so bad, was it?

Then Dads who hold the receiver with the hand that Moms didn't crush, first calling the Tunisian relatives and rejoicing and then Grandma and asking to speak to Grandpa. Then Dads who come home whistling in the dawn with his eyes ringed in black and his beard rough. And you who have become a big brother.

The next day Dads button on their work tie with little SL logo and put on loose creased pants which shine in the sun and you share a little Paco Rabanne and Dads say: We will remember this day for always. Dads are right. You take the subway and stop at the newspaper stand, Dads choose a bouquet while you get to pick bulk candy, and Dads say: Throw in as much as you want! And it's a lifelong dream that's being fulfilled, you start to fill the bag with all kinds and all colors and it's mint chocolate and Ferraris and fried eggs and Turkish pepper and chalk licorice and raspberry boats but also big toffee squares and whips and salty suckers, which you know Moms like. Then show the bag to Dads and the scale arrow spins far and the cashier guy laughs because it comes to almost a hundred crowns. You prepare yourself for putting some back, but Dads just smile and pay and shout: Today is a party, no penny-pinching! just like the dad in *Emil in the Soup Tureen* and soon you're out on the street again and it's Dads with the best bouquet and you with the biggest bag in honor of Moms and you munch and of course you have to try one of each on the way up to the hospital.

Dads tell you that the photos for the Sweden Picture competition have been sent in and now you just have to wait, soon we'll have the perfect seed money to start a studio! And you listen a little bit but you're mostly concentrating on the candy because there are so many that look suspiciously poisonous and absolutely must be tested before little brothers accidentally get poisoned by boob milk. You go up the hill toward the hospital and it's fall sparkle sun from the sky and water gravel in asphalt cracks and taxis that line up and right before you take the revolving door in, Dads say seriously: We are the men of the house now.

Then you go in and Dads scratch off their Djurgården scarf and spell your last name twice to get the right ward. Then taking the elevator and your stomach that's starting to feel weird and hospital floors with yellow stripes and hospital smell and rough hospital blankets. And then, then it's pale Moms with dried spit in the corners of her mouth and shiny hair. Sleeping when you come, with her head bent at an angle a little like a crash test dummy. When Dads wake Moms with pattering cheek kisses, Moms stretch their hands like sunrises and smile the mom smiles that only they can make and nothing is nicer, especially not new little brothers who have skin like rotten old Indian men and small nails which are barely hard and sticky eyes and not even any hair on their yucky scaly heads.

But you still want to hold one of them, show Dads that you can, carefully against your shoulder, feel the little body near yours, the shoulders banana-soft, and the little nameless one sleeps and you watch the head, smell the baby smell, which is talcum powder and a little used diaper and a little newborn neck sweat. And then, when no one is looking, you pinch him as hard as you can in the back of his knee, mostly just to see what happens. And he screams himself blue in the face and almost has trouble getting air and you give him back to Moms, who shh and cuddle him quiet.

Before Grandma and Grandpa come, Dads want to take pictures with three sons at the same time; the nurse is called in and she smiles at Dads' pride and immortalizes the mustache that is a big black double-u and you with your tongue stuck out and little brothers' sleeping wrinkle faces. Dads are happy like a child, while you have grown up, have a stomachache from candy, and wish you were back at day care. Dads' faces aren't like everyday again until perfumed Grandma and crooked Grandpa can be seen in the hall.

And you remember the following time of sunny weekend breakfasts and Dads who make tea and cut pieces of fruit and curl croissants from dough that comes prepared out of tins that are on sale at the Hötorgshallen market. When the morning smell starts to spread, it's Dads in striped pajama pants with leaking elastic who call to Moms and sons that now it's time and you crawl up out of beds and land heavily on kitchen chairs while Dads whistle and cool the tea by pouring it from cup to cup again and again.

Moms sit at the kitchen table with gritty sleep eyes and she is still weak but still manages to read the paper;

she makes circles around courses that should be perfect
for Dads. She hmms when Dads say: Soon the results
of the Sweden Picture competition will come, darling.
Moms circle Swedish courses at the Workers' Educa-
tional Association and programs to become a home language teacher and Dads say: If I can just have enough
time I promise that my new collection is going to
change everything. And Moms who fill their French
voices with ultimate irony: Yes, time has really been in
short supply. You've only lived here for . . . seven years.

Six years, darling.

Seven years, darling.

Moms look down at course catalogs and Dads suddenly look nervous. The silence around the table is
thornier than usual; Moms puncture the croissant with
a knife a little like she wants to murder it and Dads clear
their throats kind of deep down in his stomach. No one
says anything and you understand that it's best to keep
quiet.

Then it's as though they both want to start a fight on
purpose to get it over with and they start talking about
names for little brothers and Moms want two nice classic Arabic ones, maybe Fathi or Muhammad, or why not
Faizal after Grandpa. And Dads say definitely not. If it's
going to be Arabic it has to sound Swedish and work
both ways; my sons are not going to be jobless and end
up as mafiosos or riffraff . . .

Or subway drivers? Moms ask kindly and Dads'
throats swallow forth a compromise:

What about Camel?

Moms who laugh.

Would you want to grow up in France and be called
Chameau? Why not . . . Ali? And Dads: Why not Gösta,

like Grandpa? And Moms: Gösta is an old-man name, darling. And Dads: Ali is an idiot name, darling. And Moms sigh and Dads sigh and their sharp eyes are aimed right at each other. Then Moms: What about Malcolm, then? And Dads: Like the radical Negro in the U.S.? On my gravestone . . .

And what started with a lovely weekend morning ends with seriousness and French swearwords and Moms who refuse to eat and emphasize every word with her teaspoon like a pointer and Dads who get up and look out onto the balcony walkway and suddenly swear way too loud and little brothers who wake up and wake each other up and now they're both screaming and neither Moms nor Dads move, both just stare, both play the waiting game, and it's like a chicken race but in a kitchen version and finally you get up, go to the bedroom, and stuff double pacifiers in double little brothers' mouths.

Then comes the day when *Current Photography* finally presents the winners of the contest and Dads come in to you with nervous steps and ask you to translate. You, who have just started to learn to read, spell your way through the text while Dads walk around around in circles. They say that they were flooded with answers and that's why the results have been delayed, and Dads shout: Forget that, who won, who won? Read the explanation! But in any case here they are, the hundred winners of the contest "The Sweden Picture." And Dads come closer to you and together you flip pages up and pages down and there are pictures of sack races and blue-and-yellow flags, there are butterflies in close-up and naked children in summer wreaths, there are two photos of blades of grass with backlit fuzzy raspberries, there are misty lakes in the dawn, naked-bottomed night swimmers, rainy picnics, folk-costumed fiddle players. There are rainbows, travel trailers, handwritten kiosk signs, and three waddling cows. But no levels, no day-after vomit frozen in the snow, no iced bikes.

Dads swallow.

Dads page through one more time to be absolutely certain.

Dads go out and don't come home for dinner.

Then comes the year when Dads need breaks from the stress of family life more and more often. Dads say: We're just going down to the city to look for jobs a little and practice a little Swedish. And Moms look up from the chaos apartment where drying cloth diapers drape everything in white and double little brothers scream and poop and throw up and do everything but sleep.

The Dynamic Duo doesn't wait for Moms' answer.

The Dynamic Duo has more important things to do! The Dynamic Duo goes into the city and while Dads photograph flaneurs on Drottninggatan and extol the sunshine on the Åhléns clock, you collect redeemable bottles and sit waiting patiently on bike racks. Only once some drunk men yell: Damn oil Turks! And then Dads show you exactly how one carefully plays deaf, pack up his tripod, and wander toward Central Station.

Dads' new friends are sitting gathered there, the gang that's already got its own nickname: Aristocats. They're sitting bent forward with pointy backs like dragons, and their smells are strong tobacco and their cheeks are prickly beards and their upper lips twisted mustaches. There's the cook Nabil with shoulders as wide as castle walls and there's Aziz, who you recognize from SL. There's Mansour with the small round glasses

and Mustafa with hippie braids and a little leather pouch
on his belt. Everyone is extra nice because you are the
only kid and they offer you throat lozenges and tickle
and turn your cheeks red by showing you pictures of
missing-teeth daughters and joke-planning marriages.
Soon you slide down under the table and sit among
grown-up legs and play Ghostbusters while Dads on the
top side drink refills and billow smoke and tell about
someone who was assaulted by racists in Skåne and
Nabil's cousin who was refused a residence permit and
Mustafa's voice says: It's only damn Iranians who make
it in this whore country . . . then you hear a magnificent
voice that clears itself and shouts: But hello! You can't
forget Refaat! And you squat there under the table and
hear Dads' proud voice tell his friends about the
almighty gifted businessman Refaat El-Sayed. Haven't
you heard of him? Is it true? The Egyptian doctor of
chemistry who borrowed money and bought a pharma-
ceutical factory that was in danger of being shut down.
Then he got convertible stock for his employees and
now the stock value has gone up eleven thousand seven
hundred percent. In two years! What do you say about
that?

And you hear mugs that clatter but no one who answers. And Dads' bubbling voices say that Refaat recently
gave the Swedish state one billion crowns to start a foundation that will support young inventors. ONE BILLION!
shout Dads and your table roof shakes from his fist
thumps. This is a man who has succeeded! And if I could
just find someone . . . anyone . . . who could give me a
small, small loan, then I could follow in his footsteps.
Just some temporary support to start my studio . . . Does
one of you maybe . . . ?

When you creep up to table level again, the ashtray is volcano-shaped and the atmosphere is different. Nabil looks at the clock and Mansour tells about the idiots in his institution at the university; Aziz arranges rolled-up bits of paper into patterns and Mustafa gets up to get a refill.

Dads slowly peel their smiles off.

And right when you write these words, you wonder if it wasn't Refaat who was Dads' most important source of inspiration. Because of course there were all the photo books and photographer quotes and classic pictures in the lab. But maybe it was Refaat's successes that meant the most for Dads that year when suspicious tenants' associations declined to call, when banks rejected loans, and when Dads' application to the Art Grants Committee disappeared in the mail. Because it did, right?

The next memory is from the time when Dads have started to develop some sort of allergy to the polyester in the SL uniform, and Moms have recovered from the double pregnancy and the exhausting maternity leave. You have started the first grade and during the morning break everything is normal, with playing alone and stair-fossil counting and gravel-bandy watching and keeping a lookout for that cute South American girl in the other class. And then suddenly Moms are standing there in the hall! And everything is imaginary, of course, because Moms don't belong in school halls and Dads have explained how important it is to tell the difference between real and imaginary. Thus you ignore Moms' waves in the hall. Up until Moms come up and grab hold of you and repeat again and again that Grandpa has died and finally you understand that Moms are real and that Grandpa really is dead. The hall gets fuzzy edges and Moms hug you and ask if you want to come along to the hospital. Of course not, because it's almost time for students' choice and after that we'll probably draw pictures about it and besides, I feel a little weird. But Moms just smile with wet eyelashes and whisper: I still think it's best that you come along. You'll regret it otherwise.

Then you take a car to the hospital, and you don't remember who is driving, maybe it's a taxi. It's the exact same hospital where little brothers were born, but in only a few years that light in the waiting room has dimmed and you use the same entrance but a different elevator and a different corridor and end up in a waiting room with more modern sofas. And it's you and Moms who wander farther toward the hospital room and Moms' hands are coldly scaly the way they get in the fall and Moms let you balance on the marking lines on the floor and touch everything that's yellow because on some days childish systems like that, which you've actually outgrown, are super-important to follow.

Then open the door with a hissing sound and into the hospital room with tremble knees and all the Swedish relatives are gathered there. Grandma shaking in the corner with a crumpled handkerchief. Consoling aunts and bear-sized uncles who collapse like card houses and throw themselves, crying, at dead Grandpa, who's lying stiff in the bed. And only you understand that everything is a fake, that it's not Grandpa at all lying in the hospital bed with his stump arm and gaping grimace and yellowed nails. It's only you who understand that Grandpa is only a shell, more like a forgotten juice packet with pale skin and nothing is as scary as you had thought because it's plain as day that Grandpa left his cancer body a long time ago and is now hanging out in heaven, playing two-armed sun tennis with old road-worker friends, drinking fancy punch and jet-skiing and laughing at his memories of the sign shop. Still you try to tear up your eyes; you think about sad movies and the final scene in *E.T.* and you succeed in pressing out a little sadness. But then you see Grandpa's empty shell and sunburned Grandpa smiling under a parasol at the beach with flip-flops and totally undamaged hands and it's flirting bikini chicks and banana-boat-hopping angels at sea and a bunch of dead movie stars who are saying that the evening's ice cream eating contest is going to be eternally good and then Grandpa looks at you and smiles and says: I'll wait for you here. And you can't share the others' sadness and you think that maybe it's a family thing and maybe you have to be fully Swed-ish to get it.

Then it's going home to your apartment and Grandma, who for once doesn't say anything mean about Dads' framed photos, and Moms, who make a little coffee without saying anything about how coffee causes anxiety, and two bears of uncles on the sofa with large-pocketed work pants and tears constantly flowing, shoulders bobbing, and legs so long that their thighs are leaning up toward their knees.

And you try to join in and carry in the milk and fetch the blanket for Grandma but then Grandpa is there again in the sun chair with a Miami shirt and Hawaii shorts and a straw hat and he toasts toward you and shines his eyes and says something you can't hear and you smile back when no one is looking and help Moms in with the coffee thermos and serve uncles' clinking mugs and fetch the digestive biscuits even though they're really supposed to be saved for the weekend. And then, just when everything has calmed down, you can hear Dads in the hall. And there's Dads, coming in whistling with shopping bags and a wave of the hand, Dads, who don't know anything, Dads, who this very day have bought a bunch of canned goods at sale price from some Aristocat.

Dads drop the bags on the hall floor, hug Moms, and don't joke for several minutes. Dads stand strong like never before and don't ask about the inheritance and act exactly like he should. Up until Dads want to comfort Grandma by offering her a can of food and then ask: And by the way . . . please I am sorry . . . but do we know please what will happen to *la boutique?* Moms yank Dads with her into the kitchen and whisper: Please, for once, can't you at least try to sense the mood?

Then it's only a few days before Dads come home with triple surprises. There are the drawings of Grandpa's sign store, the signed contract, and Dads' detailed shopping lists. There's the contract giving notice at SL and the going-away present the SL boss gave him in advance. Dads' voices are bubbling fireworks when he tells about the building that will become a studio slash atelier slash gallery. The light can be made ideal with a little renovation and the distance to the commuter train station is only five hundred meters and there are three small rooms and a storeroom, excellent! Then Dads switch voices and read out loud from the song list that's printed on the edge of the SL cassette and there's "Gösta

Gigolo" by Ingmar Nordstroms and "Fly Free" by Kikki Danielsson and "Go Where the Pepper Grows" by Leif Hultgren, and then Dads switch voices and languages again and say that the building needs a little renovation but we can do it, it's no problem, and look here, look what they gave us at work, SL are crazies, and Dads read song titles like "The Convenience Store Cashier," "It Still Smells Like Love," and "Friday Evening Blues" by Alf Robertson. Aziz was furious when I showed him; he talks about quitting, too, but I don't think he . . .

Quitting? ask Moms.

Yes? How else could I open a studio? With this place EVERYTHING is going to change, darling. I'll be able to have my own exhibitions here, and now I can get started working seriously and soon there will be Picture of the Year awards en masse and papers that will call me and stars who stand in line to have their portraits taken.

Shouldn't we have discussed this first? ask Moms. What is there to discuss? laugh Dads and hug you and kiss Moms and you think: Those poor kids who have normal dads, dads who don't still have their child eyes and who can't make magic with either words or cameras.

Dearest greetings!

Anxiety heaps my breast after the reading of your latest e-letter's depressed tone. How can I tempt you back to the path of joie de vivre? How can I get you to forget the insultations of the hate letter? Jonas: You are NOT a camel-fucking Muslim negroid ape who should be sent home or shot. You are a reasonably talented author who, thanks to me, has been delegated the chance for a secondary book.

Here come two self-strengthening directives; write them out and publish them on your refrigerator as a reminder vaccine:

1. I will NEVER let myself be infected with my father's paranoia! The whole world is not "out to get me" at all.
2. I will NEVER be silenced into speechlessness or deceit. Silence is a loss. Silence is the escort of death. Silence delegates victories to idiots who happen to have tongues.

Now to your delivered text. Praise it with roses and wreaths! The section is interesting and a progression of your talent can be noticed and applauded. See the affixed document for my comments.

The reading of your text has made me secure with one thing: the insight that even authors can form a text that is . . . not perfect. Much work remains. This maximized my inspiration and the writing of the continuation of your father's history was written almost on autopilot. Affixed you will find first the translation of the letter your father wrote me in December 1985, which put to sound the silence which had characterized our relation since our rendezvous in Tabarka in 1984. The secondary document forms my rendezvous with Sweden, your family, and the Swedish language. Let these events terminate the book's triangular section. You are invited as usual to inject your potential memories. Just memorize not to remember too many details—there is a big difference between one-eyes and books. One of them is helped by expanded thickness and length; the other is not. Do you know which is which? If not it is truly time to try to find a girlfriend . . . ☺

Your virtuoso friend,
Kadir

Stockholm, December 27, 1985
Greetings, Kadir!

Let me first ask your excuse for my letterish pause. Pardon me. Many things have been modified in my life since we last met.

For example, my family has wandered from a trio to a pentangle! My wife has borne me two further sons in twin form! I was informed of her pregnancy after my return from Tunisia, and considering our economic situation at the time, this was very complicated information. We directed our traditional procedure where I tried to convince her to descend to asking her mother for financial support and my wife yelled neverneverneverne all night. A tingling unease began to grow me for my future responsibility as a fivefold-family provider.

The economic situation, however, has been renovated thanks to my beautiful-father's tragic death. My dear beautiful-mother, Ruth, has generously delegated me both his store and an advancement on our future inheritance. I believe she regrets her initial antipathy toward me. Now she expresses that "everyone must get an honest chance, particularly in these times." In this she is entirely correct, because the climate of Sweden is truly beginning to be modified. One can feel it in the atmosphere of the streets. The looks. The comments. The frequency of immigrants is rising in step with the Swedes' suspiciousness. In this year's election commotion, the Conservatives' master, Ulf Adelsohn, expressed: "A Swede is a Swede and a Negro a Negro." He has also said that of course the Swedes' eyes sting when immigrant children take limousines from "upper-class Östermalm apartments" to sumptuous home language lessons, while Swedish children must hike. Even Sweden's socialists are starting to fly their kites in the same foreigner-antipathetic wind. Sometimes my soul is unsecured. What am I doing here? How will my three sons grow successfully in this country? How will their brown skin and black hair find success in a context where neo-Nazis have begun to manifest openly in the streets and refugee homes are attacked with firebombs? My certainty is far from securitized, but I know one thing—my sons must NOT be attracted to being outsiders. This shall be my life's true priority! I must be very careful not to follow my wife into soaping my eyes in the suds of politics.

But not everything at this time is coming up nettles! I bear a strong belief in the improvement of the future! Let us focus on the indications that are positive to us in the end of 1985: Halley's Comet did not crash our earth! Reagan and Gorbachev managed to find time for a rendezvous! More and more Swedes decorate their coats with antiracist plastic hands on which the text spells, "Don't touch my friend." And most important of all: I have terminated my slave time at SL, offput my horridly scratching polyester vest, and will soon have my own studio!

Today I was exposed to another two positive pieces of news. Number one: My oldest son has turned seven! He has now carried out his first half year in school. He bears a very expanded intelligence and his speech is now almost normal. He has also learned to control his imagination, so he less frequently attracts the looks of passersby. Several weeks have passed since I last came across him speaking aloud to his frequent imaginary friends. Observe also his artistic quality! What ordinary seven-year-old can draw pictures of equal talent?[14]

My relationship with my son is very close. I am his great idol and he often seeks my glance to verify my attention. Together we spend much time and I have already begun to prepare him for the vital weight of grades. I indicate him that his grades must NEVER be under the best one. My son always nods me seriously and prom-

---

14. Your father included three drawings in the letter. Here he is maximally generous . . . In actuality, your speech pattern was a long way from normalcy. And your drawings? Well, of course you know how they looked . . .

ises his attempt at maximization. My wife sighs me and thinks I present my son with entirely too much compression too soon.

"He is only in his premier class! He is seven years old!"

But I respond her:

"It is NEVER too early to absorb knowledge. This is my philosophy. Particularly in Sweden, which already bears an increased suspicion against those who do not bear skin of the pink color."

"And your own knowledge of Swedish, when will that be absorbed, exactly?"

"Is your voice traced with sarcasm, my darling? My Swedish will soon be perfectioned, you know that."

"It has taken considerable time."

"Time is a worldly thing."

Certainly my wife is correct—the learning process of Swedish has to me been complex and protracted. Do you want to sense the motive? In Sweden one is received very different depending on one's language. To present an Arabically broken Swedish attracts angry expressions, demonstrative "what?"s, and a negative atmosphere. If one instead speaks English or French one is smiled and receives an automatic nearness in relationships. Consequently, it is not bizarre that my temptation to the Swedish language has been filled with gaps, a little like the Advent calendars that are sold here as Christmas traditions. For a long time I also practiced the mistake of spending my time in the company of other exiled Arabs. My friendship with the Aristocats will now be reduced in favor of a future expanding Swedish.

The day's secondary happy incident met me with the evening news. While Pernilla fell the twins to sleep, I parked my tired, pounding head in front of the news program *Rapport*. There it was reported that Refaat El-Sayed was electored to Swede of the Year! That Egyptian man whom I detailed you about in the previous letter, right? This expanded my happiness to new volumes. Everything is possible! One must truly be the chef of one's own happiness! Just like Refaat, one must be ready to risk to achieve success. The roads are open for those with super-rugged diligence!

I am writing you now to present an offer. Are you tempted to afflict Sweden to assist me in renovating my studio? I promise you a prompt repayment of my borrowed economy as well as a well-formed salary as my assistant. What do you say? Can you remain six months? Or one year?

My hope is for your prompt acceptance and our prompt reunion. For what is the happiness of a reunion in comparison to those other water stations that exist in the marathon we call life? Very delicious!

Abbas

I remember how I already nodded my head with the decision of affirmation during the reading of your father's letter. The experience of the journey tempted me at least as much as the economy.

In January of 1986 I terminated my occupation of Hôtel Majestique and flew toward the northmost of north: Arlanda, Stockholm. My memory is photographically clear to me. Everything is memorized. The passport inspection, the well-founded customs inspection, the rosily red-haired policeman who tested my shaving cream and carefully smelled of its odor (and very seriously welcomed me to Sweden and returned my packing, unaware that his close smelling had rewarded him with a very humorous white nose). The icy wait for the bus, the conductor's friendly "hello hello," the journey through the deserted forest, the spruces, the shadows, the Welcome to Stockholm sign. Then the ghostly empty streets, parked cars blanketed in snow, nightly dark even though it was five o'clock in the afternoon. Then the sound when my forehead crashed the plastic window of the bus at the first view of your waiting family.

There you all stood! My antique best friend, Abbas! With a pale front, black-hooded half coat, corduroy pants, and a modernly colored scarf. In his arms your double brothers, two blanket-hidden baby sausages with matching hats. Your mother at his side: Pernilla, that young, shining beauty on the beach in Tabarka. Now slightly more trivial with an out-of-date blue hippie shawl and elephantically wide jeans.

My hands banged the bus window, my tongue roared happiness, my steps stamped out onto the sidewalk, my arms hugged your father, my lips cheek-kissed your mother, and it was everyone's voice at the same time with Arabic mixed with French. Did your trip go well? and How are you all? and What has happened since last time? Oh, they're so cute, and Gootchie-gootchie-goo, and your father repeated my welcome and your mother, who smiled politely, and your father, who suddenly yelled: But where is your baggage? and then rush into the bus again to manage to tow out my suitcase just before the bus started. Then standing there laughing on the sidewalk again, hugs and cheek kisses, your brothers' newly wakened screams, and your father's glittering glad eyes.

"And where is your oldest son?" I interpellated.

Before your father had time to respond I followed his turned head and focused you. You sat with crouched legs in the shadow of the terminal and poked your fingers deep into a sewer grate. You had pleated jeans and a glowing red hat, your nose glittered the snot of transparence, and your cheeks presented long streaks of tears. I heard how you seemed to be speaking with someone down in the sewer hole and my first thought was actually this: "Wow, I wonder which of his thin parents has inheritaged him this expanded corpulence." (Pardon me, Jonas.)

"He's a little sulky," your mother explained in French.

"He's a little spoiled," your father added in Arabic.

"What did you say?" your mother interpellated.

"That our son is a little tired," said your father.

"Where is the car?" I asked in French.

"We don't have a car," responded your mother. "The metro will transport us home to the apartment."

"The car is being repaired," your father said in Arabic.

"What did you say?" your mother interpellated.

"That I love you," your father responded. "Welcome, Kadir. It is a great happiness to me to see you. Now we'll just pacify my prima donna of a son and then we can go."

My arrival soon replaced your melancholy with shyness. On the metro's way home you clung your mother's legs and hid your face in shadow. On instruction I had invested Pez candy for you and this present identified me as your immediate favorite. The entire metro's way home you munched Pez squares and said, "Thank, Kadiw. *Shukwan*, Kadiw," over and over again.

You memorize this, right? That you still, in this seven-year-old phase, lacked the capacity to express those letters which are so vital in all languages, *r* and *s*? Although you happily passed your free time in the world of books and although you wandered smoothly from French to Arabic to Swedish, you had this serious speech impediment, which roused your father's irritation more and more often. But generally your relationship was very fine. I was impressioned that you were your father's while the twins became more your mother's.

Now comes the scene that we can call "Kadir's initiation to Sweden." Together your family and I delight everything that Stockholm's wintery spring has to offer in 1986.

Let us here change the tone of the book and present this sequence in the musical form of the medley (with your father's photographing clicking sound as a steady beat-drum).

Stockholm, oh Stockholm! CLICK! Show how we transport ourselves into the city and wander wharfs and superficially iced lakes. CLICK! Your proud father with your little brothers in the terry cloth double stroller and his frequently fired camera. CLICK! You with the demand of crying for ice cream despite the cold and your mother with attempts to guidance of historical rarities. She constantly ignores churches and castles and points me instead the Battle of the Elms. CLICK! And the block of the Mullvaden occupation. CLICK! And there is the street where the police once attacked her brother's friend with biting dogs. CLICK! CLICK! I who wander alongside with my gaze hungry for erotic Swedish women and my teeth aching after the surprise of a cool apple.

Show our shared weekends where we afflict hippie festivals on Långholmen. All your mother's friends, softly smiling Swedish women with Indian bands in their hair and bells around their arms, hibernated hippies with white sheepskin vests and well-worn pipes. CLICK! We sit on tangled blankets, delight steaming thermos coffee, nostalgizing the humanism of the seventies and listening to protest-singing guitar men. CLICK! We intake bean porridges that are offered in trade for feeding Africa's famine children. CLICK! I realize that my Swedish courting status is differentiated from Tabarka's by complimenting a woman's hair flower and collecting a resounding ear smack. SLAP! CLICK!

One Saturday I invest a hypermodern purple suit with imposing shoulder pads and deep double-breasting. CLICK! One Sunday we stroll gravel paths out to the Museum of Modern Art of Skeppsholmen. CLICK! Your father clicks his camera all the time while you in your rough orange coverall collect leaves and want to start a war with me, your "favowite uncle, Kadiw." CLICK!

At the Museum of Modern Art we inspect a gigantic and very popular retrospective exhibition of the celebrated Swedish photographer Christer Strömholm. Then write:

"My father notes Strömholm's photographs as standardized and unimpressive. Still, is it perhaps this visit which will influence so much of my father's future? Why? Read on and you will receive knowledge!!!"

(This is a so-called planting in order to feed the readers' curiosity.)

Here we will die away the musical medley and normalize the form.

It was afternoon and we had parked our bodies in the café at the Central Station of Stockholm. Your mother was home with the twins and you shared our company, munched sweets, and played on the floor under our table. Your father ignored your sounds, drank his coffee, and partook my cigarettes.

"Hadn't you terminated that habit?" I interpellated.

"In principle," said your father and borrowed my lighter.

Then careful calculations with budgets and forms, floor plans, brochures from photo companies, and sketches of alternative studio names were presented from his bag. Your father seemed to have spent many months in hidden preparation.

Even long before your grandfather's death he had telephoned numberous banks with the ambition of getting economic assistance. For several years in a row he had sought but been refused the Work Stipend, Travel Stipend, and Project Stipend from the Swedish Art Grants Committee. Frequent were the authorities who refused his inquiry about assistance in order to begin his career.

"It has been very complicated to receive trust as foreign-born in this country," said your father, looking at his thick bundle of papers. "Likewise to localize a location that is not suddenly rented when they hear my foreign accent. But now all of that is behind us."

No experiences seemed to have grown your father's frustration. Instead he exposed me to the contract for your grandfather's store, where the landlord had detailed in a particular handwritten paragraph that we were NOT allowed to start a pizzeria or a mosque or a café or any other enterprise that could attract an "undesirable clientele."

"Kadir, my happiness to have you here is very well formed. Nothing can compete with two collaborating friends. And one can never be successful if one works for someone else. By the way, have I related you about Refaat? That magic man who—"

I interrupted him, sighing.

"Hmm . . . let me think. Not more than perhaps every time we have discussed the details for my visit on the telephone."

Your father did not notice my ironic tone.

"Refaat! One of Sweden's richest men! He started with two empty hands! Now he bears a close relationship to the Volvo master Gyllenhammar! Despite his millions, Refaat still lives in his ordinary Million Program apartment. Just like . . . Who do you think?"

"Uh . . . you?"

"Exactly! Me and Refaat! The exact same. He is the premier Arab who has succeeded in finding his success in this oblong country. And do you know what was acted a few weeks ago?"

"No."

"Refaat was electored to Sweden's most excellent badge of honor."

"The Nobel Prize?"

"No."

"The position of Swedish prime minister?"

"No."

"The position as master of IKEA?"

"No."

"The position of ABBA singer?"

"Are you pulling on my leg?"

And in that second, I finally recognized your young father. The father who exploded his rage at the Greek photographer. The father who never chose the drama of falseness, who burned the heat of life and would never be able to graze the thought of giving up a lifelong artistic dream to photograph for finances. His eyes burning black, eyelashes vibrating, his jaws scraping each other.

"Respond me, Kadir. Are you pulling on my leg?!"

You were woken from your games and periscoped your head up from the floor.

"No, no. Forgive my excuse. What has Refaat been electored to?"

Your father slowly transformed his rage to a smile.

"Swede of the Year!!! You must admit what an illuminated success it is! An Egyptian as Swede of the Year! A Brazilian German as queen! This country is unparalleled to me!"

I masqueraded forth my surprise and praised the luck of Refaat. Your father happily creaked his back against the equivalent of the chair.

"Well . . . there is luck and there is luck. It is not about luck. This country offers all potential possibilities. For those who do not choose the road of laziness, Sweden is a country of a thousand free paths, just pick a path! Together we will now pass the coming time by renovating the store."

"How large will my economic compensation be? Besides the finances I have loaned you?"

"Hmm . . . it will be atmospherically large measured in Tunisian standards. Much wider than at Hôtel Majestique."

"And how great is the salary in Swedish standards?"

"There it is . . . what the Swedes call *lagom*. Not too large, not too small. Exactly *lagom*. What do you think?"

"Okay. Let us vow our promises and pray for your studio's prompt success. I would be very sad by being forced to return without the economy you have promised me."

"Our success is no doubt already our fact. I want to remind you of one thing, however: I will NEVER bend my artistic ambition. With this studio I will have free hands to support my family in order to then simultaneously maximize my artisticness. Understood?"

"Yes. Why are you detailing me this?"

Your father did not respond me. His concentration had been broken by some Arabs who parked themselves at our neighbor table. Your father nodded them grimly. When their bodies levitated toward the counter to invest coffee your father turned to me and sighed them audibly, side-shaking his head.

"Observe them, Kadir. I call them Aristocats . . . Look at that one . . . Mustafa. A real loafer. He didn't invest his own coffee! He just took a cup and paid for a refill. It is people like that who infect their bad reputation to the rest of us Arabs. They will never succeed in Sweden. NEVER! I, on the other hand, have perfect chances."

"How so?"

"Thanks to my wife I have succeeded in transforming my mentality so that it has become almost entirely Swedish. Some one hundred Swedish rules are now my routine."

"Like what?"

"Oh, it is complicated to remember them all. But let me try. I stand to the right on escalators. I brush my teeth evening and morning. I offtake my shoes before I invade apartments. I use the seat belt even when I sit in backseats of cars. I will soon begin to understand the logic that retired relatives should be isolated in so-called nursing houses."

"And what else?"

"I express triple thanks each time I invest a newspaper. I never haggle in stores. I can discuss weather and wind for hours with the precision of a meteorologist. Each time I am about to greet my neighbors I restrain myself into silence by thinking of the proverb 'A Swede is silent.'"

"And what else?"

"If I dine at a restaurant, I make sure that the woman pays her share of the bill. Those times when I imbibe alcohol, I do not stop before unconsciousness is near to me. I never expose anger if an alcoholic Swede on the metro happens to insult me."

"What do you mean, 'happens to insult'?"

Your father hacked his throat.

"It happens very seldom."

"But what do they express?"

"Only in the case of exception has someone perhaps whispered names like nigger. Or damn Turk."

Then he neared his empty coffee cup to his lips and pretended to drink.

"Praise my congratulations," I said, and did not let the irony shine too strongly.

"But! There is also another vitality that separates me from the Aristocats," your father continued with recovered hope. "I will never accept the ambition of living at the expense of welfare. The laziness that colors so many other immigrants will never infect me! Instead my studio will offer expanded support and long-term economic security. Let us now discuss the title!"

Your father presented me his name sketches and smacked his mouth happily. While I observed the competing studio names, I noticed a sorrowful emotion in my chest. Where did it come from? Perhaps it was based on the insight that something had succeeded in modifying your father. Something indicated his transformed mentality; perhaps it was his condescending method toward his countrymen, perhaps it was his brilliant smile when he found a five-crown coin on the café floor. Perhaps it was the whisper that your father, despite his guarantees, would find it difficult to combine his artistic ambitions with economic maximization? My certainty is unsecured.

The next day we initialized the renovation of your father's building. We gradually transformed the store from a forgotten sign shop in a suburb south of Stockholm to a professional photographic studio with an added vernissage room. Though still in a suburb south of Stockholm.

We cleaned out the meticulously filled storerooms, where your grandfather seemed to have saved all of everything in an infernally historical chaos. That Gösta must have been a true collector. In his stockroom were not only the antique signs, which we soon sold on to a connoisseur.

There was also Gösta's collection of Ping-Pong paddles (18 of them), water towers for antique train lines (7), scrapped refrigerators (5), milk white firemen's helmets (4), aquariums (3), crutches (3.5), old world maps (some twenty rolls). There was his collection of bottle caps from that kind of antique soda that was called "small beer" (3 bags!) as well as his not particularly well formed collection of stuffed scorpions (1). Your grandfather must have had a very complicated relationship with cleaning and throwing away . . . Fortunately enough, we did not partake this nostalgic disposition.

After emptying the rooms, we tore out shelves and filled wall holes with stiffening cream. The shabby yellow wall color was disguised behind a neutral white. We invested a complete photo lab with chemicals and copying machines via used advertisements. We invested lamps, furniture from IKEA, cord extenders, fabrics as back walls, and reflecting mirrors, as well as quantities of props (plastic fruit, candelabras, humorous crowns). The ring-spotted marble of the windowsills was hidden with pots, and the spiderweb cracks of the window panes were camouflaged with flowering curtains delegated from your grandmother.

In the stairs down from the courtyard, we taped posters from your father's bathroom lab. There was Capa's desperate soldier on D-Day, Avedon's shaky, sweat-splashing Louis Armstrong, Eisenstaedt's sailor who is celebrating peace with an unknown woman's kiss, as well as Yousuf Karsh's classic portrait of Einstein. The main room became the studio's combined atelier and vernissage room. The inner room was transformed to a black-colored darkroom with insulated light barriers, wires on the ceiling, special-colored bathtubs for different chemicals, clothespins, and, like the dot that transforms a stick to an *i*, the orange lightbulb.

Because your mother had pointed out your apartment's present crowdedness with cyclical repetition, I was offered lodging farthest back in the store's special storeroom. There I partook my home with a mattress as well as many quantities of material, film canisters, developing fluids, and fixative drums, as well as the carton in which your father hid his secret whiskey bottles (your mother opposed all forms of daily routine drinking). As a stimulant your father delegated me your black-and-white fourteen-inch TV. Pretty soon I could visualize the room more as a temporary home and less as a suffocating, cramped, windowless cave.

Are you impatiently anticipating your return in the story? Do not worry. Now it is time. During the coming months, two exterior happenings were acted that presented a strong influence on your father's future: Number one was initiated when Björn Gillberg published his article that auctioned that Refaat El-Sayed's doctoral degree was not complete.

Refaat was apparently not the doctor of chemistry he presented himself as. The consequence? The Swedish journalists attacked Refaat, punctured his reputation, and his career fell in time with Fermenta's share prices. The Volvo relationship was broken and Refaat was fired, indicted, erased, pulverized. Your father read the newspapers' headlines with rising dismay, side-shook his head, and mumbled:

"It can't be true, it can't be true; they can't do this, they can't."

But they could. Do you remember this?

Of course you remember, and there's Dads, who are sitting in the kitchen, and its green wallpaper and big black table crack that's perfect for hiding tiny things like grains of rice and Playmobil pistols. There are Dads' feet with holey socks and you can hear Dads' dark voices and this must be the first memory of Kadir because Dads have a friend visiting and at first you think it's someone from Aristocats but then you understand that

it's one of Dads' oldest friends from Jendouba, who has
jeans with patched knees and a squeaky leather vest.
He's given you Pez candy and pinched your cheek
kindly and you remember his voice when he comforts
Dads and says, *Inshallah lebes,* Refaat will survive, Refaat
always survives. And Dads say: Of course, Refaat always
survives, but why are they doing this, why, he's given a
billion, a billion! And then Moms' sleepy slipper feet
that shuffle in from the bedroom and they ask for help
hanging up cloth diapers to dry and then Dads, who
answer that they actually have other things to think
about right now.

And as they say: A tragicness often comes in stereo. Our renovation of the studio was almost finalized when projectiles from an
unknown pistol penetrated the praised prime minister Olof
Palme's chest. Sweden fell into a national sorrow and it took several days before your ragged mother got back a glimmer of joie de
vivre. Not even your muddleheaded memory could have forgotten
that day, right?

Of course you remember that too, but it's a strange memory because it's as close as you can get to a collective
experience because you are doing exactly what everyone
else is probably doing that Saturday morning. You crawl
out of bed and even though you're almost grown up you
happen to be carrying the stuffed seal you call Snorre
with you, and Moms and Dads are sleeping and you
sneak toward the TV and stand on tiptoe to press the button to check exactly what time *Good Morning Sweden* is
going to show cartoons. But instead of the schedule text

there's a fuzzy picture and a blocked-off police picture and you spell your way through the text easily but the pronunciation is still hard because your tongue just rolls itself. It says that *Good Morning Sweden* is canceled because of . . . and you read it again and again so that you don't make a mistake . . . the muwdew of the pwime minithter Olooof Paalme! and you yell loudly toward the bedroom and Moms grunt in reply and you yell again that Palme has been murdered and you're so happy and proud because you were the very first to find the news and you smile toward Moms' horror and you are just about to say it again when Moms' wailing sounds cut the apartment in two and little brothers wake up screaming and Dads wake up screaming and everything is chaos and in the middle of it all is you, who finally understand and who try to comfort Moms by letting Snorre nose her streaming tears. You climb up on the sofa and get down the framed picture of Palme and Moms hold the frame to her breast and rock back and forth and Dads comfort and you comfort while little brothers just scream and scream.

No name had yet been fixated on your father's future studio. But I strongly remember the spring evening when your father's brain was sparkled with the name idea. It went like this: Palme had been dead for a few weeks and your mother had recovered her failing strength. A visit down to your overfull cellar had presented your father with a gigantic amount of photos that he wanted to present in his new display window. Now we were sitting and resting in the fumes of the paint with aching shoulders and tired backs. I polished my nails free from color while your father paged through his large collection of photos. He bathed in negative cards and photo-

graphs; with a magnifying glass on his eye he examined hundreds
of photos. Then he said:

"Avedon is really correct in his citation. Pictures have a reality
that people lack. It is through my photographs that I know
people."

I never knew what I should answer to such citations. So I kept
quiet and shined my nails. Your father continued.

"The question is which studio name will tempt Swedes the
most. I mean . . . I will never compromise about my talent. But
the name of the studio must be safe and simultaneously tempting.
It should feel curious but also experienced . . ."

The quantity of the options was many. They wandered between
"Pernilla Khemiri's Studio" (as an appeasing for your mother, who
called the studio too risky), "Studio Khemiri Inc." (professional
aura), "Khemiri Art and Photography Studio" (artistic flourish),
"Khemiri's Wild Strawberry Patch" (Bergmanesque and appetiz-
ing), "Atelier Palmé" (as an homage to Palme), and "Extremely
cheap family portraits!" (as a temptation for the stingy old people
at the nearby nursing home).

Suddenly your father levitated to a standing position with a photograph stretched toward the sky like a sweaty Wall Street worker.

"I have it!"

The motif of the photograph was a deliciously beautiful black-
haired woman, Brazilian and German in original birth, yellow skirt
and blue waist with embroidered flowers . . . There she stood,
Queen Silvia, photographed by your father on a flag-filled stage at
Skansen, spring 1983. The stylish, bouclé-haired King Carl Gustaf
is visible, blurry in the background. Silvia's hand is frozen to eternity in its sideways wave, her smile politely distant, and both her
eyes precisely half closed like a pupil-exempt demon's.

"Of course!" shouted your father. " 'Studio Silvia!' That's what
the studio will be called. 'Studio Silvia, Khemiri's Artistic Photo
Studio.' "

That very evening your father projected his plan for how we would invite the Swedish queen to the studio's opening ceremony. With fresh coffee, wine, colored balloons, and crackling artificial fires, the journalists and art critics would interview the successful man from Tunisia who had left SL and started his own photographic studio.

" 'Photographer gets grand visit' . . . That's what the headlines will spell! 'The queen on a photo visit!' 'The queen's new court photographer.' That will show those damn idiots . . ." (my certainty is not convinced whether your father was referring here to your mother's family, the refusing gallery owners, his ex–SL boss, or the landlord of the store [presumably all of them]).

Equally as much as your mother loved your father, she detested his suggestions for studio names.

"You cannot be serious!" she auctioned on her premier visit to the soon-renovated studio.

"Why not?"

"Ugh . . . 'Studio Silvia'? It sounds almost pornographic. Besides, Silvia gives me the willies . . . She looks like a vampire . . . Our dear Nazi queen! It's a very bourgeois photograph, extremely antidemocratic and noncommunistic and imperialistic! Please, localize it in the trash room instead of the display window."

But your father maintained her faux pas.

"It gives the studio extra-fine class!" he expressed proudly and pointed at the goldish frame he had invested for the Silvia photo. "Besides, it will tempt customers. Young and old. This is my certain conviction."

Your mother observed your father and, though she wanted to, could not hold her serious front. She attracted her body toward his, bent her back, and let her soft lips nose his neck.

"I get so tired of you," she whispered in French, but her intonation bore a warmth that spoke of a diagonal opposite. Here I remember that you and I imitated each other. Both of our cheeks were reddened by the kisses that were shared between your parents, and we took our shelter out in the courtyard until the danger had passed.

Your mother's protests against the studio's name were both retarded and unmotivated. "Studio Silvia" became the name we wrote on the wooden sign that swung its squeaking sound outside the door. Underneath it said in leaning letters: "Khemiri's Artistic Photography Studio." Your father embellished the sign with some mountaintops at the bottom.

Before the opening, your father formulated an elegant letter on the finest stationery with your smiling mother's assistance. It was addressed to the royal palace. Your father praised Queen Silvia's cleverness, wisdom, and loveliness, congratulated her choice of new homeland, and invited her majestic form to be present at an official opening ceremony addressed to her honor.

Studio Silvia opened its doors in April 1986. It was a magnificent Saturday. The walls of the foyer presented the best of your father's photographic Sweden suite. There was the series of snow-frozen day-after vomits in extreme close-up. There were dried leaf poles and piles of empty beer bottles. There were several photos of proper-suit Swedes standing on sunny street corners with the exact same serene expression. There was a black-and-white blur picture of a Volvo Amazon that had crashed a softly bent street sign at Sankt Eriksplan. There were three colored-over levels and the Silvia photo in blowup. Farthest in the corner there was even a photo with your father's initial favorite motif: a powerfully snowed-over, brown-rusted bike with punctured tires, frosted handlebars, and icicles erected from the seat.

Our preparations had been meticulous. All the Swedish papers had been invited with personal exhibition cards, and neighbors had been informed with leaflets. Swedish houses of publication had been invited because your father wanted to inspire them to do a book about Swedes in the same format as Robert Frank's

The Americans. In *Current Photography,* under the heading "What's Happening," everyone with an interest in photos could look up the page before the last and read: "The photographer Abbas Khemiri exhibits 'The photo that should have won the Sweden Picture' at Studio Silvia in Stockholm." The announcement found its position right between information about an exhibition in honor of Arvika's seventy-fifth anniversary and the Sven Wingqvist Secondary School's student exhibition at the Photo House in Gothenburg.

Your father greeted all the guests with wine and coffee in plastic cups. Balloons adorned fluorescent lights, pretzels filled bowls, and your whole family was present, even your grandmother, who greeted me politely, shared me a cigarette, and gave me a very kind impression. Soon the studio was piled with generous laughter and billowing cigarette smoke, flowers and shouts of "hooray," praisings and hugs. In order to be able to court his guests, Abbas delegated me his compact camera and comically named me "the photographer's court photographer." I accelerated myself in order to document all the guests in attendance. In one corner, your mother's political friends. One could recognize them by their ample lunettes, their antinuclear brooches and beige trench coats. They waved their coat belts and incited politics while they scratched their mustaches (both the men and the women). Near the entrance: the retired ladies from the nursing home who were tempted by the free coffee. They drank with birdishly quick sips, pressed their handbags against their stomachs, and exposed suspicious line-mouths. The hippie friends parked themselves on the floor, men in soft sandals with socks and women in ponchos and newly created nicknames like "Sundawn" or "Light Reflector." In the other corner, the Aristocats installed their bodies around a table and by habit turned their backs on the rest of the guests: the old ex-boxer Nabil, Mansour with the square portfolio, and Mustafa with the little tinfoil packet whose contents your father directed him to smoke outdoors (after getting himself a little sample).

Aziz was responsible for the music; soon the volume was levitated and the party was our fact. Just as your father had prophesized, a great quantity of alcohol was needed before the Swedes left their sphere of politeness and attacked the dance floor. But when they did so they bore a frenzy and jerkiness which can most closely be called epileptic. The hippies made circle movements with their hands and limbered their heads like pendulums. The political friends bounced their bodies first unwillingly and then frenetically until the sweat dropped from their nonimperialist beards. Even the Aristocats were attracted to finger-snapping cries of jubilation when Aziz invited your grandmother to dance. Ruth first declined repeated times, but then she suddenly said yes and everyone's applause claps accompanied Aziz's instructions for typical eighties dances like the pirouette, the hand clap, the caterpillar (connect-both-hands-together-and-undulate-them-like-a-wave), the mime (pretend-to-walk-into-an-invisible-wall-which-is-then-lurched-to-the-side), the hand shaker (shake-your-hands-above-your-shoulders-like-they-contain-small-dice), and the famous "Michael Jackson owl" (move-your-head-very-quickly-sideways).

Who else was there? I am ransacking my memorizations. Raino, of course, permanently positioned at the bar, toasting solitarily. And those two Chilean brothers who had been welcomed to Sweden after the coup and now projected a theater society localized on the green metro line to the south (unfortunately I remember neither their names nor the metro station's). And that beautiful friend of your mother's who had studied in Cairo and attempted to converse me about your father's "ironic work with the Swedish self-portrait." While I attempted to discuss . . . entirely different, considerably more erotic subjects.

In the photos I have from that Saturday, your father's nervous form is in the majority. First in the morning: updressed in a pressed mint green suit and patterned tie, correcting his cravat pin, and water-combing in front of the mirror in the hall. Then happily smiling with you, draped in a white shirt and overalls. Then his arm around his beautiful wife with a gold-decorated dress and coral necklace. Then distributing a hug as thanks for a bouquet. Then thumbs-up in front of the Silvia photo. Then a photo where his back is marching the hall away toward the storeroom. Then a later photo when your father is standing back in the studio, most of the guests have gone, the dance floor is deserted, some balloons are lying air-free and punctured on the floor, your father's cheeks are red, his smell a shade modified, filled up by a certain confidence of drink and unnoticing of your mother's furious background eyes. Then the last photo, when he tipsily waves farewell to the last guests (Aziz and Raino supporting each other like a capital A). Here your father's smile is strapped on like a fighter pilot's gas mask, his sweeping movements reduced to two blurry thunderclouds; his voice echoes forth the promise that everyone who wants to will get future family portraits at a reduced price. The opening was a complete success. Right? Who didn't come?

The journalists.
The publishing people.
The art critics.
The queen.

The most important ones seemed to be conspicuous in their absence.

Here follows a section that we can call "Studio Silvia awaits success." We wait patiently for the attention of journalists. We observe newspapers in hope of praising reviews, we correspond yet another series of invitations to art critics. The result? A monumental silence.

Three weeks after the opening ceremony, your father received a letter from the Swedish palace. The envelope bore the king's official seal and the queen's typed "thanked for the congratulations." Your father framed the letter behind glass and placed it in the display window, to the right of the photograph that sparked his brain with the idea for the studio's name.

My official task at Studio Silvia was soon transformed. From photo assistant and makeup-responsible to coffee maker, backgammon player, and general waiter.

Your father tried to putter parallelly with a new artistic collection, but he had difficulty finding inspiration. He noticed that time was limited, that he had invested his wife's patrimony in an uncertain photographic studio. The future suddenly seemed to glide uncertainly like a water slide.

In the summer of 1986, your day care was annulled to save economy. Instead you spent your time down in the studio in our company. Do you remember those summery days? Do you remember how your child arms helped us spread leaflets in the newly built shopping center, where many retail spaces still stood unrented? Do you remember how we let you sneak into the nursing home and nail leaflets onto the bulletin board? You worked very effectively, although your age was that of a child. And although your father perhaps did not pronounce it in your presence, he was very proud of you. Very, very proud.

Do you remember how we partook our lunches? How we assisted your father when he apart-took his camera? How we began to roar rude Arabic insultations after the customers who invaded the studio, encountered your father's welcome greeting, and then for some bizarre reason returned out to the courtyard with a regretting exterior? And do you remember how you often imitated your father when he nervously drummed his fingers against the perpetually silent booking telephone; you drummed your small fingers in the exact same rhythm and your father lost his train of thought, silenced the drum, and regarded you, a copy of himself when young, the same suspect imagination, the same speech-related problems. He lovingly patted your cheek. But the telephone continued its silent rest.

And you remember the silence, the ticking of the kitchen clock, the gaze from the blown-up Silvia portrait, the framed letter, and Dads, who drum their fingers, the sun which moves over the courtyard and filters through the curtains, and Dads' friends, who drink coffee and billow cigs and play backgammon, joke about cheating at dice, and sometimes borrow the bathroom, and once Kadir, who wants to fix the washer in the dripping faucet, the faucet that's bothered Dads for several weeks but that now they want to keep.

The economic success for Studio Silvia bided its time like a patient meter maid. Your father said:

"Do not worry, Kadir. This is a premier phase. Swedes bear a certain initial suspiciousness, particularly toward us Swedes who do not bear a Swedish appearance. But soon, anytime, our business will take off. In just a few weeks they will realize my artistic talent. Soon there will be lines and guest lists in order to access my photographic services."

"What shall we do until then?"

"We wait."

And you remember the waiting and the faucet dripping which continues and Kadir, who again offers to fix it: It's simple, it can be done in a few minutes, but Dads don't want to, Dads refuse to let him repair the faucet: I want to keep the dripping! shout Dads suddenly with a slightly too loud voice and you remember that in particular but don't really understand why. It's the summer of 1986 and the studio is empty of customers and you're starting to hang around the neighboring courtyards, starting to explore the shopping center, starting to chat with the drunks and becoming friends with the dry cleaner. And then sometime in the middle of the summer you catch sight of Melinda. And the first time you see each other you both just watch suspiciously from a distance and the second time Melinda shows you her homemade Super Mario belt and the third time you play Indian tiger tamers with extra-long whips and specially made tranquilizer darts. And doesn't someone get angry at you because of that very game? You don't remember. But you remember that Melinda soon becomes your first real best friend because Melinda is just like you. Melinda gets why you can think imagination games are fun even though you've begun elementary school and Melinda also has a bunch of imaginary friends who really exist but can't necessarily be seen by regular adults. Melinda agrees that you can play Super Mario Bros. even if you don't have that new TV game called Nintendo and she just gets mad that time when you suggest that instead of being Mario she should be the princess who must be rescued.

And we waited. With the ambition of patience we let the hours tick on while waiting for the assault of customers. To pass the time your father and I started to layer our backgammon games with nostalgic discussions. While you found your friendship with the neighborhood children, your father portioned his memories of his father and the lostness he felt from having been abandoned. I also remember how he very poetically related his longing for his father despite that this father had never been his actual knowledge.

"Is this not bizarre, Kadir? That my soul feels perpetually hollowed. It has only become worse since I became a father. I thought the consequence would be diagonally opposite. How can a hollowness arise even though what I miss has never been experienced me? How can an emptiness cause pain? And how can one cure the pain that is caused by an emptiness?"

"I do not know. Have you tried exchanging these thoughts with your wife?"

"It does not work. I can't. I do not know why. She still believes that Cherifa and Faizal are my real parents. And she knows nothing about the loan I owe you . . ."

Here we were interrupted by your storming income. With sweaty forehead, bare chest, and a long whip made of a string you whistled down the stairs and took shelter behind your father. A second later the door was opened by the master of the nearby flower shop. Furiously he sought after "the Turks who chased his grandmother's cat with darts." Your father hid your body effectively and pointed out that anyone who likened his son with a Turk would be afflicted with rumbling fists, understood? The flower master mumbled that "this neighborhood is really going downhill." He excited the studio and you crawled, smiling, from your hiding place.

"Where were we?" I coaxed. But your father did not want to continue. He signaled in your direction and made me understand that this was NOT intended for your ears. Your father varied the subject:

"Anyway: I am very glad to have your company here in Sweden, Kadir. But I have to reveal you one thing. I have no possibility of returning your economy. Unfortunately. Not right now."

"That pains me to hear."

"It pains me to admit."

"But my salary?"

"I will outpay your salary, I promise you that. With a certain delay. This studio's success has perhaps not become as I had hoped. But I want to present you an offer: If you agree to postpone the repayment of the loan, I will offer you a golden exchange."

"What? Free passport photos?" I sighed.

"No, much better. The possibility to learn the foundations of Swedish!"

"How can that benefit me?"

"Well, imagine. Swedish is a Germanic language with many international loan words. If only you know Swedish you will soon know German and Dutch and after that almost English."

"So?"

"If you want to cultivate a future as a hotel owner you MUST learn many languages, particularly Swedish. Then you can return to Tabarka with perfect prerequisites for hotelish success. By the time I repay you my debt you can open the doors for your own hotel that tempts Nordic tourists. And Nordic touristettes. What do you say?"

"Well . . . I would probably rather choose to obtain my promised economy."

Your father presented a face that looked so miserable that I immediately regretted my words.

"I lack that possibility, Kadir. Unfortunately. However, I can teach you the foundations of Swedish. This will further your future. And mine. Pernilla is frustrated that my static Swedish is never glistened to gold. And Swedish is the only language that works in Sweden. No other country I have afflicted has tied a greater worth to the perfection of language."

"But . . . which other countries have you actually afflicted? Besides Tunisia?"

"Many upon many."

"Which ones?"

"For example, Pernilla's relatives in Denmark last summer. What do you say?"

"Okay," I sighed.

Accompanied by the summer's transformation into fall, your father and I begin to repeat Swedish personal pronouns, the intensifying of adjectives, and the mystery of prepositions. We memorize how all Swedish words referring to people and animals are noted with the indefinite form *"en,"* with the exception of *"ett barn,"* a child. We tame our tongues to the mystery of Swedish pronunciation, where there is a big difference between *u* and *y*. Migratory birds leave Sweden, green leaves become firishly red, the ground is frosted, the sandbox sand stiffens, and Stockholm loses its delicious odors. All while we note that some call Swedish "the language of twenty-nine letters" or "the language of breathing," because *h* gives an actual exhalation instead of the muteness of French, and the inhaling sound with suck-formed lips indicates an affirmative response.

I want to describe what occurred with the following words underlined in a different form of text:

Magic!

Swedish filled me. Expanded me. It harmonized every bodily particle.

Where did this emotion come from? Perhaps from your father. It was he who passionately spoke of the Swedish language. It was he who led my process, who delegated me his antique handouts from *Swedish for Immigrants*, who praised my encouragement and honored my storming progress. Sometimes he mumbled:

"You learn very easily, Kadir, very easily," and this seemed to fill him with a big dose of happiness (spiced with a shade of jalousie).

I said to your father:

"My conviction was first that you just wanted to teach me Swedish in order to postpone the payment of economy. But now it feels like I have waited my whole life to get to speak this language. It is as though my tongue is made for this. Not Arabic. Not even French. Swedishness is my destiny and my studies go as quickly as a dancing feather in hurricane winds. Don't they? Is the learning equally simple for you?"

Your father hmmed forth his response to this question. This last part may surprise you but I must admit it: Sometimes I was given the emotion that your father learned more slowly than I. That something in his experiences blocked his learning.

The studio continued its empty echo during the fall. Your father's invested photo equipment glistened almost unused, the telephone waited in silence, spiders wove webs in the darkroom. The studio's photographic activity lay quietly in hibernation, and not even your mother's friends left their beloved Södermalm to support the studio despite their eagerly expressed curiosity for what they called "the colorful, multicultural suburb." I never really understood the meaning of this expression. The neighborhood in the vicinity of the studio was not particularly separated from the neighborhood in Hornstull where you localized your lodgings. The same rectangular box houses, the same brown house colors. The same brightly shining mailboxes, the same Konsum grocery, the same Apoteket sign. The same red-nosed alcoholics who sat mumbling on the benches outside Systembolaget. The same Assyrians who started the same pizzerias with the same clever Italian names. Sometimes I noticed that people from Södermalm truly enjoyed pointing out every crucial difference between "the suburbs" and "downtown." Sometimes I thought that the situation was similar to when tourists in Tabarka enjoyed pointing out the crucial difference between "the mystique of the Orient" and "the stress and pressure of the Western world." And sometimes I was heaped, like your father, to frustration by people's constant ambition of focusing on differences between people. Where does this infection come from? Can your memories of that fall offer any response?

Then comes the fall, with the usual fall routines, and there are no more weekend picnics at Trekanten and no more demonstrations and Moms stop mourning for Palme and Dads stop mourning for Refaat. Moms start working as nurses and Dads leave little brothers at day care every morning before the studio. You start second grade and conduct yourself excellently and become one of the best in the class and come home with a special diploma that time when the elementary school has a competition with times table work sheets.

At the same time it's a split time because the others at school aren't like you because most of them have cars and brand-name clothes and their own video games and cable TV and fancy country cottages and Christmas lists that are pages long. And sometime maybe you say that by the way you have cable TV now too and then some-one asks what your favorite channel is and you think and think because you know that there's some cool channel that plays music videos all day long and just before it's too late you remember the name and say it proudly: My favorite is that music channel where they play very much disco. Yeah, you know, Disco-Very. And they look at you and laugh and you don't realize your mistake until much later.

Then it's safer to go out to the studio in the after-

noons, share a snack with Dads and Kadir, and hang out
with Melinda in the courtyard. You have just started to
say "want to hang out" instead of "want to play." But
then you still see each other every day and play play
play. No one else understands life like Melinda because
Melinda has the world's yellowest Pumas and a fluorescent gummy smile and a hairstyle that's the school's
flattest flattop. And one time Melinda tells you that
some sixth-graders set their milk glasses on her hair
and told her to balance them over to the counter and she
did it but then she ran home to the courtyard and rushed
into the hall crying (fake tears of course) and a second
later her sisters came rushing out of their rooms, the
Melinda sisters who were already notorious in the area
because there were four of them and they were gigantic
in size and they all looked the same, with dimple thighs
like logs and powerful biceps and stonewashed sus-
pender jeans. They fought like no one else and it was
total uproar when all the Melinda sisters tried to get
their shoes on first and they raced to the school at full
speed and Olayinka still had her hairbrush in her hand
and Adeola rolled up her sleeves as they ran and Fayola,
who was the quietest and had the best grades, ran farthest back and mostly came along to stop the others.
The Melinda sisters invaded the cafeteria and went
from table to table with the question: Was it you? Was it
you? Was it you? And when they finally reached the
right table with the right gulping sixth-graders came the
question: Was it you? And the answer: Who did what?
And that was all the Melinda sisters needed to hear and
Monifa kneed groins and Olayinka punched and Adeola
gobbed spit and Fayola tried to·calm them down and
pull them back but then some sixth-grader said some-

thing about bananas behind her broad back and then the roles switched and Fayola became the one who was winding up and Adeola got in the middle and tried to stop it.

You're sitting wide-eyed in the swing next to Melinda's. What happened then? Then the janitor and the beefy shop teacher came and the fight was stopped and the sixth-graders cried and said: They're totally damned crazy! And the Melinda sisters went as one body out of the cafeteria and someone happened to frisk a jacket and someone happened to overturn a hall table and Melinda was right behind them and you remember that when Melinda has finished telling she smiles in that way you only smile when you see your family succeed.

On the way home you think about how you don't have a sister army, you don't have any relatives who can come to your rescue, you don't have uncles who play records at the Afro-pop club at Sankt Eriksplan, you only have Dads and Moms and a worn-out Mickey Mouse Pez dispenser that lost its dispensing power a long time ago. And little brothers of course, little brothers who are growing quickly; the nights are less screechy, but shopping is extra heavy, with milk at bulk price and canned food three for ten crowns. And soon you'll be buying juice without pulp and then a few months later just juice concentrate and then just juice on the weekends and then only on Sunday mornings, no more than one glass per brother. And soon, written clearly on the shopping list: "Cornflakes—Eldorado, NOT Kellogg's." The finances are starting to waver and Dads spend more and more time in the studio and sometimes Moms say with her opposite-loaded voice:

It's lucky there are two of us contributing to the household money, isn't it, dear? And another time, a little later that same fall with the same reverse voice: What would we do without your dad's brilliant sense of economics?

And in the same second you write the word "economics" and then the question mark you remember that it must be this fall that Dads formulate their new strategy for the studio's survival.

When do Dads present the idea? You don't remember, maybe you're sitting in the studio in the company of Kadir and a quietly silent customer phone? Maybe it's the same day that Mansour has visited and shown you that article where the *Svenska Dagbladet* journalist Erik Lidén wrote that Refaat was certainly unique in Swedish industry because he "with his Arab origin has a totally different view of truth and life than regular Swedes." Yes, presumably it's that day, when Mansour has put on his glasses and left the studio in a heavy fog of smoke and Kadir is sitting silently and Dads mumble: This country is very bizarre to me, first you're an Arab and then you're Swede of the Year and then you're an Arab again.

You take the commuter train home together and Dads sit silently. Then over dinner Dads look at Moms and say: I have made up my mind. No more not-Swedish. You are right. Starting now we will ONLY speak Swedish. Both here and in the studio. The twins will not be confused by the multitude of languages! No more French, no more Arabic. I must make my Swedish seriously impeccable in order to guarantee my studio's continued survival!

Moms who applaud and you who protest and Dads

who suddenly pretend not to understand either Arabic
or French objections. Swedish, my son. Now we speaks
Swedish!

Dads change languages.
Dads shrink a little.

I am resuming the rudder of the narrative in order to describe the
next phase in our Swedish learning. It was acted in early spring
1987. Your mother had pointed out that perhaps it was not ingenious that your father taught me Swedish (and I him). She noted
the likeness to the myth of "the blind leading the blind" and rec-
ommended us to cultivate the assistance of an outsider. Who did
we select? Exactly. You.

Your father interrupted you in your games in the courtyard,
called you in to the studio, and pronounced his desire:

"We need your assistance. Instead of spending your time with
childish friends you shall be our guide into the Swedish language.
Daccurdo?"

Your father explained that we were in need of explicit linguistic rules that define the structure of Swedish and you nodded
your head and had a very difficult time concealing your glowing
pride. The next day we initiated our lessons. When you reached
the studio, which was empty as usual, you had prepared certain
notes and together we parked ourselves at a table with the ambition of illuminating the dark cave that we can call the Swedish
language.

During the following months you did your best to act grown-up
and assist the formulating of our rules of grammar. Here you can
write in the memories that detail for the reader that it was thanks
to your father and Kadir that you were infected with the ambition
of an author.

And you must admit that Kadir actually has a point because it is in the formulating of the rules of grammar that you see Swedish from the outside in for the first time. And maybe this is where your linguistic curiosity is wakened? Dads who decide that there is a system to language and ask for your help and what is bigger than dads who ask sons for help? The whole spring you go directly to the studio after school. You help with grammar, practice pronunciation, and correct their texts with dictionaries. You do your best to make up simplified rules of grammar, which Dads collect in the black wax notebook. And you remember how strange it feels to know more than Dads for the first time in your life. The feeling intoxicates you, takes over, and maybe sometimes you correct mistakes that are really correct and maybe sometimes you make up rules that aren't exactly right, but Dads continue to write in the wax notebook and Kadir continues to imitate your pronunciation and you have a power that you've never had before. Soon you feel how the language opens up, how the linguistic structures are everywhere, how you are always on the trail of the truth. You collect more and more rules with a huge amount of examples. Until the day when Dads suddenly take the notebook from you, hide it in the *mémoire,* and forbid you to continue collecting rules. Why? You don't remember. But you remember that you keep going in your head because not even Dads can control the inside of your head and in there you build new systems and new structures for how Swedish is constructed. And just one time, right before Kadir returns home, you try to convince Dads that Swedish is actually a total Arab-hating language, and Dads, sighing, ask why, and you only have time to give one example: What about the expression *pyramid scheme*? What's more Arab-hating than that? And Dads whip around and the cuff on your ear burns your cheek red and Dads hiss: *You're* Swedish, you goddamn bloody idiot!

Right now I'm sitting here behind my reception with the black wax notebook with our rules of grammar in front of me. Its exterior is worn, the shine is lost, and a brown coffee ring tattoos its first page. Still it is very grandiose to me in its nostalgic value. What fun we had when we together became each other's astronauts in the universe of the Swedish language! Was our togetherness not delicious? Everyone received compensation: You practiced your tongue to say *r* and *s* (finally!!!). I prepared my hotelish CEO proficiency. Your father practiced his Swedish in order to be able to wait on photo customers in the right language. Do our rules of grammar justify their position in the book about your father? I believe so. Below I have translated the text from the booklet, approximately how we wrote it (spiced with a little extra metaphoricalness). And by the way, before I forget: If you persist in bringing up a certain cuff your father happened to delegate you I want to remind you of the truth. It was a "cuff" that we can sooner call a "pat softer than a sweater present on Christmas Eve." And it was for your own sake, memorize that.

KHEMIRI'S (& KADIR's) RULES OF GRAMMAR
Formulated While Waiting for Photo Customers, Spring 1987

INTRODUCTION

Swedish is the language of the Swedes. The Swedish mentality bears a great interest for different phenomena. This mentality is reflected in the Swedes' language. This is vital. In order to understand the Swedes and their humor and their bizarre manner of discussing the weather and nodding forth their refusal we must understand Swedish. The mentality and the language are linked together, back and forth in the mirror of eternity that is symbolized by two mirrors put up facing each other in a sweaty changing room.

Jonas—this is my decorative introduction with a poetic metaphor stolen from your father.

Who, then, are the Swedes? Let us describe them and relate their language to their mentality.

MNEMONIC RULE I

Swedish is the language of loans. When in doubt about a Swedish word—choose the French equivalent. Or English. This saves a lot of time in the learning of vocabulary. Swedes are a people with quick influences from the world around them.

This was our initial linguistic rule. In the composition book we collectioned a monstrous quantity of correspondences between Swedish and French and English in order to effectively build our vocabularies. In double-column form with linked arrows are nouns like "chauffeur," "avenue," "premier," "voyeur." The adjectives include words like "maladroit," "excellent," "vital." A particular page has been dedicated to the verbs of quantity; there are "pronounce," "terminate," "disregard," "march," "respond," "lodge."

MNEMONIC RULE 2

One can also visualize Swedish as the language of melody—when in uncertainty, notice the nuance of intonation. Swedes love song and music. No people sings in choir more than Swedes. Incidentally, Pernilla has taken music classes. Swedes sing songs on holidays, birthdays, and before they drink alcohol. Someone who does something well has "struck the right note" and people who disagree are "out of tune." Everything in Swedish is music.

This was our secondary rule, formulated in order to try to differentiate between words that in Swedish are confusing copies with only the vital difference of tone. We expose examples like "bass" (partly the guitarly, partly the fishly). The baby's "mobile" is compared with a book"mobile" with the city of "Mobile." The "Polish" (from Poland) compete with "polish" (for shoes). "To reject" is mirrored against "to be a reject." It also says:

> You can eat chili and be chilly.
> You can sit on a board and be bored.
> You can hit the brake and take a break.
> See also hail, fall, hit . . .

Your father and I carefully practiced the tones of pronunciation to the correct Swedish melody before we onwent to the next rule.

MNEMONIC RULE 3

Also, when the melody is exactly identical to us, the poetic ambiguity of Swedish can deceive. Be wary of the context!

Swedes are, for example, extremely amorous about payment to the government. Thus "the Treasury" takes one's stately tax compulsion and "treasure" is a precious chest of riches.

Here many pages are dedicated to equivalent examples. At the end your father celebrates one of his Swedish favorite words: "drive."

Oh, that magnificent word which in the form of symbols shows the poeticness of Swedish! By context, "drive" can bear three diagonally separated meanings. There is to "drive" something through, as in firmly advance a particular politic. There is to "drive" as in controlling a moving vehicle. There is also to "drive" someone up the wall in the aim of annoying.

And then, just when your father was done, you said:
"And then driving as in the meaning of driving snow!" and your father nodded happily and added it in the book.

MNEMONIC RULE 4

Swedes love music and particularly birds' song! On the radio there are intermission birds, and the vitality of birds is mirrored in hundreds of Swedish expressions.

Here we noticed how you began to be more interested in our language discussions. The day after the formulating of that rule you came back to the studio with a long list of examples:

To "rule the roost" is to be the leader, and "pecking order" describes the ranking of colleagues. When something is "scarcer than hens' teeth," the rarity is very intensive. When one "wings" something, one is improvising. One is free as "a bird" and watches like "a hawk," and to arrange a home is to "nest." To admit error is to "eat crow," and the ideal saver of time is to "kill two birds with one stone." The reddish spots of itchy disease on small children are called "chicken pox." The coldness of skin is related to "goose bumps," and one provokes by "ruffling feathers." Information from a concealed source is from "a little bird," cowards are named "chicken," and an unlovely person is named an "ugly duckling." And knowledge about the oldest art of love is of course related in "the birds and the bees."

Jonas—I know that you collectioned even more examples but perhaps these are sufficient?

MNEMONIC RULE 5

For that matter—let us reformulate; not only birds are vital for the Swedish mentality. ALL of nature is constantly present for them. They are alone in the celebrated Everyman's Right. Nature is EVERYTHING for them.

Here you began to spend more and more time with our rules. You began to read dictionaries and snickered yourself through your father's old Swedish-French gems. Then you formulated this rule and presented us examples in quantity. Your father was impressed and encouraged you. Initially. Which in turn only seemed to feed your hunger rather than to satisfy it.

A "happy camper" is someone very content. When two people are extremely similar they are "two peas in a pod." An evil person is "a bad apple," and one who is silent at a party is a "wallflower." Life is compared with "a bowl of cherries," and a bad thing is "the pits." The Swede's ideal is "down to earth," people are the "grass roots," a mysterious person is a "hard nut to crack."

Nature is always near in the phase of reproduction as well. The beautiful woman is called "a chick." She is stroked on her bosom, or her "melons." Soon her "bush" is moistened. She is fertilized by the man's "wood" when he sows his "wild oats." Together the woman and the man then carry out the act called "a roll in the hay."

These phrases wakened great humor in the three of us. The space for this rule ends here, but a few pages ahead the enumeration of nature continues . . .

For that matter—let us not forget the Swedes' names. What can trace the influence of nature better than the last names of celebrities? There is the pianist Lars Roos, like a rose; and the pop star Lasse Berghagen, "mountain pasture"; the author Astrid Lindgren, "linden branch"; and the skier Gunde Svan, "swan." There's the architect Asplund, "aspen grove"; the director Bergman, "man from the mountain"; the skier Stenmark, "stony land." The journalist Lagercrantz, "laurel wreath," and the politicians Palme, "palm tree," and Björck, "birch." And last but not least: Magnus "Här-en-stam"— "Here a log." The Swedish nature is near to us everywhere! Sometimes also in first names! What other people name themselves Stig ("path") or Björn ("bear") or [x].

Here I cannot really decipher the handwriting. We continue with . . .

MNEMONIC RULE 6

Hmm . . . My son says: Of course NATURE is vital, but is it not IN PARTICULAR the forest that the Swedes idolize the most? The forest and in particular the trees. Swedes are the Forest People! Sweden is the Land of Trees!

Here you began to be entirely too overactivated in your collection of linguistic examples. One can see more and more often that your fingers have taken the pen and themselves written in wordish examples.

Among other things, it reads:

> Everything on a tree can become a new word in Swedish. The frequent customer of a bank can go to a "branch," and we are "rooting" for the studio to succeed. A Swede removes his body and "leaves," a perplexed person (or a political speech) is "stumped," someone in love "pines." To redecorate is to "spruce up," and a complicated situation is "sticky." Comedy is "slapstick," a policeman has a "nightstick," a child plays with a "pogo stick," and you light a candle with a "matchstick." The ideal of life is often to "turn over a new leaf." When a Swede is on the wrong track he is "barking up the wrong tree." Oof, my fingers are getting tired.

. . . you had actually written that in the notebook . . .

> You can also "go out on a limb" and "put down roots." To snore is to "saw logs;" to go insane is to be "barking mad." If someone is scared they "shake like a leaf." One is poor because "money doesn't grow on trees."

When we had written this I hacked my throat and coughed a few loud times . . . Your father ignored me.

> And what can be better proof of the Swedes' tree fixation than this: Their capital city is called STOCKHOLM! And their economic currency is called "CROWNS"! (The stock bears up the tree, and the crown, of course, sways above.)

Then follows a section that we can exclude because it is crossed out. In it you wanted to convince us that Swedes are the Alcohol People. Under the lines one can decipher "the ideal is to be 'in high spirits' or 'drunk with joy' or 'intoxicated by life,'" and farther down, "a Swede who doesn't express feelings 'bottles them up,' something small is 'pint-sized,' and . . .". Then your father seems to have stopped you in the middle of this rule and taken the pen back.

MNEMONIC RULE 7

What do the Swedes love more than products from the dairy? Nothing! Their milk exists in a majority of differentiated variants, and they drink it like water. They are the Dairy People, mark our words!

In the notebook it says:

The Swede with importance is called "big cheese" and something that is too sentimental is "cheesy." When we photograph, the customer says "cheese." Something that works smoothly is "like butter," and someone who is angry is "cheesed off"!!! "Don't cry over spilled milk" is called scornfully at someone who is upset over a triviality, and when one takes full advantage of a situation it is "milked." And, and . . . there is more, I am convinced. YES! What is the ideal in the world of the Swede? To find the type of success that is called being "the cream of the crop."

Somewhere around here your father got the task of photographing a newly deceased senior citizen's home of death at the nursing home. Your father carried out the task with brilliance and precision. In the darkroom he took me separately and whispered:

"Am I exaggerating if I say that my dear son seems to be a little . . . special?"

"No, but in which respect? His late speech or his corpulence or his persistence in discussing with himself?"

Your father angrily hacked his voice.

"Watch yourself, Kadir. I am referring to how he invests so much time in our rules of grammar. Haven't you seen him? He yells, 'Wow, my theories just grow in expansion—Swedish has surrounded me, I see the patterns, knowledge is swirling me! My theories are developing with the heat and speed of a forest fire!' I am alarmed by his development! It is not positive that my son has the tendency to grow his passion for things with such a strong strength."

"I just think he is reminiscent of you."

This made your father quiet his voice. We continued with the darkroom work. From your father's position I heard him say:

"This does not prophetize well about the future."

Here follow two empty pages (a mistake?) before the next rule is presented.

MNEMONIC RULE 8

The Swedes are also the Climate People? Right? Well, perhaps. YES!!! Snow and ice are central to the understanding of the world of the Swedes. When the Swedes are extremely occupied, they are "snowed under." After one's day of death one hopes to reach the heaven that the Swede calls "paradice." Even the winds are important. A success "takes something by storm." One shouts, "Okay, we will do it—let us throw caution to the wind!" A solution is discovered by "brainstorming."

Here your father began to say that you should devote more time to homework than to linguistic rules. Simultaneously I began to project my journey home. The letters in the notebook now cease to relate examples in complete phrases. Instead the words are presented helter-skeltered in chaoticness.

MNEMONIC RULE 9

In addition, let us not limit the Swedes' interest for Nature. The fablish world of animals is also central and vital. To bother is to "badger" and to imitate is to "ape," and the police are called "pigs" and one's love is complimented with "love bug," even though to annoy is "to bug," and when one struggles it is called "floundering" and having to "grin and bear" something makes no one happy and one feels "happy as a clam" or one feels the opposite and "clams up," and there are "scales" like at the grocery store and "scales" like on a fish and insectly "bees" and "bees" for spelling and that was great and thus "a whale of a time," and a distraction is a "red herring" and a pain in the leg is a "charley horse" and a snitch "rats" someone out and one drinks "like a fish" and the "donkey work" is boring and a scream sounds like "a stuck pig" and to ignore is to "play ostrich" and nervousness fills stomachs with "butterflies" and the pants with "ants" and something unusual is "neither fish nor fowl" and one "squirrels away" like a miser, and when one is hungry one "could eat a horse" and one can "go ape" and "have a cow" and have free reins and sit on "high horses" and live "high on the hog" and . . . (height essential—Swedes v. tall!).

Here your father began to spread active irritation about your constant talk of wordish rules. He said to you:

"Twist your focus to your homework instead! Go out and play soccer! Be a bit normal! I wanted to formulate these rules with a gleamed eye, not with the passion that you seem to show. I do not want to see hide nor hair of you here!"

And do you know what bizarre you respondered? You sat with the yellow pencil chewed between your lips, pondered, and then pronounced:

"Even this can be salvaged as a rule of grammar! 'Hide nor hair' is like 'scarcer than hens' teeth.' And who cares about hair more than Swedes? The contours of truth are near now!"

Your father side-swung his sighing head. On the next page is the tenth and terminating rule:

MNEMONIC RULE 10

The Swedes are also the Hair People. Hairstyles bear a great weight in Sweden; the work of hairstylists exposes a well-formed status and also this can of course be noticed in the Swedes' linguistic use. Absent is when one has not seen "hide nor hair," of something, a neat person does not have "a hair out of place," something subtle is as "fine as a hair," something uncertain "hangs by a hair," something that makes one tough "puts hair on one's chest," finding subtleties is "splitting hairs," to be anxious is to "pull your hair out," and to inspect carefully is to use "a fine-tooth comb." Do not touch a "hair" on my friend's head and do not give yourself "gray hair" in your attempt to "let your hair down" and a "hair-raising splitting of hairs does not make a hair's breadth."

These were our ten rules. We can conclude the section with your father's recurring praise of the poetic excellence of Swedish (this is actually not in our notebook). Do you remember it? He would say something like this:

Let us now ring out our cry: Swedish is the language of loans, melody, the dairy, nature, animals, fine as hair! And of optimism! Swedish is the language where the narrow end of the alley is not a "dead end" (like in English) or the "rump of

In April of 1987 I chose to return home to Tunisia. My breast had shrunk my belief in your father's economic talent and grown my longing for Tabarka's touristettes, the daily life of Hôtel Majestique, and my nightly poker partners.

My emotion for your family's status had also begun to distress me. Your father's dirty shoes and holey beret, your mother's tired nurse exterior, your constant economy-size packages from the cheap stores in Skärholmen, your magnet-attached three-crown rebate coupons on the refrigerator, your TV with a taped antenna cord, your little brothers' hand-me-down rompers, your room with your father's home-constructed bookshelves. Everything filled me with the tragedy of aversion. For certainly it was not this your father projected when he left Tunisia?

Your father closed the studio and escorted me to Central Station for me to say farewell. Before the departure he delegated me a certain reduced salary plus our joint linguistic-rule notebook:

"Here, a souvenir. You may as well take it so that my son escapes confusing himself even more in the fog of his imagination."

I accepted the book. And then pronounced a phrase that I would probably regret and draw back into my mouth with the same suck as in the Vicks cough drop ads of the time. If I only could.

"Thanks, Abbas. Good luck for the future. I hope you succeed in your ambition of not infecting your son with being an outsider."

"What do you mean, infect?"

"Well, certainly it seems being an outsider wanders in inheritance from one generation to the next? And simultaneously infects those who are near? A little like a contagious disease?"

This was a thought I had polished in my solitude and I felt proud about, for once, being able to sprinkle your father with a new insight. Your father nodded his head.

"That is the most intelligent thing I have heard you say for a long time, Kadir. Being an outsider as an infection. I will memorize that. And if you ever come across an idea of how I should grow

my studio's success, then contact me . . . I guarantee to pay my borrowed sum with added interest as soon as it is possible."

We waved our farewell. This picture, of your unshaven father
who grimly waves me through the glass on the airport bus, is to me
a strong memory. This was the last time I saw your father and automatically recognized him.

PART FOUR

Dearest greetings!

Naturally I am gladdened by your athletic ambition. But I am darkened when I do not understand your insinuations. You write: "Isn't it true that you and Dad had a huge beef before you parted? That you had a big fight with yelling and scuffling and uproar?" What kind of knickknack is this? Is it your mother who has said this? Is a "beef" equivalent to a fight?

I will unmask something: Your mother may be a woman unique from the generality of ALL other women. BUT her interest in your father's friends was never bigger than that of a puddle. She constantly mixed their names, and when your father named them Aristocats your mother soon began to name them the Aristoidiots. She was irritated by their drinking habits and would probably rather see your father's relations with her secure communist circle. This is my truth and you can verify it with your mother.

That you do not remember my friendly farewell or all our linguistic rules surely doesn't mean that they have not existed? I have the proof before me this very second. Write me, by the way . . . What do you remember of the moon landing or the Olympics in Mexico or the summer of '74? Not much, right? Do not let the precariousness of memory swirl our focus.

On the other hand, you are possibly correct that the rules would uptake too many pages in our book. In order to shape a global master opus the alternative that these linguistic rules are injected ONLY in the Swedish version is presented. In the French version we can let your father applaud the Eiffel Tower, Jacques Brel, and nuclear tests in the territory of others, enjoying a Brie-filled baguette. The Australian version can fantasize forth a customer who invades the studio and tells of his time as a kangaroo hunter. In the South American version an Indian can play a melody on a pan flute. Indian readers can be served your father's recipe for curry; to yellower Asians we can introduce a passage where your father expresses himself positively about small, cute stuffed animals, video games, raw fish, sumo wrestling, industrious men, and obedient women. What do you think?

Now we will initiate the book's quadratic section, and once again it is time for you to invade the story. You must be rather hungry for revenge after your latest defeat. Naturally you will get a new chance; no one is infallible, not even Dr. Phil. (Except maybe in his master opus *Defining Your Authentic Self.*) Let us now show how your father succeeded in rousing his studio to a success story. Let us simultaneously hope that you have grown your talent since last time. I affix you an adequate introduction with added headings in order to guide the book in the correct angle.

Your biding friend,
Kadir

ps: The global world net just informed me that Jean-Marc Bouju has received the World Press Photo of the Year! Can you keep a very secret secrecy? Jean-Marc Bouju is one of your father's anonymous aliases! Your father shot the photograph in question in March 2003 in an American prison camp near the Iraqi Najaf. Have you seen the photo? It is painfully arresting. An Iraqi prisoner sits with bent back on the ground, draped in a white coverall behind curled thorny wire. His head is confined in a black plastic hood. In his embrace he has his crying son. The anonymous man is enclosing his son, resting his hand on his forehead; the plastic hood is gleaming in the sunshine. The photo constantly moves me to tears. And now as I am writing you these phrases the tears are coming back. Just the thought of the father and the son makes everything blurry, the keys, the letters, the computer screen. I miss your father so terribly much. I hope and pray that he soon will return from where he is now. But perhaps it is too late.

Initiate section four as follows:

"Let us be honest. Studio Silvia's first year of life attracted only a minority of customers. My father's talent sprinkled some passport photos and a local shoe-factory owner's advertisements. Sometimes he was engaged by immigrants who had met Swedish women and were now lured into marriages. In order to convince the ever stricter Swedish authorities of their honest intentions, Abbas was commissioned to create historic nostalgia photos from vacations and family gatherings and everyday balcony dinners that had not had time to exist. Abbas documented charter-trip love and New Year's kisses and picnic smiles, always with a virtuoso camera talent that heaped the photos' authenticity. In New Year's pictures one could see sparklers, wine-flecked tablecloths, and a blurry couple in love who showed typical red eyes and sufficiently puffy pale faces. The sandy beach photos were accompanied by umbrella drinks, coolers, and fictive grains of sand in the camera. As the finishing touch my father ordained that the Swedes' shoulders and noses should be greased with ketchup mixed with milk (which resulted in the stinging red shiningness that characterizes Swedes on charter vacations).

"But these commissions filled neither my father's photographic talent nor his wallet. The lucrative photo commissions still lay beyond my father's horizon. What to do? Abbas realized that he must formulate a new strategy in order to reach success . . . here is how it happened . . ."

In the next scene, your father wanders his sorrowful steps away from his studio. It is a slushy day in the twilight of the eighties. He notices that the neighborhood around Studio Silvia is beginning to be modified, step by step. More and more of the neighboring buildings' balconies present shining white satellite-dish ears, which listen in satellitish TV waves from around the world. Children of frequent colors play in the sandboxes. The local tobacco shop where before one could purchase classic pipes and expanded cigarette paraphernalia in polished wood has been replaced by a video rental with a separate corner for horse gambling. Instead of the classic hairdresser salon that was decorated with gliding-around spiral advertising, antique sensational magazines, and brown-and-white photographs, there is now a modern salon with orange-sponged walls and an English title. The pharmacy has disappeared. The post office has disappeared. In place of the paint store a Chinese restaurant has opened its door with "Super Lunch Asian Buffet" for fifty-five crowns.

Your father's massive steps wander farther toward the commuter train station. On the square, the Swedish alcoholics have received the company of a group of older men with rosaries and an Indian family who sell neon-colored sweat suits and sequined tops.

Your father waves to one of the denim-vest-draped alcoholics and thinks: "Håkan is still here, in any case; not everything is modified." Abbas' smile is reduced when he discovers the multitude of posters that have been pasted on the pillars above the escalator to the train station. They say, "Do YOU want YOUR children to face MECCA?" and, "Out with the RIFFRAFF," and, "Stop the MASS RAPES, stop the MASS IMMIGRATION," and there are even more slogans, which your father blocks out of his brain and refuses to let himself read.

While waiting for the train into the city, your father catches sight of you. Instead of being in school and doing your lessons you are playing with some friends over by the abandoned commuter rail tracks. At first you're standing solitarily and discussing loudly with yourself while at the same time scratching yourself frenetically on the stomach and back. Just when you have shouted: "I need a hit!" up pops that skinny Negro girl. With suspicious shoulder glances she delivers you . . . a stick. You pay her with some leaves, strike a few blows on your own arm, and then place the stick against your arm bend. Then you slowly doze off while your friend inventories your pockets. Then you fly up, laughing, and you switch your roles.

Sighing over his son's bizarreness, Abbas transports himself into the city. He aimlessly wanders all the streets, which he knows as well as his pockets. Kungsgatan. Up Drottninggatan. Down Odengatan. But his mood is still as cloudy as the gray clouds that roll the sky. His best friend has traveled home. The success of his career far away. The rent for the studio stings his wallet. The family's economy threatened. A son with bizarre habits who risks being infected by the virus of being an outsider.

Suddenly, at Sveavägen's intersection with Odengatan, he is roused out of his lethargy by a loud shout:

"Abbas!"

It is your father's antique companion Raino, who, smiling, waves his hand. Raino's hairstyle is neatly trimmed, the walrus mustache shaved smooth, the signs of alcoholism reduced. The two photographers greet each other amiably and exchange each other's résumés while Raino's leashed dog noses your father's hands. In his humorous choppy Finland Swedish, Raino asks about your father's career. Your father tells about his studio and Raino says:

"I conkratchulate you! What is your specialty?"

"I photograph everything!" Abbas smiles.

"Putt . . . you must specialize yourself. You can't photokraph EFFRYTHING. Either you are an artist or you photokraph foot. Either you to ats or shoot tocumentaries. Fint your specialty and then work to pecome pest at it."

"How is it going with your career?" Abbas interpellates, in order to change the angle of the discussion.

Raino details that he has recently reached his success; he has just presented some of his food photographs at a Scan Foods–sponsored exhibition that is touring Europe and in addition he is in love with a twenty-three-years-younger meditation instructor. He notes life as euphoric and their sex life as heavenly. Then he is interrupted by your father, who congratulates him but says that he is suddenly in a big, big hurry, excuses himself, and withdraws in toward the City Library. He stands there in the entry, recovering his breath with his gaze out toward all the gray. Heaped with that bizarrely maximized sorrowfulness that is installed after a rendezvous with an antique acquaintance who is unexpectedly euphoric.

Your father decides to invade the library. He steers his steps toward section four. The smell is wet umbrellas, book pages, bearded stamp men, and female students' perfume. Abbas parks himself near the photographic section. He pages photographic opuses and tries to feed his inspiration. He reads about photographic giants who also confronted hurdles in the dawns of their careers. Cartier-Bresson. Karsh. Halsman. Before he goes, he returns, of course, to the biography dedicated to his biggest hero of all: Robert Capa.

Your father pages all the photographic motifs he knows by and with his heart. The soldier in the Spanish Civil War who has been captured in the middle of dying. The siege of Bilbao. The eleven photos from D-Day that weren't ruined by that poor shaky-handed lab assistant.

Abbas sighs his lungs. His vitality is trickling out of him. He thinks of the sixty-one photographs from the invasion of Normandy, lost forever. He visualizes the poor lab assistant. He thinks: Some are created for great achievements and others are not. Perhaps I am one of the latter?

Then his eye is captured by a name: "Endre Ernö Friedmann." Abbas reads the name again. Friedmann, born 1913 in Hungary's Budapest. As a povertous Jewish refugee he crossed borders, localized himself in Paris, and tried to start a career as a photographer. He met the disinterest of silence from picture buyers and the establishment. What became his response? In the hour of desperation he formulated a new name, a more adequate name, a name that contained his true ideal.

Which name did he formulate?

Exactly.

Robert Capa!

Prepare your surprise when I write you that Robert Capa has never existed! Capa is in reality the result of the myth that Friedmann created. The name referred to the director Frank Capra and soon Parisian tongues began to whisper about this mythical Capa, transparent and difficult to meet, presumably American in origin, few equal in his beauty and with impressive photographic talent. Capa's photos began to sell, his success grew, Friedmann fed the myth with anecdotes and rumors up until he exchanged his official name and identity. Friedmann was transformed to Capa, fantasy became reality, and Capa said: It was like being born again, without hurting anyone.

The idea flashes your father unexpectedly, like a flash of light-ning. Hmm, that metaphor was not sufficiently excellent. Let me try again: The idea flashes your father unexpectedly, like a very, very energetic lightbulb. (Then let a real lightbulb daz-zle both the air above your father's head and the librarians who hush your father's mumbling.) Abbas suddenly stands up, the chair falls backward, and the library's silence is broken by the words:

"Of course Capa's strategy will be mine! My Arabic name must be MODIFIED!" (ied . . . ied . . . ied . . . echoes section four).

Back in the chair, your father begins to fantasize forth adequate artist names. Should he perhaps inventory the American photogra-pher George MacDonald? Or the Italian photographer Ferdinando Verderi? Or should he perhaps present his work under the name Papanastasopoulou Chrysovalanti? A homosexual Greek photogra-pher who documented genuine Arabic culture in Jendouba with borrowed fezzes? The ideas storm your father's brain until he stands up again and auctions:

"No . . . my photographic alias shall be spelled . . . Krister Holmström Abbas Khemiri! And my specialty will be . . . DOG PHOTOGRAPHY!!!"

("SHHH" is heard from steel-gazed librarians.)

The idea of transforming his name came from Capa. But where did the idea of taking photos of dogs come from? Can we blame Raino? Or perhaps your linguistic rules? In any case, it is not your father who excites the library. Instead it is Krister Holmström Abbas Khemiri, the dog photographer, who in the nocturnal darkness of the afternoon glides down the staircase and wanders his happy steps toward the metro. A strange light follows his steps, and his thoughts whisper: "A name is much more than a name . . ."

Just days later your father has fabricated a new studio sign and begun to paste the light poles of the dog parks with fringed advertisements: "Are you looking for a photographer to take pictures of your beloved darling dog? Call Krister Holmström Abbas Khemiri! Cheap animal photographs by an internationally famous animal photographer!!!"

Was your father's new name a coincidence? Of course he knew of Christer Strömholm, world-celebrated photographer and receiver of the Hasselblad Prize. But with the voice of honesty I inform you: Your father did NOT have the ambition of parasiting upon Christer's customers and reputation. Rather, he wanted to maximize the distance between himself and those prejudices that degraded Swedish Arabs. Therefore he selected a name that he considered attractive, professional, and well known. (In the book, you can inject a verbose insultation of the other Christer's obnoxious lawyer, Hallerstedt, who initially pursued your father with threats of a summons.)

So . . . now it is up to you to continue the story. Do not rouse my disappointment. I launch the following chapters:

1. Your father's success
2. More details of your father's success

3. Your growing confusion
4. The happy summer of 1989
5. Abbas' departure from his friends

YOUR FATHER'S SUCCESS

And you remember when Dads fix the new studio sign that says "PET PHOTOGRAPHER KRISTER HOLMSTRÖM" in big letters and "Abbas Khemiri" with small cursive ones underneath. And soon Dads' customer phone begins to ring. Dads book a black terrier on the twelfth and a Great Dane on the fourteenth and the weekend after next a dachshund society that's having a competition in Södertälje. Dads start to fill the calendar with appointments and no longer have time for games of backgammon, discussions of language, or photography quotes.

The Dynamic Duo is split up, and it's lucky that there is Melinda. Every afternoon that spring you meet either in the shopping center near the candy shop or down by the abandoned tracks. You play train robbers and Indiana Jones or Super Mario Bros. or drug addicts and dealers. And sometimes, when you are in the mood for sports, you do your self-invented septathlon (run around the courtyard, springy-horse rodeo, small park-bike throwing, one-hundred-meter park-bench hurdle, standing long jump from the swings, shopping cart rally through the shopping center, senior citizen relay tag).

Everything is total bliss until Melinda tells you that the Indians who sell synthetic clothes on the square have a son who is "pretty cute." You both sneak off to spy and of course you point out that the son is about the ugliest person you've ever seen because he has an underbite and glasses and is the fattest in the world, with dorkily big baggy jeans. Besides, downy mustaches like that are really ugly, Melinda, don't you think? But Melinda keeps spying and doesn't answer. Then you switch to spying on the fatty's sister because she is actually also VERY CUTE (and you say it out loud so Melinda will stop staring at the fat Indian). The little sister has her hair in hard-as-steel slanting bangs and is blowing shiny pink Hubba Bubba bubbles and returning your looks with total nonchalance. But it is obvious, of course, that she wants you.

One day the fat Indian comes over and gives Melinda a salty sucker and another time he asks if you want to listen to his Walkman while he's helping his parents close up, and of course you say yes and with one hand each you hold tight to the yellow waterproof Sony player and together you push the soft play button and together you are shot up into space by NWA's album *Straight Outta Compton,* the world's best album by the world's best group.

Since that day the fat Indian is one of you. And pretty soon you stop calling him the fat Indian and start calling him his real name, Imran. And pretty soon you get that he isn't Indian at all, he's Baloch, which is about like Arab or Iranian only better (according to Imran). And soon after that you actually start to like him as a real friend, because you realize that he and Melinda are by no means going to fall in love and leave you alone, because Imran succeeds in saying all the things Melinda has heard for her whole life and therefore hates more than anything else. ("At first when I saw you I thought you were a guy. Were you born here? Do you get even darker when you sunbathe? Why are you so skinny and your sisters so fat? Shit, you're strong. For a girl, I mean.") And Melinda just sighs and makes it into a fun thing to smash Imran to pieces in your own septathlon. You're the judge and you do your best to be impartial and not smile on the outside when Melinda outplays Imran in event after event.

Maybe it's because Imran wants to play something where he knows the rules beforehand that he suggests on a rainy Saturday that you play Dungeons & Dragons. Role-playing? Isn't that for huge nerds? But Imran says that it's pretty much like playing but more grown-up. And maybe you don't dare? Maybe you're chicken? Of course not. You're voted game master and soon you're under way.

While real customers with real pets start to ask their way through the shopping center to find the pet photographer Krister Holmström, you hang out by the deserted commuter train area. Melinda and Imran each build a character while you prepare adventures, draw maps, and plant treasures in dragon-guarded bunkers. In reality the adventure should be placed in historic time and in reality one can choose between being a knight or a magician or maybe an elf. But Melinda says that if she's going to play she wants to be called Miss Super Zulu Sister and be a monster-strong medicine woman from black Africa who has a poisonous Afro pick in her hair and an AK-47 hidden between her breasts and a bunch of medicinal brews that grant maximum magical skill. And in that case Imran wants to be MC Mustachio, a Baloch super hip-hop prophet from Compton who has a sharpened Raiders cap, magic Air Force Ones, and battery-powered nunchucks. His mustache is also super long and can be used both to box enemies and to caress girls. You let them stretch the rules and soon you're under way.

While Dads finds a home in the studio, you find a home in the role-playing. Nothing can beat the feeling of being the master of everything. You invent adventures that make Imran and Melinda sweat, roar, cry, and once, when MC Mustachio loses a battle against a CIA-trained giant amoeba, Imran takes his dice and chucks them away over the tracks, almost all the way to the platform, where regular people discover you and wonder what you're really up to.

During the summer, Dads's customer phone keeps ringing. Dads's calendar goes from totally empty to three shoots a week to the time when Dads has to say no to a commission for the first time, because of lack of time. Soon all of Dads's hours are dedicated to work. At breakfast Dads sits with magnified eyes and checks contact sheets. In the morning there are shoots and at twilight, the darkroom. Dads shoots a retired general in uniform with his German shepherd, a smiling lady in strawberry shorts with two Rhodesian ridgebacks, a wheelchair guy's Labrador. While you sit out by the train tracks and toss dice and fight against amphetamine-junkie elves.

It is soon obvious that you are something of a gifted game master. At first, of course, it was mostly fights with black orcs and princesses with hard-as-steel slanted bangs and Hubba Bubba gum who must be rescued. But soon you learn more about the world. You read up on monsters and their characteristics, you learn everything about Cerberus and Evard's Black Tentacles, ice dragons and hydras. Imran has played with four other gangs of friends before, in three different cities. But no other game master has created adventures like you. No one else has let all times be mixed together into one, no one else supplies rakshasas with mini-Uzis or basilisks with mirrors (so that their petrifying gazes can be sent around corners). No other game master lets two-winged dinosaurs attack on those air skateboards from *Back to the Future*. And only you persist in never letting the adventure end. Because right when the head boss is conquered and Miss Super Zulu Sister and MC Mustachio are catching their breath and doing high fives and are about to take the treasure, some extra-hungry hippogriffs or some manticores with newly sharpened claws and rocket packs always show up. And Imran shrieks in fury and Melinda threatens you with a real beating but that's life, manticores are monsters like everything else and you haven't finished your task until you've gotten out of here, so what do you say? Who's going to attack first?

The final battle begins and it's always just the right level of bloody; Mustachio throws his razor-sharp vinyl records and Zulu Sister peppers with the AK-47, and the manticores attack with their tail spikes. Just when it seems that the lion monsters with the human faces have the advantage, you let Mustachio get out his Forty Ounce beer grenade and the manticores flee and Zulu and Mustachio fall down to the ground half dead. But alive. With yet another treasure. You did it! Again!

And you have just written "Again!" when you're struck by the fact that "manticore" is like *monte* and you think about the Kroumirie Mountain Range and Dads, who says that you're *monte*-men, and Moms, whose name was Bergman, and as usual you're tempted to see a pattern, proof that nothing is random.

~~But then you suddenly remember the summer of 2001 when you were in Tunis to study Arabic and had just started seeing Faiza, the first since E. who really meant something. And you two live in that run-down apartment with the piss-smelling stairwell, and of course you tell the story about your parents' first date and the symbolism of their names, Moms Bergman and Dads Khemiri. And Faiza laughs and lets you look up the letters of Khemiri in her Arabic dictionary and you look up *KH* and you find *KH-M* and you find *KH-M-R.* And you realize that the consonants without their vowels mean . . . drunkard. And you remember that then, sitting there on the brown sofa with round cigarette burns, you think that nothing is a pattern, that everything is random, and you promise yourself to stop looking and stop missing Dads.~~

~~You contemplate whether you should really keep the chapter above.~~

~~You are still contemplating.~~

~~Now you have decided.~~

~~You push control *s* and paste in the next heading from Kadir's mail.[15]~~

---

15. Congratulations that you have succeeded in attaching yourself to the reality of truth. But I still propose that you suppress these memories from Tunis. Remember: We are MAXIMIZING the mysticness of the story, NOT degrading it.

MORE DETAILS OF YOUR FATHER'S SUCCESS

What else is there to tell? Dads finally get customers. But instead of artistic photographs that capture the fleeting spirit of time, Dads capture the cairn terrier Matilde in the middle of a jump. Instead of documenting the landing in Normandy like Robert Capa, Dads document a conductor's bulldog in a humorous high hat. Instead of summarizing impressions from his new homeland like Robert Frank, Dads summarize impressions from the Scandinavian Sealyham Terrier Society's annual special exhibition, where the dog Torset Temptress wins both Best Bitch and Best in Show.

Dads buy economy packs of dog treats, print real business cards, and promise discounts to owners of standard schnauzers. Dads rescue the family finances and soon Moms can stop cutting their hair and Dads can afford squeaky brown leather jackets from Rocco Barocco. Soon you start buying juice for everyday use and Kellogg's cornflakes instead of those crispier Eldorado ones. Soon you start having whole-grain bread instead of rye bread and one time you have Skagen shrimp salad at home and it's a weekday and it's just sitting there in the refrigerator and there's not even a note about "for the weekend" and you think that this, just like this, must be what it's like to live in the rich part of Söder and have vice president parents. But at the same time, Dads have gotten so busy. Dads always have to work late and never have time for anything and instead of photographer quotes, Dads start to mantra the lines from the pilot film *Top Gun* where the instruc-

tor says with a steely voice: This school is about combat. There are no points for second place. And Dads
agree: "Remember that, my son, in life there are no
points for the second. You always have to be the absolute best."

When it gets too cold out you move your role-playing
into Kadir's old room, the storeroom in the very back of
the studio. You sit on the soiled mattress and make a
game board from old boxes and you always close the
door carefully so that your friends won't hear how Dads
answer the telephone with his enthusiastic almost-
Swedish voice. Hello-this-is-Krister-you-have-the-animal-
I-have-the-camera . . .

Because for some reason it's hard to hear Dads, who
have given up his beautiful Khemirish where all the
languages were blended with all the others until no
outsider could understand. In order to instead start
stumbling over consonants, abusing prepositions, and
taming his tongue to approach the melody of Swedish.
In the studio it works, because here Dads soon have a
routine of fawning his voice and presenting himself as
Krister and shooting the wind, petting cocker spaniels,
and angling the reflector so that the pets' eyes have the
exact right Disney shine.

But outside the studio it's another world. There it
only takes one single mini-mistake for Dads to be met
with the obnoxious smile, the smile that smells like dill
chips, uncooked meatballs, and egg farts, the smile that
has hidden fangs and pats his head condescendingly and
whispers clever idiot and trytofitinbutyoucan'tfoolme.
The smile that laughs deep down in the belly but can't
be seen on the outside, refuses to understand Dads'
questions, and, at the same moment Dads clear their

throats to try again, turns to you in order for you to act as interpreter. Explain now what Dads' tongues can't. But Dads don't give up, Dads learn that it's called Magnum's "annual" instead of "annuary," "deposit slips" instead of "deposition papers," "olive oil" instead of "oil olive," "macaroni" instead of "potties."

Dads learn everything that there is to know. But still. One single wrong preposition is all it takes. A single *en* word that should be an *ett*. Then their second-long pause, the pause they love, the pause that shows that no matter how much you try, we will always, ALWAYS see through you. They enjoy taking the power and waiting waiting waiting until just when Dads think they are defeated. Then they point out the right way with vowels that are quadrupled as if they were talking with a deaf imbecile. STRAAAAAIGHT AHEEEEAD, then to the LEEEEEEEEEEEFT, okay, then RIIIIIGHT. You're welcome. And Dads say thanks politely and bow and you're standing alongside and feeling how something is bubbling inside.[16]

YOUR GROWING CONFUSION

You're not sure what Kadir means by this. Confusion? Sure, the role-playing takes over that coming winter and

---

16. What is bubbling? Do you have gases in your stomach? Here you can properly introduce a little more information about your father's success. You can tell how he expands from only photographing dogs to shooting all sorts of pets: cats, cockatoos, snakes, aquarium fish. He photographs rabbits and walking sticks. And one day he is tasked by the popular youth magazine *Okay* to afflict Ben Marlene, the singer in the celebrated pop group Trance Dance, to document him with his three purebred Dalmatians. (Your father later sold this photo again to a photo agency for an elegant price.)

sure, you spend most of your time in the stockroom with Melinda and Imran. But confusion? You remember that Dads start to come in and complain that you're disturbing his clients. You apologize, tell Melinda and Imran to sit down again and try to keep the volume of their battle cries down. But soon MC Mustachio and Zulu Sister are attacked from the back by four tree leeches with poisonous yo-yos and cockatrices with solar-powered crossbows and Mustachio is trapped in a cage and tries to pry himself free with his superstrong mustache but everything looks bad until Zulu Sister remembers her hidden voodoo dolls and starts pricking them into pincushions and the dice are hit and incantations are called and in the middle of the heat of battle the magic is broken by Dads, who come roaring in: That's enough! and overturn the game board and force you out to the courtyard.

Why? You suppose that Dads are probably just jealous that you have new, real friends. Friends who are your age, who are just like you and who understand that if you aren't allowed to play role-playing games you can just as well go together to the mountain on the other side of the train tracks and play mountain climbers and smash icicles. The first time you do it you remind yourselves that you're not playing, because you're too big for that, this is also like role-playing only like in real life. And the second time you've made up your own mountain climber names and your own special characteristics and the third time you've brought along hockey helmets and ropes and a hammer and a Phillips screwdriver and Imran has an empty backpack and Melinda has plastic glasses and looks a little like that construction guy in the gay band YMCA and you laugh at her until you see yourselves in the plate glass of the video store and realize that you look at least as funny as she does. But you don't give up, now all the damn ice must go, a mountain clearer got to do what a mountain clearer got to do. You climb up the slope, secure ropes, and bang icicles and have gotten about halfway when a hat man stops his car and yells: What are you doing, damn niggers? You always have to destroy! And you just turn around and pretend that nothing happened and are ashamed, because that's what Dads have taught you to do. And Imran does the same. But in the corner of your eye you see how Melinda is bending down and weighing a chunk of ice in her right hand and then she chucks it straight at the man and she's not far from hitting him and the man shields himself with his hands and roars about the police and slides himself back toward the car and you let the icicles rain over him as he accelerates himself away in a panic. You're still standing there laughing on the edge of the mountain and you've won your first battle and the next time some senior citizen says something you're ready with a supply of particularly throw-worthy icicles.

When you're not hanging with your friends you go to school or help with Dads' shoots. You angle reflectors according to Dads' instructions, you fetch photographic props, you bring out the just-bought background paintings that depict dark, drab forest paths, cloud-filled skies, or stormy wave scenery. You wipe up drool from disgusting pit bulls and take out dog biscuits for bribing. You turn on the coffee machine and welcome customers who come too early. And the whole time you keep yourself from thinking that something is wrong. Because the family is getting its finances secured, of course, and Moms regret their skepticism and one big day, one eternal day in the spring of '89, Grandma's little white Toyota stops outside the studio. A line-mouthed Grandma wriggles herself out of the car, straightens her blouse, and enters the studio. She looks down at Dads, who are bent over the contact sheets with the magnifier in his eye, and says in one breath: "Well-I-just-thought-I'd-see-how-it's-going-for-you-and-I-guess-it-looks-like-it's-going-well-that's-great-Gösta-would-be-proud-but-yes-yes-I-don't-want-to-be-a-bother-absolutely-not-and-coffee-no-no-I-don't-want-to-impose-and-you-must-be-busy-just-keep-working-good-bye-then! And Dads just look at the door where Grandma was just standing, the magnifier still in his eye as Grandma catches her breath out by her Toyota like after a marathon.

Times change. But some things are the same. Like the voices you still hear every time before you fall asleep. Like your nightly dreams and sweaty awakenings. Your way of thinking of systems for keeping fate in check. Sometimes you just have to touch yellow things and sometimes you just have to tightrope alongside a whole flower bed. Just because. And sometimes Dads get tired of all of that and make you walk right on the cracks in the sidewalk and right on bad-luck manhole covers. But only one time do Dads get so angry that you are locked in the darkroom until you silence your screaming and admit that you're not scared at all and that you have no problem at all telling the difference between fantasy and reality.[17]

---

17. Hmm . . . The reader will probably realize here that those few times you were locked in the darkroom were your father's method of getting you accustomed to your fear. It was nothing your father took pleasure in doing. Perhaps he regrets this as well.

THE HAPPY SUMMER OF 1989

And you remember how you take the bikes and it's towels on the luggage carriers and lunch bags in the bike baskets, Dads who ride the red women's bike and Moms who ride the blue one, and you who borrow your cousin's little red one. Then the whole happy family, first on the forest path with the pine smell and pinecone mashing and then the gravel road past the outdoor pool with real salt water and Dads' and Moms' legs move so slowly but their wheels so quickly while your legs are bouncing pistons and you still end up last. But they don't ride away from you on purpose, they wait for you before the curve down to the beach and then you go on together with the sea breeze from the side to the secret sand dune that only you know, where the wind is on the lee side behind the rose hip bushes and you can drink juice and eat grapes and cheese sandwiches with peppers without anyone seeing and Dads and Moms who once kiss each other on the lips even though you're there and of course you look away and check out ants and check out the sky and those clouds aren't on their way here, are they? Then comes the rumble and the first drops of water, which land heavy on the plastic bags, and it's quick packing up but it's already too late because the drops are falling and you can hear them landing and the light sand dune sand is becoming dot-

---

It will be perfect that we contrast the dark of the darkroom with your memories of the delicious summer of 1989. Because you remember that last happy summer, right? When your father had succeeded in his career, your parents' love was rediscovered, and the sun shone like in orange juice ads? I know that your father often remembers that summer with the painful smile of nostalgia.

ted dark brown and the bike seats are already wet and all the dips are puddling and soon you stop biking fast because everyone's jeans legs are already dark blue wet-through and everyone's hair is loose and stringy and you taste the fruit flavor of the hair gel and Dads and Moms start to laugh and yell and you almost get a little scared about being alone in the middle of an empty beach in a rainstorm with two psycho parents but they keep laughing and one time they hold hands even though the diagonal wind makes it hard to balance and then you do the same, laughing and yelling, and the rain roars while the whole happy family rides the beach road, the gravel road, and the forest path back up to the house.

And you remember summer days that are called workdays and everyone, absolutely everyone, helps with the raking and the outhouse painting and the cleaning of the creek and the sawing down of shading pines. And you remember Dads, who stand on the roof and clean the gutters, Dads with a borrowed lawn mower in the area that used to just be for compost, Dads who chop wood in the dusk until uncles come out and say that the woodpile was full a long time ago. Dads with bulked-up arms and a V-shaped upper body in overalls with paint flecks, who fix flat bike tires and repaint window frames and fell birches with cracking sounds. Dads, who bend down with the rake to fill hundreds of plastic buckets with needles and pinecones, Dads who suddenly stop and call your name because the back pain has come and you have to support Dads into the house and their face is grimacing when they slowly slowly stumble along and lie down on the sofa. And then Grandma's voice, murmuring from the kitchen:

So convenient. And you who don't really understand what she means.

And you have just written " . . . what she means" and put the period when you realize that you're mixing up summers. Because it can't be eighty-nine when you borrowed your cousin's bike, right? Because you saw it a year or two ago, rusted out and tiny. And the creek was already drained in eighty-seven and Dads' back pain must have been when little brothers were newborns because Grandma would never say that in eighty-nine. You must remember wrong. The summer of eighty-nine, what really happened then?

This is the summer when finances for once are not the family's constant concern. It's the first summer that Dads don't need to work extra at either SL or a restaurant. Dads come along to the country and Grandma makes an effort to not clear her throat over Dads' strange ways of making bread and killing mosquitoes by throwing hand towels at the ceiling and his even more suspicious way of cleaning off tartar with a razor blade. It's the summer when Hallandsås for once doesn't serve up weeks of rain and little brothers have gotten teeth and learned to run and can follow instructions to build Legos. It's the summer when you take sunset walks on beaches like real families and sometimes Grandma comes along and sometimes Grandma and Dads agree that the day was nice but that the sunset was really more beautiful the day before. Dads pull little brothers in the wagon proudly like a real dad and in the evenings you can maybe afford mini golf or arcade games in front of the downtown kiosk or soft-serve from the ice cream bar or bulk candy for watching track and field on TV. And Dads are nice and polite, Dads eat their kassler and speak their Swedish and don't even start a discussion when Moms' aunts comment on the hundred-meter race and the camera shows the waving Kenyan (he looks dangerous) and then the waving black American (wouldn't want to meet him in a dark alley) and the waving Irishman (oh, he looks nice). Dads just swallow hard and look out at the chopping block and soon the extra shed has so much wood that it will last for the next four summers.

It's this summer that you meet Patrik, who's a few years older and has premature pimples and legs bent like parentheses, and together you spy on uncles' wild midsummer parties and taste schnapps when no one's looking and discuss who is prettier, Madonna or Paula Abdul.

But pretty often you are homesick for Melinda and Imran, because sure Patrik is great and stuff, but at the same time you're very different, because Patrik's parents are totally Swedish and Patrik has another country place that's near the Riviera and they have sunny balconies and waiters as servants there. You sit on the beach and Patrik tells about his luxurious school in Täby and his sister who got to go on a language course abroad and his jeans are real Levi's and he has a bought tape of Guns N' Roses and . . . what do you counter with? How can you answer? You who live in a Million Program box in the city and have secondhand jeans and not even a single video game? You who have never been the richest and never been the poorest but instead have always been the constant in-between. You just take Patrik by the forearm and lead him up from the beach to the sunset light where long-shadowed Dads are standing, still, a whole afternoon later, with paint-flecked overalls and

the whole yard full of billions of raked-up leaf piles.
Dads with a bare chest and a slightly bigger stomach
than previous summers but with the same just-worked
smell and the same eternal greeting: Hello, you damn
fools! And you don't bother with introductions, you just
ask Dads to do the knuckle-cracking trick and Dads
raise his hands and crack his knuckles, one after the
other, and the sound echoes forth as it always does and
it gets white around Patrik's pupils and on the way back
to the beach Patrik is finally quiet.

But it's also the summer when you're on the way
home from Patrik's and you take the beach road with
your Walkman loaded with Imran's NWA tape. It's
washed-up jellyfish in the dusk and sea-grass-covered,
hard-packed sand and you are the biggest badass in the
whole entire world because you're walking in exact
rhythm with Dre's beat and you are Ice Cube in the
first verse and MC Ren in the second and you're just
about to become Eazy-E when you see your shadow in
front of you and notice the car that's following your
steps. And because cars are allowed to drive on the
beach it takes a while before you notice that this Volvo
doesn't want to pass but would rather drive really, really
close. And you stop and turn around and behind the
blinding of the headlights you see the silhouette of two
piggish sneers and the one is shaved and the other has
long thin hair and there are more sneers in the backseat and their music is white Viking power and white
revolution without mercy and you're standing alone
there in the car light on an eternally long beach and the
sun is going down out by the horizon and they're staring at you and idling the engine and revving the motor
and you're waiting each other out and you swallow and

they sneer and you get ready and they roar the gas and you throw yourself to the side and they disappear laughing off toward the downtown kiosk. And it's a red Volvo with a license plate you'll always remember and they've made it twenty meters when someone on the passenger side sticks a *brännboll* bat out the window and you see the silhouette of the *brännboll* bat when you, like the world's least-badass, run like a rabbit up to the cottage and you get rid of the tears in the woods but then they come back when you tell Dads. You expect fury and uproar and a nighttime expedition to find the racists. Moms swear in long strings about idiotic farmers while Dads get a wrinkle in his forehead. Then he says: How do you know that they were racists? Maybe they were just joking?

And you think that this is the last time that you'll try to get Dads to understand.[18]

ABBAS' DEPARTURE FROM HIS FRIENDS

Here you're once again a little unsure about what Kadir means. His departure from the Aristocats? Or some other departure? You remember, anyway, that the Aristocats' visits to the studio become more and more rare,

---

18.   Here your phrases are excluding the reality of truth. Because do you know what your father did when you had fallen asleep? He sat isolated alone by your crackling fire while your mother tried to discuss him. Then he suddenly levitated himself, left the cabin, and set off on a solitary expedition in your grandmother's Toyota. For two hours he spied streets and all-night kiosks in the ambition of seeing a red Volvo with racist inhabitants that he would bomb with kicks and box to historic time. Why did he not tell this to you? Perhaps because his greatest fear was that the infection of outsiderness would infect you.

and that the only time Dads speak Arabic is on the telephone with people in Tunisia. Sometimes it's with Amine and then Dads speak so loudly that the windows rattle, and sometimes it's with Cherifa and then Dads promise to come down soon with the whole family. But most often it's Kadir. Kadir, who's started to call more and more often at stranger and stranger times. Sometimes early in the morning, three times in a row, and sometimes in the middle of the night and sometimes on the customer line, again and again until Dads, sighing, unplug the phone. With Kadir, Dads' voices are quieted to a hissing. They talk about money and finances and *chamsa mie* and *attini flous* and then Dads who suddenly slam the phone down and say to you, sighing: You must be very careful who you choose as a friend. You can't trust anyone. Remember that. And you nod and promise. Then Dads: By the way, why do you only play with that Melinda? You should call that boy, what is his name, who you met last summer? Patrik!

Why? You ask and Dads say: He seems very, very nice. He would be better for you . . .

And you remember that your pursuit of Dads' approval is so great that you actually call Patrik. You go out to his Täby suburb where the houses are villas instead of square and boxy, where people have gardens instead of courtyards and their own basketball hoops instead of the one at the park. Patrik has lawyer parents and his own Atari in his room and you play the skyscraper game with double joysticks and Patrik shows you his model airplane collection and you play Ping-Pong in the basement and in the fridge they have three kinds of juice and cola that you can drink without asking permission. You realize that this is true luxury and what Dads have achieved is just a warm-up for what exists out there, because Patrik's parents talk angrily about Social Democrat politics during dinner and say that they're planning their sun vacation to France this summer and sit politely silent when you say that you thought their country house was on the Riviera. Then they ask you about your parents and you say that Dad is a photographer and Mom is more or less the vice CEO for Swedish hospitals in the county council and despite their smiles you feel minimally insignificant.

Late at night you watch Mafia films and eat cheese curls and when the credits are rolling Patrik says as though by chance that his real dad is from Chile. Is that true? Of course it's true because Patrik's middle name is Jorge and the Swedish dad is just a stepdad and in the same second you hear that, you realize Patrik must also be the same sort as you, Melinda, and Imran, and you tell him so, you say: But then you're a *blatte* too! And Patrik considers this and scratches his elbow and says: *blatte*? You say: Of course. *Blatte!* And Patrik smiles nervously and doesn't seem to know if he should be happy or sad.

Before you go home you let Patrik record the NWA cassette and you show him how you can hear the difference between Eazy-E and MC Ren and you teach him how you can rap along with all of *Straight Outta Compton* and carefully switch out every "nigga" for *"blatte."* And you remember how the change is visible on the outside, how Patrik gets another kind of pride in his body, how with half-open eyes he rhymes in time in pretend English and how he says good-bye with a finger-twisted West Coast sign when you part ways at the subway.

You, you go home and are met by Moms who shush your greeting because Dads are lying with a moistened towel on his forehead. The migraines have started to come more and more often and little brothers have been sent out to the courtyard and you also have to be quieter than quiet. So you sneak into your room and turn on the music extra low. But extra low is not low enough because during the refrains you happen to turn up the volume and you CAN'T listen to "Gangsta Gangsta" quietly and soon Dads are standing outside your room and banging on the door and roaring. You connect the headphones instead. And think: Are Dads working twelve-hour shifts in the studio for this? Are Dads dead tired and falling shoulder first into the hall in the middle of the night with unbuttoned leather jacket, dirty shoes, and smile long gone for this? Have Dads lost contact with all his old friends for this?[19]

And you remember that time when you and Dads are going to go to the city and look for Christmas presents and the year must be almost the nineties because Dads' bodies have gotten rounder and rounder in the waist and Dads' hairlines have started to retreat.[20] It's the final reprise of the Dynamic Duo, an awful remake with badly dubbed actors. You have your new jeans that hang

---

19. What do you mean by these phrases? Do you not realize that your father sacrificed everything for the economy of his family! It was for YOUR sake, of course!

20. I suggest the more veracious "is impressively muscular and virilely hairy from top to toe."

just so, and in your earphones of course you have the new NWA single and Dads look at you and ask: Are you on the way to the circus? What do you mean, circus? Well, you are dressed like a clown! And for the first time in the history of the world not even Dads laugh at their own jokes.

Dads' eyes seem colorless and the migraines seem to get worse every day and Moms want Dads to see doctors and take medicine but Dads say that medicine is for wimps and promise that everything is fine, it's just a little trouble at home. What kind of trouble? No trouble. But you sense that something has changed because Dads have stopped sleeping at night and sit awake and call ten-digit numbers again and again, without ever getting an answer.

On the way into the city you suggest a classic visit to Central Station before you start the hunt for presents and then you add that "present hunting" is a funny word in Swedish, I mean you're looking for Christmas presents and then of course it's the same word as the word for witch-hunt, you know just like in a huge perse-cution. But Dads don't react to things that have always been Dads' ultimate humor, Dads just nod absentmind-edly and get up to get off at Slussen, realize his mistake, and return to his seat.

At Central Station, of course, the Aristocats are sit-ting as though rooted to their corner table and it's been a long time and hugs are given out and cigarettes are smoked and daughter pictures in wallets are shown. They're the same photos as before but now the daugh-ters are almost grown up and want to go to discos and apply to art schools and they laugh scornfully at poor Aristocats' sudden attempts to cling to traditions they themselves have almost forgotten. It's the same friends and the same Dads with phrases that have become trite. Instead of crawling down under the table and playing Ghostbusters you sit on the chair, and instead of pastries you force coffee with milk and double sugar into yourself like a real grown-up. Dads sit silently in the corner and everyone notices that they're different but no one says anything. Instead they talk about V65 racing bets and the upcoming European Cup. Then Mansour starts a conversation about racist Sweden and as usual everyone agrees that all the universities are racist and the businesses are racist and the doormen are racists and store security is racist and security cameras are racist and Swedish Television is racist and journalists are racists and the telephone company is racist and Systembolaget is racist and the referee in the last European Cup match is racist and the horses in V65 are racists and Aziz says this last one and everyone laughs except Dads, who sit quietly, resolutely, fingering their berets and twirling their cigarettes. When Mansour says for the third time: But, but seriously . . . racism at the university is still the worst, because now my dissertation . . . he is interrupted by roaring Dads. Damn it, go home then! You damn idiot! What are you doing here? Get out! Go home! Do you know what the most racist thing is? It's those electric doors over there, do you see them? They are so incredibly racist, you have to like go up to them for them to open! Look, what damn racists!

And Dads do everything in one movement; stub out their cigarettes, put on their berets, and knock over your water glass. Then they say good-bye and disappear toward the exit. You don't really know what you should do because if you stay sitting it would be wrong but if you go it would be wrong so as usual you do the in-between thing and sit for six seven eight seconds before you say excuse me and bye and ahem yourself away toward the exit.

All the way to NK Dads walk a step ahead of you, mumbling that Pernilla is right in saying that the Aristocats are Aristoidiots. And it's slushy snow and winter wind but you still hear how Dads say that they are lazy immigrants and they should help themselves instead of just sitting on their asses and complaining.

Inside in the warmth of NK Dads take out their wallets, which have a new American Express, and Dads look at you with the smiles from before and say: A party is a party, no penny-pinching! And just that quote makes everything a little like before because the Dynamic Duo is going to work together but instead of driving subways or looking for bottles or standing in the darkroom it's Christmas present hunting. And for you Christmas present hunting is the simplest child's play because you're Muslim so it's okay to buy all the presents on the same day. You laugh because you're the only ones this close to Christmas who don't seem to have present panic and stress faces and long, well-worn wish lists of things that sold out the first week of Advent. For you everything is simple—double Turtles for little brothers, check, insoles and tennis socks for uncles, check, deluxe bath salts and round green candies for Grandma, check. And for Moms a blender for several hundred crowns that you can make drinks and shakes with, check. Then the Christmas presents are almost done and Dads nod, pleased, and say: There are advantages to being Muslim, aren't there? What do you want?

You go up to the CD section and you get to pick three discs, anything you want, and you take Eric B. & Rakim's *Paid in Full* and Public Enemy's *It Takes a Nation of Millions to Hold Us Back* and Eazy-E's solo album and when you're standing there in line Dads inspect the discs and ask: Why are you just listening to black music? Huh? Why are you just listening to a bunch of yo yo nigga bitch? Do you want to be black?

And you answer: Isn't Otis black?

Dads sigh. Otis is a totally different matter. Otis is love and soul and the pain of the heart. Not a bunch of bitch this and nigga that.[21]

On the way down the escalator you try to find your way back to the good mood. What do you want for a Christmas present, Dad?

Me? I don't want a Christmas present. I am content with my sons' love. And maybe a . . . Prada tie.

But you're Muslim, you joke, and Dads continue the joke just like you used to do. I will say what Zola said: You cannot say that you have seen anything until you

---

21. Why did your father say these angry words about Negro music? I believe it can be explained by his expanded irritation with other immigrants. He was frustrated by immigrants' incapacity to abandon their traditions and feared that lazy immigrants would limit his sons' future chances. He was ached by the growing number of veiled women. He was alarmed about Sweden's modification. And most of all he was irritated by the growing number of Negroes. Eritreans and Somalians steadily increased their numbers, they echoed their unabashed laughs on the metro, they lazyboned themselves at suburban cafés, they repeated their songs of complaint about the racism of Sweden. BUT: Note carefully that your father was never racist (despite your accusations). Write: "My father did NOT think that Negroes are less worthy than other races. As you know, my father loves Otis Redding! My father is convinced that all races bear an identical worth. This is true independent of their talent for rhythm and dance, their athletic capacity, their hunger for bananas, or their laziness. That a certain race might resemble monkeys does NOT give the consequence that they should be treated like monkeys."

have photographed it . . . and in that moment, when you're laughing there on the escalator, everything feels a little like before again and you remember that you think that Dads' temper is like a mogul course.

You hop off the escalator on the second floor and Dads lead the way into the clothing department. From a distance you can already see salesmen who scan you with eagle eyes. They notice your arrival. They watch your movements. They look from the bottom up at Dads' rolled-up green corduroy pants and brown leather jacket and dirty Djurgården scarf. They swallow their perfumed throats, walk to the register, and lift the telephone. Soon you see the guard who's rushing his steps to get there. Then he stops, meets the eyes of the salescunt, which reflect him on to you. And what do you do?

Dads do not let themselves be bothered. Dads slide his fingers along suit hangers, check the expensive interfacing and the hidden inseams. While the salesmen circle like sharks and the guard nervously fingers his walkie-talkie, Dads point with gleaming eyes at the monograms on the Eton shirts and the underseam on the Clark shoes.

Sometimes a salesman comes up and folds shirts right beside you and sometimes they block the way and say, Oops! as though they hadn't seen you. Sometimes they take out a spray bottle and start polishing mirrors but of course the mirror is directed at just the right angle for them to be able to watch your every move.

But Dads don't notice anything. Dads are entirely too busy. Dads just say: No thanks, when the next salesman glides up and loud-voices out his: May I possibly . . .

help you with something? Dads cruise on, feeling the quality of Armani jeans, holding the Prada tie up to check the color, and demonstrating the Boss coat with wrist buttons that can really be unbuttoned, just like tailor-made ones from London. And Dads don't let himself be provoked even when the guard is tired of waiting and stands right in front of you and sort of stares daggers. Dads just keep checking price tags with hmm sounds and running fabric qualities between their fingers.

Come on, let's go, you whisper between your teeth and drag Dads toward escalators.

And it's then, when you turn around and see the guard whore smile at the salescunt, that you feel the hate. That rage you've never felt before, the hate that links store racism to red beach Volvos to Dads' mood swings, the hate that turns everything red and that beats exactly in time with NWA's "Fuck tha Police." One second later the rage has rushed you up the down escalators, back to the salescunt where he's standing and play-flirting with the guard, and then you give a hellish roar and throw fists at store bosses and crash salesmen faces with the tie display and rub luxury shirts in guards' faces, you shout: Fuck tha police coming straight from the underground a young *blatte* got it bad cause I'm brown, you feed them combinations and box them into unconsciousness, you are a hurricane, you are their worst nightmare, you are the maximal reach of skinny arms, you are quick feet that smash coatracks to shards, you are the overturner of dressing rooms who knocks down walls like dominoes and half-naked rich Swedes in brand-name underwear howl and the storeroom explodes and the fire alarm goes off and the sprinkler water destroys silk ties forever. You don't stop before Dads come hurrying, grab hold of your arm, and rush you down the escalator. It's the end of the eighties; something is happening but you're not really sure what.[22]

---

22. Write me, Jonas. Why are you relating this return to the clothing department? This is a lie! I know for certain fact that all you did was show your erected tongue and your stretched-up middle finger to the guard. And he did not even see you! Who are you trying to dupe? And why? This does not prophesize well . . .

PART FIVE

Dearest greetings!

Are you reading this in a sitting position? Good. For euphoric news comes from having been presented to me: Your father is alive and in excellent vigor!!! Two hours ago I received an e-letter where he excused his expanded silence with that during the past time he has prepared an anonymous project that will most likely securitize his position in the exclusive photographic bureau Magnum! I congratulated him heartily for not being murdered. Right now he is apparently back in New York after some very stinging weeks in Rwanda, where he has documented the trail of genocide. Among other things, he wrote about a woman whose pregnancy was terminated in the seventh month by two soldiers who gambled about the sex of her child; they knifed up her stomach, defined the sex, and left her to die in the puddle of blood. Your father is gathering his strength in his roof loft and trying to decide if his next target should be the landless Brazilians or the Untouchable Indians.

He terminated with the note that there are many times when, despite his great success, he misses his wife and his children. Is that not a bizarre coincidence? I have, in accordance with your directives, not informed him of our relation. Perhaps you can still try to telephone him? Even if you seem certain in your declaration to "fucking never make the first move," I inject you the number to his Tunisian portable telephone. It works globally: +216-********. In case you change your mind. Nine years of silence between a father and a son is really rather nine years too long. And regardless of whether you capture him at a peace conference or in an intellectual tête-à-tête with Tariq Ali, I promise that a call from you would grow his gladness to hurricanish strength.

Now to your delivered text. I realize that you do your extreme to extract literary talent from yourself. You are learning. But are still not totally stable. Carefully inspect my affixed footnotes for a complete survey of those times that you injected too-large glides of truth. Why have you named the document *Montecore,* by the way? Perhaps you have spelled wrong? Do you want to refer to the manticore, the lion monster from your role-playing? Or is Monte Corps intended, as in the army of the mountain? Or Monte-cœur, as in the heart of the mountain? Calm my confusion.

Are you now ready to terminate the book? Is your stomach fluttered by as many butterflies as mine? It is time to form the turbulent time that we can call Sweden's nineties. I am letting you bear the relay rod of the narrative and inviting to you to formulate yourself freely. On the condition that in this section you allow my commentary to compete on the same level as you do, somewhat in the form of a duel. *En garde, monsieur!* Let us try together to understand how the conflict between father and son grows to the radioactive explosion that motivates your modern silence.

Your affirmative friend,
Kadir

The first thing you remember is the basketball court in Melinda's courtyard, just three gates and a pedestrian bridge from the studio, the basketball court with two shred-netted baskets where you start hanging out every day after school, you, Melinda, and Imran. And sometimes Patrik, mostly because it's cool to have someone along who always has money for candy and is always worst at twenty-one. Because in his entire life, Patrik has only ever played badminton and the recorder and his basketball clothes still have just-bought folds and his jump shot is a huge joke and once in the beginning he said: Nice triple-timer! when Melinda made a killer layup. But of course he can still hang out with you, because you're no haters and everyone have to learn sometime.

Now the time is different because spring is starting to seem like summer and Patrik has learned how to trash-talk the mothers of opponents and replaced his upper-class *i* with a believable Spanish accent where *h* is pronounced *ch* and *s* is pronounced *th*. Sometimes you're interrupted by some Swedelows in matching club jerseys who try to test you and they have a real leather ball that's marked KFUM SÖDER and it's three against three against one basket and you play center and Melinda is guard and Imran is power forward while Patrik warm the bench and twirl a towel in the air and roar WOO! every time you make a steal. Together you own the basket and it's three-pointers and blocks and alley hoops and three poor Swedelows who are sent home with sweaty tails between their legs. Then lying on your backs on the sun-warmed asphalt, with a ball each for a pillow, celebrating the victory with water from Melinda's cola bottle with a faint diluted soda taste that never disappears while the sun trickles itself down through the squares of the fence.

Sometimes you talk Dads and then Imran say his dad were a world-famous clothing designer in Pakistani Baluchistan. But then we move here and Dad couldn't get a loan to start his own brand so that why he had to do imports with synthetic tops from China and that the only reason he sells those damn sequin skirts because in Pakistan his name world-famous like as famous as Kenzo and Gucci and that Prada.

And Patrik says: My dad was an anarchist journalist who fled Chile and met Mom at Konsum when they both were reaching for the same leek and Dad was super slick and just like: If you want the leek you'll have to take me too. He and Mom fell totally in love but then she apply at like a hundred jobs at Swedish newspapers and of course she barely got interview and so she ditch Sweden and now he has own business that ships soap on the Atlantic and he's totally loaded and live in Chile on a huge lot with a white luxury house with a veranda and servants and a new wife and like three or four lovers who are models with tiny g-strings who can only dream of getting to live on his ranch and hang out by his pool. They all "please please let us come dance at your barbeque parties." And my dad all "maybe, I have kind of a lot of bitches at this particular party . . ."

There's a little pause as Melinda gets ready and starts telling her parents are educated chemists who came to Sweden on research grants from Nigeria with two minimal Melinda sisters in their baggage. Soon they stay in Sweden because they loved the calm and the security and soon Mom get a job and here, have you seen this?

Out of her wallet Melinda wriggles a photo that shows her parents standing in a lab with smiles so white their lab coats seem dirty, they look like total angels with gigantic Afros and shoes with pimp heels. Then the rest of the sisters were born and I came last and Dad wanted to stay but couldn't get a job even though he looked everywhere and spoke good Swedish and fluent French and perfect English and a little Portuguese. Then finally he get a job as a truck driver for some book warehouse in Södertälje but then he get tired of his coworkers because they were huge racists and put notes on his locker with copies from animal books with pictures of baboons and the first time it happen it don't bother Dad, you know, he's a chill guy, he never would snitch too soon. But then it happen again and again and every time he come back from lunch there new monkey pictures on his fucking locker and there were gorillas and chimpanzees and one time some goddamn fucking panda and one day he just say bye to the job and bye to Sweden and now he traveling around the world as a medical machine engineer and right now he at Singapore and we still keep in touch and last week he send a top-class black top of the finest silk. After school I swear I going to leave racist Sweden too and move. Where to? asks Imran. Melinda smiles that smile that only she has. To the castle that Dad built in Nigeria, on my mother's grave I swear it looks like the palace Eddie Murphy's dad have in Coming to America. There's elephants and tigers and gazelles and a bunch of fountains and rose flowers on the floor and we can just hang around our entire lives and never come back to fucking whore Sweden . . .

Can you get your thing cleaned by the maids, you

know like in the movie? asks Imran. Your royal penis is clean, doesn't that scene rock?

Melinda sighs: Honestly, how old are you?

It gets a little quiet. The asphalt warms backs and the water bottle is passed around. It's your turn. Wow, I mean, my dad . . . And you want to say that Dads are not at all some weak-ass animal photographer who take pictures of poodles. Dads are no old beach flirt who invented a Swede name as an alias to attract customers. Nonono, Dads are also super-educated like all other *blatte* dads. Dads also collect job application letters and thanks-for-your-interest letters in piles . . . Dads also have a totally political past and have sat in a concentration camp under Franco and been a huge threat to Pinochet and dissed Idi Amin on the radio plus pissed on the ayatollah on live TV. Dads also read secret books at night and teach you about the revolution and plan demonstrations for a free Cuba and a free Palestine and a free Chechnya and a free Iraq and a free Kurdistan. Dads collect cash in piles to start his own radio station and an intellectual bookstore and have torture scars and torture nightmares and a huge amount of hidden treasures in deposit boxes in countries we can't return to . . . Wow, I mean, my dad . . .

And you try, you say: My dad is a photographer but not just any photographer because he is super close friends with world-famous Frenchmen named Cartier and Bresson and also he's pretty tight with a guy named Capa and . . . You lose your place and say: But right now he mostly photographs pets. Everyone lies quiet, the spring sun trickles its light, and someone clears their throat.

Then Imran says his dad still has a bunch of factories

with his name on them in Pakistan and Patrik says around his dad's ranch there are certain bushes with cocaine: you can pick as much as you want and everyone gets to snort it for free at his parties. Melinda says her dad has bushes like that too and everyone nods and it gets a little more quiet before you go back to discussing the game. Seriously, bro, my block was cleaner than yours, and did you see how I screened him and did you see how I went backdoor and I swear if he hadn't been there I would have dunked 360 two hands.

Sometime in the dawn of the nineties I telephoned your father's studio as usual to inquire my finances. Your father's voice responsed my ring and the words were exchanged as follows:

YOUR FATHER *(in Swedish):* Hello-this-is-Krister-you-have-the-animal-I-have-the-camera.

ME *(in Arabic):* It is Kadir.

YOUR FATHER *(in Swedish):* Hello?

ME *(in Arabic):* Stop being silly. I know it is you, Abbas, I can hear your voice!

YOUR FATHER *(in Swedish):* Hello? Is someone there? This is Krister Holmström, can I be of assistance?

ME *(in Arabic):* Arrest this idiotic spectacle, it is me, Kadir, your only and most antique friend!

YOUR FATHER *(in Swedish):* Oh, so strange, still a foreign language that I do not control!

ME *(screaming):* Hello, you damned betrayer, stop playing me as your father played you!

YOUR FATHER *(whispering):* Sorry, Kadir, it was a humoristic joke that unfortunately lacked humor. Excuse me.

I excused your father and we smoothed our conflict. Abbas began to summarize his latest happenings. He successively filled his voice with more and more bubbly happiness, a little like a well-chilled Dom Pérignon in a silver bucket.

"I have succeeded!" he auctioned. "My studio has reached establishment and many assignments are frequent to me!"

The telephone trembled with your father's euphoria.

"Which assignments are offered you?" I interpellated.

"Can you imagine? My success is here. Soon we will probably be able to relocalize our address to the inner-city Östermalm, my children will be able to play with the children of fully Swedish journalists and politicians! My three sons will be like the generality of regular Swedes! No outsiderness will ever infect their souls! They will excel their mentalities and play tennis and practice piano and bear tidy collar shirts and be diplomaed with the highest grades and drape themselves in custom-tailored Boss suits."

"And which assignments are offered you?"

"Many different ones. Mostly artistic fashion jobs and celebrity photographing and a great quantity of similar assignments. And sometimes pet portraits."

"Praise my golden congratulations!"

"Your voice does not sound honestly happy."

"It is."

"No."

"Hmm . . . Perhaps it is explained by that your life is modified while mine stamps static holes in the same place as usual. I have encountered a VERY serious poker tragedy. I MUST obtain my loaned finances. Otherwise there could be trouble."

Your father stopped smacking his mouth with pleasurement and spiced his voice with a new solemn tone, which I did not recognize.

"Dear Kadir. I have guaranteed you your economy. Soon. But you cannot just blame your staticness on me! Do not follow the mistakes of other Arabs. Do as I did! Advance your position to the maximum instead of accusing the context."

"But . . ."

"Look at me . . . I have installed my own photographic studio. Thanks to my two striving hands."

"But . . ."

"If your ambition is to start a hotel you must wander new steps on the steep escalator that we can call your career! Understood?"

"In that case you must guarantee me the same faithfulness that I offered YOU, for God's sake!!! If you do not return home with my finances soon you will be sorry!!!"

I realized that the use of discussing with your father was less (like subtraction) and parked my telephone with a crashing sound on its holder.

And you remember another time and it's the same spring sun and the same basketball court, the same friends and the same passed-around cola bottle that still has the faint soda taste. And Imran starts the contest by saying: By the way I have Melinda's mom over this morning and it was nice because she swallowed my sperm like yogurt because she was crazy hungry, bro. And Patrik who right away wants to show that he's learned the game says: Sure but your mom was at my house last weekend and she was so fat I swear she couldn't get out of the apartment if you didn't tempt her with a huge Snickers and oil the door frame. And Melinda says: But both your moms are so fat they're as wide as they are tall! And you say: Tuskut because ALL your moms are so fat they have their own area codes! and Imran says: Shut up, whores, because your moms are so fat I swear they have the equator for waist measurements! and you say: Bitch, your mom's so ugly I swear every time I see her I think of like a huge . . . butt-ugly . . . mutant!

And then it's quiet for a few seconds before they roar their laughter and: WOOO! you lost, bro, just admit you're out!

And they continue the contest according to classic tradition. Patrik says Melinda's mom is so dumb she got fired from giving blow jobs and Melinda says Imran's mom is so ugly she should live in the zoo and Imran says Patrik's mom's teeth are yellower than butter and Melinda says Patrik's mom's teeth look like a chessboard and Patrik shows both his palms and gives up. Imran can smell the scent of victory and yells Melinda's mom is so fat she lost her watch in her fat rolls when he was finger-fucking her yesterday and Melinda fumbles, Melinda is going downhill, Melinda is counted out . . . Melinda has a brain fart and happens to say something about Imran's dad selling polyester Indian whore clothes.

Suddenly Imran stands up and his eyes are lasers behind his glasses and in one second the atmosphere has changed from joking to absolute seriousness. Melinda flies up reflexively because fighting while sitting is impossible and there are religion insults like Muslim cunt and idiot Catholic and I spit on your Muhammad and fuck your pope and then fucking Somali lesbian whore and fucking ugly cunt Indian and you and Patrik get between them and try to stop it but Imran's glasses are already off and Melinda's guard is already up and there's the first shove and there's the next coming back and you yell calm down calm down but they still both have threat stares and their breathing is like breathless divers' and they're just about to start winding up when you hear yourself yell: QUIT IT! WE'RE BROS DAMMIT!

And your voice echoes between the box houses and some birds fly from trees and both Melinda and Imran stop short as you raise your voice and afterward like this you're a little uncertain what was actually said but you remember that all those things you started to think but maybe didn't formulate all the way suddenly spray out and you roar enemies are enemies and friends are family and brothers are bros and sisters are siblings and we have to stand strong and not let ourselves be separated because there are more and more racists and fucking skinheads hang out at the helicopter platform and the Nazis own the city every November 30 and it's us against them, don't you get it!? It's white against black, it's Swediots against *blattar* and I swear any *blatte* that fight with another *blatte,* he worse than the biggest Bert Karlsson, we have to stop fighting with each other, we have to unite and spread love. And every time we see a *blatte* going by in a fancy Benz, Beamer, or Audi I swear we never play Swediots and play jealous instead we just make a fist in the air and show respect because what the racists want most of all is we fight with each other and we won't do that, shit we'll even show the fist of respect if it a cheap damn sellout Iranian who's driving a Volkswagen Passat, it don't matter, Iranian, Assyrian, Polski—*blatte* is *blatte*! Now shake hands.

Your friends look at you and you can't explain where the yelling voice came from, you just know that you have suddenly gone from a regular person to something much bigger, you're a U.N. diplomat, you are Malcolm and Gandhi combined, you are Palme reborn. Then come the laughs and they crack up and poke you in the ribs and Imran says: Wzup, Prophet! and Patrik says: Total Martin Luther King! But they do it with complete love and the best respect and Imran and Melinda make peace and they both say sorry and when you say good-bye in the dusk you feel like something has grown on the inside.

And now, afterward, when you're writing these words in a poorly lit hotel room in Gothenburg after a reading at Högsbo library, you have trouble remembering why Dads always had to be defended and Moms always made dirty. Maybe because Dads' positions were way too precarious to be tested.

Or maybe because your Dads were your eternal heroes who will never become anything else ☺?

Write me . . . You may certainly formulate yourself freely, but . . . the Swedish in the above sections seems me more unpolished than in the previous parts. Is this your intention or your carelessness?

At the parallel time I realized that your father's position was more demanding than he wanted to admit. He feared that Sweden's coming recession would threaten his studio. At the same time, he noticed how Swedes still observed him with the glances of suspicion. Despite his success they weighed him in a constant ambition of predicting his actions. He was still threatened by the smothering net of prejudices and in sympathy for all of this I forgave him the belated payment of my loaned economy. Oh, how tragically transparent are all those people in our lives who do not cement our prejudices!

I promised myself never to become one who does not forgive mistakes that people implement in their weak moments. Like a godlike reward for my amnesty, the poker cards began to stimulate me again; soon I had won back my debt, then I expanded it to a considerable profit and one evening I returned home with a capital that was adequate for investing the lot where since the days of my youth I had projected my hotel!

It's the nineties and fall when the gaze of the world is aimed at Iraq for the alliance invasion. Soon you gonna start high school and it's the time when you start reading the paper seriously and on CNN the war looks like in a film with trailers and American narrator voices and exact sights that hit exact targets and no innocents who die. On the front page of *Dagens Nyheter* is the photo of the aircraft carrier with the airplanes' burning turbo motors and arrows show the simplicity of the attack and everything is static and blood-free, about like in *Top Gun*. You sense that something is wrong and try to talk to Dads.

But Dads have closed himself in the studio and only come out on weekends with a crooked back and red eyes and a constant tension headache. Dads have gotten a different smell and become mute and refuse to talk about the Gulf War. Something has happened in Tunisia that's made Dads have to take Treo tablets until the metal tubes fill their own glass bowl in the kitchen and Moms watch anxiously from the outside.

Instead you talk with friends and in the evenings you start to hang out in the city and most often it's you, Melinda, and Imran, because Patrik is starting to have problems coming into town because his parents have become worried about the change in his clothing style and his new vocabulary.

It's you with the downy mustache that's sometimes enough for you to buy near beer at 7-Eleven, the black synthetic jacket with the blue panther print on the back and worn-down Ewing shoes. It's Melinda with a grown-out Afro and a special comb in imitation ebony, give-blood T-shirts from her mom's job, and heavy, dragging LA Gear sneakers with double laces, black and white. It's Imran with a shiny polyester shirt, red-striped bandanna, and black-and-white flannel shirt buttoned with one button at the top. Everyone's jeans are supermega-extra loose with too-big waists, perfect for highest-kick contests and secretly placed *brännboll* bat. All of you have drawn tattoos between your thumb and index finger and around your necks are just-bought bling-bling chains, which look like shining gold at first, but after the first shower slowly but surely start to change color to green rust.

Together you sit on the backs of benches or at the twenty-four-hour McDonald's and talk about all of those subjects that at that time meant more than anything. Is Dr. Dre really a real doctor? Is Paula Abdul really an Arab (as you stubbornly maintain)? Where exactly is Compton? Does Madonna have to have specially pointed boobs for them to work in that cone bra? Where do you get the cheapest fake ID? What's up after school? Is it true that you get crazy drunk if you put sugar in beer? What's the best practice for balling once it's time? (Imran: I mean, I've heard, but I haven't tried it myself, but apparently you can take an orange and make a hole in it and then boil it and then you can stick in your cock and it's supposed to like feel totally like *punani* but remember like I said I haven't tried it. You: You'd have to find a fucking huge orange. Both, with roaring voices: Yeah, really, huge-ass, super gigantic. Melinda: You are fucking insane. You: Maybe a melon would be better.)

Sometimes you get into politics and you agree that

there's something fishy about the pictures from the Gulf War and you keep talking Sweden and Melinda says she saw skinheads again at Slussen and Imran says a Swediot-alcoholic spit on the windshield and yelled Muslim whore when his mom dropped his sister off at handball practice last week. And you think about his beautiful steel-banged sister and say: Shouldn't there be an organization that unites all *blattar* that makes it obvious that *blattar* must never fight with each other but should fight the system instead? And they nod and agree and while you're finding unity Dads seem to be splitting in half.

Dads sit quiet at the dinner table while Moms try to tempt out Dads from before with wine and appetizers and her weekend face with makeup. You try to tell about basketball games where you ruled poor Swedelows and when it doesn't work you tell about how Patrik made a scene when his shop teacher read his middle name wrong and called him Jörgen instead of Jorge. Do you know what he did then? He just bent his head back at the exact right angle and yelled: *Orale vato loco!* but he did it with just the right Spanish pronunciation and . . . Moms listen and little brothers listen but not Dads and then it doesn't feel particularly interesting to keep telling.

Dads' eyes have lost their glow and Dads are starting to look like shells and Dads seem emptied of color.

Except that time when the news is telling about Saddam's Scud missiles at Israel and then Dads suddenly get up from the easy chair so the blanket flutters to the ground and yell: How can ALL Arab leaders be such damned merry idiots? And Dads' cheeks glow and his fists shake and your eyes meet.

It's the nineties and dark news bills warn of coming recession and headlines shriek about mass immigration of refugees and it's Iraqis and Yugoslavians and Somalis by the thousands and more thousands who are invading our beautiful country and robbing our travel trailers and raping our women. Soon the new party New Democracy is launched, the mass media latches on, and there are articles and public meetings and stacked crates. It's that guy Bouvin who maintains that Swedish aid is causing a catastrophe by helping African children survive (because they should actually be eaten up by wild animals). It's Bert Karlsson who says that ninety percent of all crimes against the elderly are committed by Gypsies and wishes that Bengt Westerberg's daughter would be infected with HIV by a refugee. It's Ian Wachtmeister with the fisherman's hat and hawk nose who shouts about "full speed ahead" and thinks all refugees should be tested for AIDS and no mosques should be allowed in Sweden and the Swediots laugh and the public meetings are a success and Dads?

Dads sit quietly.

And you remember the papers that form stacks in your room and you start to clip headlines about firebombs in refugee camps and assaults by racists and you read *The Autobiography of Malcolm X* and listen to Public Enemy while the attacks on immigrants wander from the news bills to headlines to articles to notices and the police call them "schoolboy pranks" and Dads?

Dads sit quietly.

The only thing that rouses Dads' second-long engagement is the immigration question. But not in the right way. Because Dads start to call the immigrants "them" and Dads say: After all, there are getting to be a few too many immigrants here in Sweden and Dads say: After all, there are still many who don't act as they should. I can understand the Swedes, because there weren't any problems like this in the eighties. And lots of immigrants are lazy idiots who just sit around and live on welfare and tightly hold on to their traditions.

And one time when you're sitting in front of *Rapport,* Dads suddenly yell that one actually MUST crap down on EVERYONE who commits a crime and refuses to learn Swedish! And you say crack down and Dads say crack? and you say crack and Dads become quiet again.

Here your father's sleep begins to become more and more sporadic. The nights become him a constant wake, a constant flow of historical pictures hover his interior and threaten his mental balance. He lies hour after hour, bathing in perspiration beside your peacefully sleeping mother. He observes her exterior. He tries to calm himself by stroking the softness of her forearm. He reflects whether the actions of his life were actually correct. Had he acted right to place his body in a country where he was not invited? Had he acted right to in addition place his sons in this context? Unlike you, he found no security in simple answers.

And you remember the headlines that scream recession and the crown falls and the politicians panic and Dads don't say anything, but whisper: Just when the studio has been stabilized the economy is going to crash, life is really typical. And by the way . . . Why do you continue to be with those . . . What are their names? Melinda and that fat Indian? Why are you never with other friends? Ordinary friends?

And you actually don't understand what Dads mean, you just point out for the thousandth time that Imran is actually Baloch and not Indian.

Up until one day when you've eaten dinner and you've told about your plans to start an antiracist organization and it's probably going to be called BFL, Blatte for Life, and Moms think it's a great idea and little brothers ask if they can be in it too, and Dads?

Dads sit quietly.

Until dinner is eaten up and Moms do the dishes and close kitchen cupboards with the angry sounds, little brothers are playing with Dino-Riders in the living room, and Dads scratch themselves on their continuously growing guts and say with flaky wine lips and stifled burps: Hey . . . by the way. Why do you only hang out with immigrants? Niggers, Indians, and damn South Americans . . . Why no Swedish friends? Are you racist? Be careful of hanging out with the wrong people. Swedes are better. Immigrants just use you and use you and then, when you need them most, they stab you in the back.

And you must have heard wrong because the enemy is out there and the enemy has boots and shaved skulls, the enemy is New Democracy and White Aryan Resistance, Keep Sweden Swedish and Ultima Thule, SL inspectors and Sweden Democrats, red beach Volvos, Securitas guards, and the riot police in Norrmalm who beat up Fayola's boyfriend for no reason. The enemy is Shell and American imperialists and Per Ahlmark and settlers and the CIA and Mossad. But the enemy can't be in your own family because then things are probably going to be more mixed-up than expected.

NB: Your father is NOT the enemy. He is only a man who is trying to guarantee the success of his children in a tradition-heavy country! He is a solitary modern cosmopolitan in a barbaric society. For this is the truth about the country we call Sweden, civilized on the surface but barbaric in the structure of thought. But he did NOT dare relate you this. He feared that you would be strengthened even more in your outsiderness thoughts. For the same motive he chose not to relate his family when his studio began to be attacked . . .

One Monday morning in the late summer of 1991 your father came to the studio and was met by black words that had been sprayed and trickle-dried on his store window. There were phrases like WHITE REVOLUTION—NO MERCY, GOOD BLATTE = DEAD BLATTE, and DEATH TO COMMUSM! (It actually said that.)

Not only your father's studio had been attacked, but also the video store, the Chinese restaurant, and the completely innocent, Swedish-owned floral shop. A professional firm was engaged to glisten the panes. Everyone promised each other to keep better supervision of suspected individuals. Then Abbas closed his studio early and went home. Without informing his family of the attack.

Then comes August 2, 1991, and the student David Gebremariam is shot on the Tropp Path in Stockholm and there's already talk of a red light the next day and the papers dub the perpetrator Laser Man. Soon afterward Moms and Dads sit in pale TV light and watch election results and precisely what Moms joked about turns out to be exact reality. The conservatives take over and New Democracy enters the Parliament and they have the balance of power and a tear runs from the Palme picture on the wall and Refaat sighs in prison and Mansour still hasn't gotten his dissertation approved and

Aziz is still working at SL and has sold his record collection with eighties hits and Sweden is changing and your nightly dreams get worse and once when you wake up you've sleepwalked out into the hallway and are met by Dads, who look at you as though you were a ghost. You are led back to bed and Dads sit beside you until you fall asleep again and it's not until the day after that you ask yourself what Dads were doing up and dressed in the middle of the night.

Your father remembers that night well. It was a few days after attack number two on the studio. This time it was only Abbas' store window and the Chinese restaurant's that had been dirtied with political slogans. In addition, the photo studio's keyhole had been prepared with chewing gum and in front of the door stood a pink ice-cream clown statue which smilingly waved Abbas' arrival. Someone had stolen it from the pizzeria kiosk and it was not until your father had gotten all the way there that he understood its meaning. It was escorted by a wastebasket and the text that was spelled out of the smiling clown mouth was the usual: "Keep Sweden CLEAN." A text that still today can be seen on thousands of wastebaskets outside of thousands of kiosks (but which for your father bears a constantly modified content).

In the following time, your father's sleep was more and more sporadic. He was plagued by hazy childhood memories. He mourned the political loss of his parents. He was grieved by the growing political turbulence in Algeria. Instead of tumbling his perspiring body in the bed, he began to take nightly walks. It was on the way out for one such walk that he met your sleepwalking form. You gesticulated wildly with half-open eyes and auctioned that you wanted two lawyers immediately. Your father transported you back to your room and waited by your delirious side until you fell asleep. Then he patted your cheek and levitated toward the stairwell.

Then it's October and two new attacks and first it's Shah-ram Khosravi, who is shot in the jaw, and then it's Dimi-trios Karamalegos, who is shot in the stomach, and both are *blattar* and people are talking about a red light again like on a laser sight and people are starting to whisper that the Laser Man is a racist who is at large in the city and you and your friends join together and you feel how you grow in Dads' silence, how your contours become sharper, how something is growing in you that won't be able to be stopped.

During the same time, you go around town with Melinda and Imran and the security guards at Mega do their routine lookout and they follow your steps closely and smile when you walk toward the cashier to pay for the cassette tapes. You leave swearing and say that this is the last time we'll go to Whoremega. Then past Åhléns and there it's the same lookout gazes from a dif-ferent security company and when you pass the CD reg-ister, constantly pursued, the alarm goes off and time stands still and everyone stares and the guards come running and you think: Shit, maybe I took something? There's lineup for inspection and then: Shut up when you try to explain that it must be the cassette from Mega that set off the alarm. Then in a line to the special square room, stares and index fingers and someone who snick-ers and an old Swediot man's serves-them-right laugh. There's waiting and more careful inspecting and then instead of apology the girl guard who says: All right, you can go now. You're already presenting the plan for counteraction at the outer doors near the subway where warm wind is blowing and double mirrors turn you into infinitely many.

Two days later you're back at Åhléns. You, Melinda, Imran, who invade the department store with shouts and maximum *blatte* accents. You yell: Hey, bro, whazzup! to alarmed perfume fags, you mack on scared student interns, you play mini-basketball in the sports department, and try on ladies' coats in the clothing department. You fuck up signs and mess up folds and Melinda waves to the uniform guards who swallow nervously. The undercover tries to play invisible and it works pretty well up until Imran goes up and pinches his behind and introduces himself as Don Corleone. The alert is at the highest *blatte* level and you stay until you get the sign and then you sail back down the escalator and the guards escort you all the way out to Sergels Torg. Everyone lets out their breath. And of course no one has seen Patrik, who's been hanging out in skinny Levi's 501 jeans, borrowed glasses, and his stepdad's sailing shoes farther away in the same department. Of course no one has seen his homemade alarm-deactivating magnet, no one has seen his growing Peak Performance backpack. And it takes maybe a half hour for them to notice all the empty shelves where there had recently been Champion shirts, NBA shorts, and piles of genuine Raiders caps.

Patrik comes out through the warm-air corridor with his cheeks red and his mouth whistling and you race away toward Kungsträdgården to split up your loot.

. . .

Your father continued his nightly walks all autumn. He wandered in a standardized circle. Night after night. Mostly he interpellated himself the same repeated questions. What am I doing here? How can this country note me as immigrated after so many years of taxable lodging? And why does my idiotic son take this insultation and exalt it as ideal? The sleeplessness forced him to thoughts of the character: And why are they attacking my studio when there are so many other immigrants who don't behave properly? Perhaps it is other immigrants who are attacking me, with jalousie or location temptation as a motive!

Then it's November and Heberson Vieira da Costa is shot in the face and the stomach and it's the fourth *blatte* in one autumn and once again it's the red laser sight and this time the news becomes internationally big and there's a description of someone in a beige trench coat and suddenly every Swediot in the whole city has a beige trench coat and everyone leers menacingly and everyone's shoulders stick out in that suspicious way at the armpit like with a holster.

Then the fifth *blatte* is shot and this is the first one who dies, the student Jimmy Ranjbar, who's shot in the head outside the same student housing where Mansour lived when he first arrived and there's a moment of silence and demonstrations and torchlight processions and you remember how you start to see red laser light wherever you turn, it blinks red in the corner of your eye and what started as a funny game is suddenly super serious and you feel so threatened that Imran starts to carry a butterfly knife in his inside pocket and you and Melinda each get a CO_2 pistol and you never leave home without being strapped and you remember that night at McDonald's when Melinda accidentally drops her pistol on the floor by the register and how you run away laughing and you remember how you start to blink and startle when the green walk light turns red and you remember how the city's traffic lights take on a whole new meaning and one night when you're walking on Norrlandsgatan a car brakes beside you and the red glare from the brake lights makes you startle and almost duck and a second later you are so ashamed it hurts.

The EXACT same emotion was felt by your father! But why didn't you ever talk about your common fear? Why did you never meet in discussion? Your father began to have his studio door constantly locked, he sat hidden inside among his props, he canceled appointments, he found himself paralyzed like in a dream. He stopped functioning but could not explain why. Still, on certain nights he left his home and took his walks. Despite his terror of nocturnal shadows with beige trench coats and aimed red lights. Everything was better than passing more sleepless hours in solitary battle with invading thoughts. And perhaps there was some bizarre part of him which he will never be able to explain that almost longed for a confrontation. He does not remember much more of that fall.

And you remember January 1992, and it's teenage emotion with sore forehead pimples and chafe-inducing jack-off habits. It's the time when Dads start to get fuzzy contours, Dads are practicing ballet, Dads jump through burning rings in a leotard, Dads photograph pets and smile gratefully at the audience's thunderous applause.

Dads refuse to choose a side.

Dads are cowardly betrayers.

Dads come, Dads go, and only Moms endure.

Because it's only then, when Dads start to fade away, that you rediscover Moms. It's as though Moms suddenly materialize themselves out of anonymity. Moms who have taken on the real responsibility, Moms' invisible battles that have made everything possible. It's Moms who hold down the fort, it's Moms who never give up and who never betray. But now Moms are starting to get tired and sometimes you hear how she cries in the bedroom and sometimes she looks through Dads' jacket pockets and one time she asks if you think Dads have a mistress. But it's also Moms who still have everything under control and who only let her weakness show when Dads are in the studio or out on one of his ever longer "walks."

Why "walks" instead of walks? What are you suggesting? Detail like this instead:

"That my father might have had parallel mistresses is of course an unthinkable thought, like that the sun might wake in the west or that Benny Hill might be uncomical."

Hmm . . . this formulation would have piled me with pride in the beginning of our book. Now it just piles me with sorrow. Abduct it if you wish.

The Laser Man is still sitting with his laser sight ready in movie theater balconies, huddling in front car seats, hidden behind light poles. There he is, you see? . . . No, there! Always behind you and to the side and sometimes it actually feels like you're going crazy. On January 22, the student Erik Bongcam is shot in the cheek and the day after the bus driver Charles Dhlakama is shot in the stomach and right after that the economist Abdisalam Farah is shot in the back of the head and the civil engineer Ali Ali and SHNEYA LASERMAN?! EVERYONE knows it's a conspiracy, it's going around the city that it isn't one laser man but a gang of laser men, a group of racist combat soldiers who have banded together with the Security Service and the Norrmalm riot squad and the fucking Silvia whore in order to make all *blattar* super paranoid and make them leave Sweden. Dads sits quietly and it's you, Melinda, Imran, and Patrik against the world, you against them, or fuck YOU, it's WE, WE who wander through life and together are exceptions, WE who together refuse their rules and eat their pigeon-holes, WE explode their categorizations because we aren't Swediots or immigrants, we are the perpetually unplaceable. Our dads come from Chile and our moms are Swedish Moderate politicians and we are born and raised in villas in Täby. Our parents are chemistry experts from Nigeria and we have four sisters who are the world's most immense bodyguards and our dads send fancy silk blouses from Singapore. We are born in Pakistan, we have steel-rimmed glasses and red-checked bandannas and dream of being the first in the world to rap in Balochi. We have Tunisian dads and Swedish-Danish moms and we are neither totally *suédis* nor totally *arabis* but some other thing, some third thing, and the insight about not having a simple collective grows us into creating our own pigeonhole, a new collective without borders, without history, a creolized circle where everything is blended and mixed and hybridized. We are the reminder that their days are numbered. We are the ones who take your disgusting language and turn it around. We are the ones who will never accept a language that's designed to screen us out (and which moreover calls the most beautiful part of the breast a *wart yard*). We are the ones who *jet* instead of leaving, we *own* instead of triumphing, we *bang* instead of making love, we say *five-o* when you say police, we *shine* while you rust, we soar while you land in the marsh, we sit on the back of benches and spit seas onto squares of sidewalk while you sit where you're supposed to and sigh, we're the ones who get that it's actually called *an* assist in basketball and that *mecca* has nothing to do with bingo and that a *fine cat* has nice *boudies* and definitely no fur or pedigree. We are the future! and it's Melinda who says this last bit and she smiles her glittering gummy smile and you remember her silhouette there in the dusk on the basketball court with her tangled Afro and her worn comb and it's so cold that you're playing with cutoff mittens and it's right after her sister Fayola has died of cancer, she was twenty-two and Melinda rarely talks about her but even cancer is Sweden's fault and more and more often Melinda says things that Fayola said to her and mostly it's quotes by Frantz Fanon and it doesn't matter that you don't know who that is, it doesn't matter that Melinda just repeats Fayola's words, it doesn't matter that you pronounce Frantz Fanon as though he were a Norrlander and Aimé Césaire as though he were an antique Caesar.

Nothing matters more than that you're building symbiosis and instead of dads who are willing to fight you have each other.

January 28, 1992: The hot dog stand owner Isa Aybar. Five bullets, one to the head, two in the right, and one in the left arm. The Laser Man continues to shoot *blattar* while Sjöbo politicians smile and the Norrmalm police take it easy and the politicians enjoy silence and skinheads celebrate through the night with cheers and *heils* at the helicopter platform.

January 30: Hasan Zatara. One bullet to the head at Hägersten and you've all bought candy at his kiosk and Zatara loses the ability to speak and is paralyzed and the spring wanders on in constant terror and constant suspense.

Finally there are certain parents who choose the Fight. Some take a stand and roar their rage when Friggebo and Bildt want to join hands and sing "We Shall Overcome" in Rinkeby. Some arrange demonstrations and lead torchlight processions and organize national immigrant strikes. Some make their last names invisible in the phone book and say to their children: Study whatever you want as long as you can do it abroad because this whore country isn't going to want to have us here in ten years, study medicine, study economics, then we'll get out of here, start a big business in Great Britain, and laugh at our memories of this uncultured land of barbarians.

And then there are Dads. Who continue to smile kindly at Swedish masters who want their Pekingeses photographed. Who refuse to be a part of the *blatte* fight. Who just look at you with sadly cowardly eyes when you do your best to rouse their engagement.

"Do your best to rouse their engagement?" Allow me a capital laugh for a whole line:

HAHAHAHAHAHAHAHAHAHAHAHAHAHAHAHAHAHAHAHAHAHAHA!!!!!!

You did not attempt to rouse your father's engagement. Your mission was to shatter his pride. Do you remember, for example, the February day when you came downmarching into the studio with your lousy loser friends? It was a tragic parade. First you: jeans adequate for five legs, a Mercedes star around your neck on a chain, and on your upper body an illegitimately obtained Champion shirt. Then Melinda with her microphonishly large hair and her billowing sweatpants suit, which reduced her body to the size of a blackhead. And Imran last, fat as a Japanese sumo, draped like a hip-hop tent with matching colors. All of you had the same caps with the gangster sign of the LA Raiders.

Without any respect for the customer who hired your father's talent, you auctioned with a loud voice that your father immediately, from this second forward, should annul his work for "Swediot customers." Your father excused himself toward the customer and sighed forth his response.

"And why would I do that?"

"Haven't you heard? There is an immigrant strike! All immigrants are stopping work today."

"I am NOT an immigrant! Why does everyone name me an immigrant? How long should I migrate? I am Swedish. I have passed half my life here . . ."

"It doesn't matter. The strike is going to show Sweden."

"Show what?"

"I mean like that there's a whole lot of immigrants who like . . . work. I mean . . . Why should you work for the slave owners? Why should you let yourself be exploited by Swediotic racists?"

(Here your confused friends shouted out their support in the form of bellowing hip-hop sounds: "Yo, yeah, word up, cowabunga!")

"I do not let myself be exploited!" shouted your father with screwed-up volume. "I only try to live my life in peace and kindness. Why does no one let me do this? Why do you persist in inflicting your behaviors on me? Just let me live!"

With force, your father conducted you and your sad friends out to the sidewalk. Then he locked the door and returned, sighing, to photographing the Chihuahua, whose master wanted it to be formed in an egg carton because the dog's name was Eggy. The customer commented the incident with a single word:

"Teenagers," he said, and smilingly sidewound his head in an attempt to shape sympathy. Your father responded him in the same way and they smiled each other's understanding.

Write me . . . Do you realize now as an adult that you dealt in the logic of racism? That you and the racists exposed the same terminology when you embraced everything blattish and they everything Swedish. But your father was . . . yes, your father? He was solitary in his solitude. He stood isolated both interiorly and exteriorly.

This turbulent day was not over. After your discussion in the studio, your father lacked all lust for a journey home. He did not have the strength to invade the sphere of the home to find himself trapped there between your grandmother's accusations of fundamentalism and your accusations of betrayal.

Without inspiration, he spent the long night with his work. He sat parked at the studio table with a carefully locked door and weakly echoing night radio in the background. He sipped a whiskey while he polished up a project for the Swedish domestic ferret society. He inspected photographs of the society's directors (wearing happy smiles with their beloved ferrets). He tried to focus his thoughts on the task. It went well. In thirty-second phases. Then hounding thoughts invaded his head.

Finally he raised his body from the stool, knocked out the lamps, and wandered his steps toward the commuter rail station. It was a wintry night with that special silence that encapsulates Sweden when the snow lies driven into masses. Your father wound his body into the leather jacket and squinted his eyes to steel his body against the cold. The air roused your father and he had almost regained a little of the former vitality of his steps when from the

bush at his side he noticed an aimed red light. He froze his movements like a frightened animal. His head was turned slowly
downward.

There on his shoulder . . . A vibrating red dot of light . . . Your
father's heart stopped.

With the naïve reaction of a child he attempted to brush the dot
away but the light only smiled at his attempt, wandered on from
his shoulder to his center, down toward his stomach, hip, thigh,
then a hop up to his chest; this blinding laser dot shone against
your father's heart, and your father's body throbbed with the real-
ization that his life was seconds away from termination.

He just stood there, let himself be searched by the laser beam,
and awaited the sound of a shot.

But instead smothered laughter could be heard from the bush,
which was suddenly shaken to life, the dot disappeared, and two
jokers scampered their steps toward a door. Your father remained
standing with the throbbing of his heart, the stickiness of his
mouth, and an aching cramp in his head.

But no Laser Man crime, no exploded jaws, punctured
stomachs, or paralyzed store owners affect your family
more than that night in April '92 when someone breaks
into the studio from the courtyard, breaks the storeroom pane, and climbs in through the window. They
wander around in Dads' studio and break things at random, the copy machine crashes to the floor, binders of
negatives are tossed from the bookshelves, posters are
torn down. Someone discovers the dog biscuits and
starts a dog biscuit war. Someone wants to be worse and
poops in a photography magazine that Dads have con-
tributed to, then wipes the poop in long streaks over the
white studio walls. Someone wants to be worst of all,

discovers the cans of used chemicals, developing fluids, and fixer, and someone unscrews the cork and says that this fucking smells like gas and someone else presents the idea and some third person says of course and they laugh and cheer and collect all the flammable material in the darkroom, crumpled posters, Kadir's old mattress, the empty boxes, the negative binders, a dried houseplant, some unused wooden frames. Then on with the liquid and a little more, don't be stingy, there too, more, finally everything is wet and they back toward the door and it's smothered giggles, someone who has to pee, come on now, dammit, you'll have to go later, shh, there's someone out there, are you messing with me? no, shut up now, who's going to light it, you, no, I will, okay do it then, who's got the lighter, come on someone has to have a lighter, but hell SOMEONE has to have one, okay, thanks, are you with me, are you ready?

The flames that light up the room meet the poured-out trail of liquid, rush silently blue toward the waiting pile, giggling rush out to the courtyard, smothered laughter, someone who still has to pee, someone who's looking for a key to their moped, someone who says no one lives upstairs, right?

The next day Moms answer the telephone and stand totally silently for way too long. Moms don't even have time to explain the details before you have gathered your troops. It's you, Melinda, Imran, and Patrik who with tense fists and gnashing teeth jump the gates to the commuter train, force yourselves up the escalator, crash through the exit gate so it bursts, stamp your gravel-puffing steps in time through the shopping center, share silent rage when you see the police's cordon tape from a distance and the black soot marks that have lapped out from the smashed store window.

It's you who see Dads sitting alone on the edge of the sidewalk, Dads who are mumbling to himself and who have had a blanket placed over him by someone who doesn't know him and who doesn't know that Dads always have blankets over his legs and never over his shoulders.

Everything until now was practice but now it's serious, now they have pushed us too far and your friends pretend not to hear Dads' mumbling about that you can bet it was vandal *blattar* who did it, typical immigrants, they hate other immigrants who succeed and . . .

You say it kindly because not even you are ready to test Dads when they're this fragile: Why would a gang of *blattar* write WAR on the wall with poop?

Dads answer: Precisely so that we will suspect the wrong people. They are smart, you know, smarter than you'd think when you see them . . . or perhaps they were going to write . . . Varón? Maybe it was South Americans?

You never find out who's guilty, because the police have more important things to worry about, and when you ask the constable whose name is Nilsson when they are going to put out the nationwide alert and interview neighbors and dust for fingerprints and do composite sketches he laughs as if you were joking. And he must be a racist too, you can tell by looking at him, that he's been bought off and bribed by WAR, because he's totally blond and totally freckly and his pants are pulled up too high and he's totally going high-water, and what else can you expect from someone who shares a name with Pippi's monkey? Do you say this to him? No, true to form you speak inwardly instead of outwardly. But your friends agree with you, don't they? They don't contradict you, anyway.

You walk silently, you follow Dads home to the apartment, Dads' scarred hands shake and Dads take out his old lucky chestnut and put it back in his pocket again and Dads say words that not even you can interpret, and then on the train home, Dads' jaw goes up and down, up and down, without the tiniest sound.

After that day, Dads become statues in front of the TV. Dads watch *Glamour* and *TV Shop*. Dads start reciting old photography quotes in new versions. Sons are called into the living room to change the channel and to be reminded that Cartier-Bresson certainly was right: You don't get any points for second place, no points for the second pla . . . Then Dads lose themselves in the ad for the cleaning product Didi Seven and the quote dangles, severed, in the air.

Dads mix up little brothers and call them the wrong name again and again.

Dads sit alone in the living room and make comments about the wardrobe quality of the extras on *Falcon Crest* reruns.

Dads sit as though bewitched in front of the looped ads for the Abdomenizer, a totally new kind of exercise implement that sculpts your stomach muscles in three different ways at once, you can store it under your bed and work out in front of the TV and look at all these people, sitting here tanning-salon brown and face-lifted, who have succeeded in dieting themselves to new lives in just ten minutes a day.

Little brothers have started school and they're losing front teeth and learning all the letters of the alphabet perfectly and sometimes you think that right now little brothers are the same age you were when the Dynamic Duo started. And in some way it's impossible to imagine that you, who were so big then, practically all grown up, were actually as small as little brothers are now, as gap-toothed, as boyishly stick-armed. At the same time, little brothers start to ask you about Dads. They wonder why Dads have become so strange and why Dads think the girl who hosts the nature program on Channel 1 will answer when they comment on hyenas' digestion and get irritated by the obviously unprofessional cameraman. Little brothers look sometimes worriedly but mostly fondly at Dads, and when they need help with homework they come to you instead. Because Dads say that Magdalena was Jesus' woman, and Jesus was about like history's first photographer in a metaphorical sense, and the disciples were like Jesus' invisible henchmen, they were like photographer's assistants who got Jesus down from the cross and moved that stone, you know, and actually you could say that most things in life can be explained with photographers. And assistants. But despite the changes in Dads and despite Dads' stubborn refusal to go to the doctor, there is not a single time when Dads hit Moms. Neither do Dads ever make the mistake of touching a hair on little brothers' heads. However, there are times when big brothers must be shown the right way and then it's often the best of moods, with Dads who are humming along to some ad jingle in front of the TV and then suddenly change moods before anyone has time to react and the reptilian-quick surprise attack is most often with words and seldom with blows, an attack that makes clear that no matter what you do, you will always be a

disgrace to the family because you spend time with niggers, disgusting abids, sweat-stinking monkeys when
you really should be spending time with Östermalm
Swedes who play tennis and piano. But no, you have to
play basketball and ruin your life with people from the
outskirts, disgusting fat Indians and monkeys, and
Dads spit out the words and you just take it without
striking back because you know that dads will be quiet
anytime now, because the ads will be over and the episode of *Glamour* will come back on and you know that
it's not really Dads saying those stinging words because
Dads are gone, Dads have been stolen, and everything is
Sweden's fault.

Four weeks later, Dads disappear quite physically.
Moms go from rage to worry to fury to teary conversations with friends, to rage back to worry and then
just a heartbreaking sadness that pales cheeks and
makes Moms start to take pills that help with sleeping
and sometimes freeze her movements so that it can
take fifteen minutes to throw a garbage bag down the
garbage chute. The studio is burned up, Dads have
packed their worn suitcase and left family responsibility
behind.

Do you believe that your father's journey aimed for luxurious rec-
reation or visits to touristettes' backsides? No sirree, Bob! This
journey was obligatory for your father's survival. The modification
of Sweden frightened him to nightly tears, he had vibrations from
the past, and every day before the attack he saw his own death.
After the fire it was like he had been right. He wanted to be there
for you, but . . . could not. Can you forgive him?

I remember clearly that morning of dawn in 1992 when I met

your father's form again. I had spent the night in the area where I would open my hotel in the future. Now the work had been ceased for several months with financial scarcity as a motive. With the ambition of a guard dog I made sure that no nocturnal criminal kidnapped my building materials. I slept in a preliminary storage building and every snap noise roused my alertness. Suddenly in the dawn: the sound of sneaking feet. Aha, a masonry criminal, thought my brain, attracted a club to my hands, and crept my steps out to the courtyard. A bearded shadow wandered around near the street wall and my premier thought was that it was one of Tabarka's homeless beggars. I raised the club to the sky and roared "HALT!"

In the next second I realized my faux pas. "Are you going to attack me with that?" smiled your father and put down his suitcase on the gravel. "Wherever I travel, drama seems to escort me."

I was very satisfied to see your father again. Even if he took me by surprise because of his somewhat risen stomach and his bushy beard. Abbas said that he had planned a rather long break in Tabarka, and of course I invited him to my permanent home.

In coming weeks we spent frequent hours in the nostalgia of friendship. Your father detailed how his studio had now grown to a nationally known atelier in Swedish photography circles. He told of his staff of assistants, of his close friendship with many international artistic photographers, and he praised the Swedish journals' interest in his photo sessions with celebrities like Ingmar Bergman, Kurt Olsson, and Eddie Murphy.

"Wow!" I impressed. "And why, then, can you not return my economy?"

"A vital thing in the dawn of a business is to reinvest the profits. Your hotel must also follow this pattern."

"How have you found this sudden success?"

Your father stroked his wild beard and explained proudly:

"I have followed that method which my idols taught me. I have created a photographic stage name and trained my tongue to perfect control of the native language."

"So . . . which name is your name now?"

Here your father changed to the melody of English:

"Krister Holmström Abbas Khemiri is my name, photography is my game."

"Krister Holmström . . . ?"

Your father nodded his head.

"Wow, Krister is also a name of strong Christian tradition, right?" I impressed. Your father did not consider this a compliment but made his forehead into a wrinkled paper.

"What is your tongue suggesting? Why shouldn't I get to formulate my own name? Why shouldn't Capa's method be mine?"

I silenced my mouth in order to not accidentally grow your father's bizarre irritation.

In the evenings we wandered Tabarka's quays, where the growing tourist commerce had begun to offer camel tours in five-minute phases including the documentation of Polaroid photographs. We passed the old Hôtel Majestique, the exterior of which seemed weak and worn while the new, big hotels stood like long white rows of teeth down by the ocean's edge. We passed stands that sold stuffed camels, T-shirts with Coca-Cola prints, decorative hookahs, and over-colored postcards. Your father incessantly searched his eyes at all the encountered people and I finally forced the question:

"Who is your gaze seeking, really?"

"Me? No one particular . . . I am just noticing all the modifications. The world is certainly bizarre. Here in Tabarka they sell copied Michael Jackson records and *Dirty Dancing* T-shirts. And in Stockholm my son reads the Koran, spends time with niggers, and refuses to eat pork."

"What?"

"Nothing," regretted your father, and refused to discuss the subject further.

Back in Stockholm there are Moms with three sons who must be raised and a big brother who becomes an adult that spring. For real. You take on the responsibility of man of the house. You explain to little brothers that now it's you who are the Dynamic Trio because Dads are not to be depended on and in our family you have to be responsible early on. You go to Skärholmen with little brothers to shop, you teach little brothers what bread to buy where and show how to pay honorably for absolutely everything but the garlic, which you transport home in your coat pocket in true family tradition. On the way home you explain to little brothers: There are special rules for us Swedes who don't look like regular ugly blond Swedes, for us it's No points for second place, no points for place number two, we must always be number one, do you understand? Little brothers nod exactly in time, and then you continue toward home to make your invented oven pancake with baking chocolate hidden in the edges. You pick up sick brothers early from after-school care and return videos too late at Video Nord and even dare to go down into the laundry room by yourself, even though you sometimes see ghost shadows and still hear voices before you fall asleep. But soon the voices change, they go from scary phantom voices to subject matter for the stories you've begun to write, you lie on your side in the bed and hear voices tell stories and for your whole life the voices have scared you and kept you awake and woken you standing in the hall, but only now do you realize that the voices can be useful. Imagining stories keeps your imagination in check and as an adult you don't have time to lose focus, adult sons have to help Moms into the ER when the stress stomach makes Moms collapse forward onto the

kitchen floor and adult sons are always there for support when Moms show weakness, whispering strength-
ening words and promising that Dads will come back
soon and he hasn't forgotten his family at all. Because
he hasn't, right? But why doesn't he call? Why doesn't
he write? Moms' questions are childishly difficult to
answer and on her temple Moms have a scratch from
her kitchen-floor fall and Moms close her eyes when
you dab the wound and a little fluff gets stuck at the
edge and somewhere inside you a terrible rage is growing about Dads' talent for coming and going however
he wants. Just when Dads are needed the most.

Weeks became months and your father still shared my hospitable
lodgings in Tabarka. In the evenings he wandered the streets of
Tabarka solitarily. He came home at dawn with cloudy eyes. He was
not left in peace by the demons of the night here in his former
homeland either. Sometimes I thought the thought: "It is as though
he has passed from having had three conceivable homelands to
having zero."

Your father presented a melancholy that was deeper than I had
ever witnessed. I got the emotion that he would prefer to permanent himself in Tunisia (in the physical, not hairstylish, sense). At
the same time there was the longing for his family, which tempted
him to home journey. One night we took a longer walk, accompanied by hooting tourists at beach bars and a carefully lapping water
edge.

"Forgive my long silences, Kadir. But I must be honest. The latest episode in my Swedish life has not really been as euphoric as I
have summarized you."

"Do you want to portion your problems?"

"They are too many to relate. But I can try. To support one's family as an artistic photographer was more difficult than projected. I was forced to photograph pets to survive. First my wife deprecated our constantly deficient economy, then she instead deprecated my constantly expanded working hours. None of my wife's relatives laugh at my knuckle-cracking trick anymore. Cherifa expects increased economic support every summer. The temptation of alcohol has been too much for me lately. In addition, Sweden has been much modified since Refaat and Palme have been abducted. Some ten Swedes with non-Swedish looks have been shot down during the fall and spring. The racist attacks have increased with steady frequency. The country that has always been an erected welcoming hand seems me now to be formed into an erected middle finger. Or a threatening fist."

Here we stood silent for a few seconds. Your father continued:

"But still my son rouses the greatest unease."

"Which of them? The oldest? Surely he has never offered you problems other than well-growing long legs, broad corpulence, and a great appetite for sweets?"

"He has been transformed as well. He persists in spending his time with the children of other immigrants. His body plays basketball and refuses my offers of tennis. His ears listen to the hip-hop of nigger music and he dirties his Swedish language with the embarrassments of slang."

"Why?"

"I don't know. At the same time he accuses me of presenting a 'Swediot name' as a photographer alias."

"Perhaps he is just experiencing the revolt of the teenager?"

"No. His soul is as transformed. He reads the autobiography of Malcolm X and do you know what present he inquired for his anniversary? The map of Tunisia in gold to have around his neck. He does not want to study economics and he calls me a betrayer of 'Arab ideals.' Once he quoted the Koran to my face. Can you understand this?"

"The Koran? Your son? But . . . he is as Swedish as a potato! His Arabic is more innovatively comical than academically accomplished. How has this happened?"

"Do not ask me. I have no knowledge. But it is NOT my fault. I have constantly proclaimed the importance of Swedish integration and the risk of relations with other immigrants. Particularly niggers. I have been sufficiently careful of relating too much about his origins. I have constantly spoken threateningly about the path of politics. Still it is in this mud that he wants to dirty himself. He stays out late at night, he suddenly calls Sweden a racist country and plans a future move to Tunisia . . . He is crazy. Crazy, I say."

"It pains me to hear."

"It pains me to see."

Our pause was set to sound by the melodies of screaming twilight birds. Then Abbas said:

"One thing is securized, anyway."

"And what is that? That you will return my loan very soon?" I joked.

Your father observed me with an expression of second-long madness that I probably hadn't seen since his time at the orphanage.

"That I will never make the same mistake as my father. I will not let politics come between me and my son."

Here we leave the two friends where we stand straining sand through our toes while the loudspeakers at the beach bars jangle out Inner Circle's "A La La La La Long" song and the red sun lies down to sleep in the Mediterranean.

Back in Stockholm there's also the world's best grandma with cigarettes in holders and soft sun-wrinkle eyes, who, in a rage that someone dared to sully her husband's and son-in-law's place of business, starts to go on spying trips in the vicinity of the burned-down studio. When she isn't cruising around in the Toyota in pursuit of suspected perpetrators, she helps with the cleanup. It's you, Imran, Melinda, and Grandma who together get to work scrubbing away the soot flecks and clearing out the debris. Everything is thrown out at the dump except things that might be repairable, and you put the remnants of the negative binders into the storeroom. Hundreds of photo series in purple opposite colors, silhouettes of dogs and hamsters, parrots and snakes.

From Grandma's garage you fetch leftover paint, and together you repaint the inside of the studio and you remember how surprised you are at Grandma's energy. Grandma turns out to be a seventy-six-year-old revolutionary with just-wakened fighting spirit, paint-flecked Birkenstocks, and double white pearl necklaces. A warrior who refuses to bend, who now seems to regret her words about Dads's laziness. Your father is a good man, I've always said so. And it sure can't be easy to come from a third-world country and then come here and try to understand our customs. But he tried, anyway, he should get credit for that. The rest of the time she tells of memories from her life with Grandpa, how they met at that wedding in the archipelago when she was new to Sweden, how handsome Grandpa had been, how he accidentally almost head-butted her when he bowed nervously, how he complimented her brooch. And you listen, and after a while you stop pretending to be interested and you become interested for real because there's so much about Grandpa's life that's reminiscent of yours and you think: Everything goes in circles and of course Dads are good dads, after all, and of course Dads have done their best, after all. You force yourself to understand Dads' actions, you defend Dads in perpetual inner battles, you say that Dads actually had it really tough and I can understand and I promise he'll come back soon and I blah blah blah and understanding here and understanding there and you've been understanding for your entire damn life, understanding for idiot *blattar* who routine-complain about Sweden and understanding for Swediots who complain about *blattar*'s welfare craving and understanding for Arabs who hate Iranians because they always want to be better than other *blattar* (except when it's a matter of allocating themselves into the *blatte* quota) and understanding for Iranians who hate Arabs because of all the historical rubbish and understanding for Serbs who hate Bosnians and Bosnians who hate Turks and Turks who hate Kurds and Kurds who hate everyone and everyone who hates Gypsies and the only ones you've had a little trouble understanding are black Africans, because they are pretty far down in the *blatte* hierarchy but unlike the Gypsies, they never seem to hate back and you can't understand how they can't be tempted into using hate as a driving force. Because in the end isn't it the hate that pushes us on, you think when the studio is done being renovated in a new light blue color and Dads are still missing.

Six months pass.

Then you say good-bye to the understanding and hi to the hate and start to be ashamed when someone asks about your dad.

Are you serious? Do you want to write that you "start to be ashamed" of him in the book about your father? SUPPRESS this NOW! Both of us must be ready for compromises. I can, for example, imagine that you were indignant when in my earlier commentary I was allowed to say:

"The Koran? Your son? He is as Swedish as a potato!"

This has now been renovated. Instead I say:

"The Koran? Your son? He is as Swedish as herring!" Is this experienced as more adequate?

During your father's break in Tabarka, I often did my mediator and tried to overcome him to return to Sweden.

"Come on, my friend. At least call them! Respond their letters! Contact your oldest son, because I see how much it pains you to have lost his relation!"

Your father did not respond me. Then I uttered something that I suspected would have an effect:

"Return to Sweden. Or do you really want to practice the same mistakes that your father made with you?"

Some weeks later, your father booked his return journey to Sweden. His mentality was fixed: He would seek his family's excuse for his absence. He took my farewell with the words:

"I will miss you, but my hope is still that we do not see each other for a long time. I will now seek my retreat to my family!"

I wished your father's success and waved his farewell.

That same night he was back outside my door with an alcoholic odor and the excuse that something unfortunate had happened on the way to the airport.

"What?" I wondered.

"A sign of fate," responded your father and rolled up his eyes.

The postponation of your father's journey home was repeated like a tradition. The whole time it was a sign of fate that stopped his departure. The sun sifted wrong through a chestnut tree, a chestnut had clinked alarmingly against a pocket coin, a news headline had said something about a . . . chestnut? Parallel to your father really wanting to return, he could not return. Do you have this double ambivalence in your experience?

Dads disappear.

Paradoxically enough, it's in his absence that Dads' presence grows stronger than ever.

Because suddenly Dads' silhouettes are sitting there behind helicopter windows. There are Dads, hunch-running out of the rotor eddy and shaking hands with presidents and heavy-shouldered generals. Then Dads climb up to platforms, wave the cheers from the masses, promise new antidiscrimination laws that will actually have consequences and companies that discriminate will be self-destructed and presidents applaud, generals salute, the people rejoice, and sweat-runny Dads dry their foreheads with cloth napkins and are led past the troops' attention swords toward the refrigerator-cold limousine backseat.

And there are Dads training in lightbulb rooms. Dads pump iron and eat oat pasta and punch them-selves sweaty against sandbags that have Keep Sweden Swedish logos and Bert Karlsson's face. Dads measure biceps and thigh muscles with doubly extended mea-suring tapes, oil their Glocks, file their bullets (care-fully carefully) to get the right explosion effect. Dads teach their sons all the kung fu pressure points and deadly finger combinations. Dads hit the bull's-eye on skinhead dolls, they assemble a group and hunt for skinheads and Sweden Democrats and of course they will find that damn cunt in the southern suburb who shone red laser light at passersby right when Laser Man paranoia was at its height, and presumably laughed when panicked *blattar* threw themselves down on bike paths and scraped up their chins. And look there! There are Dads coming home again and opening the studio, and instead of photographing pets they start to document the police's *blatte* abuse, racist doormen, and the Sweden Democrats' tax cheats. Or? What are Dads really doing during this time? No idea.

Does the reader understand that the above passage is not the reality of truth, but rather your fantasies? Does the reader understand that your father never WANTED to leave his family, but was forced to this by the modification of the Swedish society? Does anyone at all understand anything about a story that is not their own? Doubt has begun to stretch my breast.

During the months ahead, your father supported himself by photographing tourists with a Polaroid camera on the beaches of Tabarka. He prepared himself for his journey home. He thought of your mother.

If you are brooding about how he could let himself be separated from Pernilla, I must detail you: Certainly he missed your mother. More than anyone else. There is no more delicious, more intelligent woman in this universe, this is his strong conviction. Still. But at the same time, it is the tragic fact of life that all love one day finds a normalized routine. Even love that was launched with ground vibrations and artificial sky explosions and a man who comes into a *paillote* night after night shouting: "Her name is Bergman! Pernilla Bergman!" Even love that seems to pulverize all walls just to have the possibility of existing. One day you wake up and the person who gave you a nervous tongue cling and perspirations of desire suddenly stands heavy-hipped and slack-breasted beside you in a bathroom mirror with a ghastly grimace to clean her teeth with floss. One day you wake up and the beautiful youth who cited poetry by torchlight and burned his life to modify Art is suddenly a somewhat corpulent photographer of pugs. Such is the tragic passage of life and your father accompanied such thoughts in preparation for his journey home.

In the end, what got your father to pile his courage and return was a letter from your mother. She wrote that she had stifled her rage, that she partially understood your father's going away, but that a divorce was now obligatory. She also wrote that she was worried about you. You spent more and more nightly time roaming around the city. One night you had been transported home by two police, who accused you of metro vandalism. Your telephone conversations with your friends were acted in more and more broken Swedish, and faced with the upcoming November 30, your mother was worried that you would participate in the traditional conflicts between racists and antiracists.

"I beg you. Come home so we can arrange the divorce. And you can talk reason with your son." Your father packed his bags, strongly decided to finally go home. I wished his success and waved his farewell. Naturally I would have stopped him immediately if I had known the tragic consequences his visit would have . . .

The year is ninety-three and Dads have been gone without a trace for a year and a half. November 30 is approaching. The happy day for racists. They will have processions past the palace and leave wreaths of flowers at the statue of King Charles XII. They will honor the Laser Man and New Democracy, they will bellow national anthems and spit snuff and *heil* and stamp their boots. In our city! In Dads' absence you've grown up and started a war. The organization Blatte for Life has been founded and we have waited long enough. It's us against them, we the unidentifiable creoles, the blend of everything, all the pigeonhole-free border people. And them? The ones who seek security in simple black and white, the ones who want to defend Thou ancient, thou free, thou joyful bullshit.

What was once Studio Silvia and then Krister Holmström Abbas Khemiri's photographic pet studio has now become Blatte for Life's meeting center, the organizational headquarters for the new generation of soldiers who will NEVER go the betraying way of Dads. It's here everything joins together, people from the suburbs meet inner-city kids, feminists hook up with dreads activists, homos with heteros, anarchists with Zapatists, niglows with Swedelows, *blattar* with palefaces, Chechenies with Russkies, Kurdish with Turkish(!), Iranis with Arabis with Jewish(!!). All on the same side, totally without self-loathing.

What was once an embarrassing pet studio is now something much, much bigger.

Write me . . . Do you realize now how comical it was that you, in your ambition to minimize your Swedishness, started to attribute such a crucial weight to the value of ethnicity? Because what is more "Swediotic" than to attach people to their ethnicities? Who does this better than Swedes? And who becomes a better pet of racists than people who accept the existence of an us and a them? Who is more toothlessly harmless than the *"blatte"* who accepts his existence as the *"blatte"*? At the time of writing I realize that "comical" should sooner be replaced by "tragic" (the boundary between them seems grayer and grayer to me).

Your father landed at Arlanda in November 1993. For the first time in his life he succeeded in passing the passport check WITHOUT attracting the looks of suspiciousness! For your father, this was a sign in a good direction. Once at Centralen, he parked himself at his antique café of habit in order to enjoy a little nostalgia. The interior of the café had been renovated, a great many types of coffee were now offered, complete with matching ciabattas and pasta salads. Smoking was strictly illegal and none of the old Aristocats were visible. Your father interpellated the waitresses if they knew news about Mansour or Mustafa or maybe Aziz. They all side-shook their heads.

Before your father dared to seek your mother's excuse for his absence, he wanted to examine the status of his studio. He wandered his steps to the commuter train, passed the barriers, and remembered his old work position at SL. On the way out of the city he nostalgized all the days you shared in the cockpit of the metro, all the weekends in Tanto, all the hours in the little bathroom lab. The train swished him farther out over the bridge with a fantastic view of Stockholm's autumnal loveliness, glittering half-frozen water, red-hissing leaf forests, and a multitude of small garden houses. The view calmed a little of the nervousness that rumbled his insides.

From a distance, Abbas noticed that the sign for his studio was abducted. He unlocked the door and gazed into the darkness. In encountering the studio's new color, your father recoiled and fanned his hand in front of his nose as though the sight were a painful scent. The state of the studio was not at all like before. Certainly it was half renovated from the fire. But instead of classic white, the wall color had become light blue! The walls were decorated with illustrations of people like Malcolm X and an assortment of hip-hop Negroes. (One was that Ice T or Ice Cube or Ice Man or Ice Cream? Your father does not recall.) The floor was filled with pillows and blankets, well-filled ashtrays, and dried apple skeletons. On a table lay worn books by names unknown to your father, like Malek Alloula and Patrick Chamoiseau.

All the ruins from your father's business had been localized in the storeroom. The traces of the fire were also still evident there. As usual, you had renovated on the surface but not managed the whole way. Your father paged through his antique material and was hypnotized by his old photographs. There was everything in a mixed mess, smoke-damaged pet photos, heat-bubbled negatives of your little brothers disguised as Batman and Superman, burned-black pictures from the dog days of the Stockholm Exhibition, yellowed motifs of your mother's goddessish silhouette exposed to a romantic sun laying. All this life that was now reduced to slowly fading memories. Your father may have teared his eyes. Hours may have passed. Suddenly a key was heard in the door. Someone invaded the studio.

Your father carefully glanced out from the storeroom and first saw only a shadow. Then an erected person in a black-and-white keffiyeh, frequent facial pimples, shaved skull, and an army jacket materialized. He stood out in the studio and hacked his throat, making notes on a pad while at the same time thoughtfully picking his nose with his thumb. It was you.

BFL has called a general meeting at Headquarters and I come first because I am the self-appointed General of the Fight (code name: I-on Carry-on a.k.a. Dow Jonas a.k.a. the Head Khmer). I'm the one with the key, I'm the founder of the network. I'm the one who's written all the regulations and decided on the super-secret knock. Soon Imran comes, then Melinda, and last Patrik. BFL's innermost circle, the central quad. We're the ones who start every meeting by updating the map of Sweden where pins mark WAR organizations and KSS centers and towns where New Democracy got too many votes. We're the ones who put up new enemy photos on the bulletin board, write battle manifestos, and write up outlines for the future.

Then we sit on the floor, roll a spliff, and plan the

evening's meeting and the night's action. Only sometimes do we send Patrik out to scout for suspicious
security police cars on the street. Melinda lights up and
the spliff is passed around. The green does its thing,
our chests get that calming chirpy feeling, and the air
clouds. We wait for the others, what time did we say?
Eight, but you start to hear the knock combinations on
the studio door fifteen minutes early.

Here they come, everyone who's dedicated their lives
to the Fight. Polyester sisters, basketball brothers, shining siblings, million-generationers. First the Melinda
sisters, waddling down the stairs, and then Imran's
whole basketball team, and then Hanin, who's the
leader of the Malmö force, and Chia, who's in charge of
the youth troops. Then some of the Aristocats' kids, Elif
and Daphne, Kai and Mine. Then Mohamed from your
grade, who has promised to dismantle the drivel of the
integration debate.

Your father heard knocks, loud voices, the door which was opened
and closed again and again. He carefully closed the door to the
storeroom so he wouldn't be discovered.

Then comes a big gang who all got the five-to-eight train:
the journalists all together, Oivvio and Lawen, Devrim
and Vanja. There's Shang waving—she's responsible
for the laws—and there's Emma and Farnaz being
welcomed—they're going to expand the theater—and
there's Pontikis, who's going to take over the film industry. There's Ernesto, who's going to infiltrate the Minis-
try for Foreign Affairs along with Davor and Julius in

data support. Macki controls the offensive on the business school, while Reena storms the political science department. There's hugging and greeting and Wzup Moses how's it going with the director post at the Royal Institute of Technology? and Kifhalek Karim! with his sights set on becoming a professor of philosophy. And there's Nadia, the future director of Swedish Television, and there's Zvonko, soon to be editor in chief of *Dagens Nyheter*. And there's Cengiz and Goran and Mustafa and Golbarg and Ksenia and Behnaz and him and her and them and you and us . . .

Finally everyone's sitting in a group on the crowded floor, the air warm and the windows steamed over. Melinda gets up and declares the meeting open. She summarizes the results of the latest actions, and everything is a success and letter bombs have been sent to neo-Nazis and nighttime visits have been made to the skinhead who assaulted the Kurd in Lerum, pinioned him, and left him in the flaming vegetable shop. The Swedish commander in chief will soon regret that he dismissed Carl Gustaf Belmadani as a chauffeur for the minister of defense for the explicit reason that he was dark and had a strange name (last name, that is). Skara Sommarland is being boycotted for having a racist owner. The paper *Expressen* is being boycotted for the news bills where they wrote: "What the Swedish people think of immigrants: Drive them out!" The racist town of Sjöbo is besieged. Vivianne Franzén is put under constant surveillance.

Everyone cheers and applauds and toasts and back-thumps.

.　　.　　.

A sweetish smell of marijuana trickled into the storeroom where your father sat hidden. It was accompanied by growing voices and then the vibrations from your roaring declaration:

"Melinda gets up and declares the meeting open."

What meeting? reflected your father. What are they actually doing out there?

After Melinda, it's Imran's turn. He gets up, tells about upcoming actions, shows drawings and maps and future strategies of how *blatte* representatives will infiltrate area after area, slowly but surely gain influence, and then force in more *blattar*.

Everyone cheers and applauds and toasts and back-thumps.

After a half hour or so, your father cracked open the door. He heard your now-hoarse voice shouting: "Everyone cheers and applauds and toasts and back-thumps." Your father collectioned his courage, turned out the door further, and looked out into the studio to see who else you had enticed along into your decadence.

Then Imran turns it over to me and I'm really just going to give the final speech, that inspiration chat I always give at the end of every meeting, and as usual it's dead quiet when I begin and as usual I give a speech that revolves around the older generation as cowardly betrayers. I say dads are fucking traitors and damn Uncle Toms and house Negroes and Benedict Arnolds, this goes for all dads, I swear if they were real dads they wouldn't be gone now because real dads never betray their children, and real dads lead revolts and don't care about finances and I end with my fist in the air and the promise that we will NEVER be like our parents and I'm standing before a field of raised fists and we solemnly promise and there's cheering and saluting and roaring and whistling and there's a choir of one more time one more time and JONAS JONAS but I decline and say: That's enough. For now.

When the meeting is over, we sing the fight song for the coming revolution, promise ourselves NEVER to give up no matter what happens, and then the troops turn toward home.

We let out our breath, close the minutes book, toast with near beer, and spill a few drops for dead homiez, a drop for Grandpa, a drop for Jimmy Ranjbar, two drops for Fayola. And soon we've built up enough strength for the evening's real task. It's a sneak attack and it's best if we do it ourselves. Even generals must go to battle sometimes.

But Jonas . . . NO ONE HAD INVADED THE STUDIO! There were no "troops." There was just you and your three lost friends. Melinda, Imran, and Patrik sat on their floor pillows while you gave a long speech in which you sullied your father and waved your hand at an invisible army. Your father crept back to the storeroom, sank whimpering down into a squat, and felt his heart melt at the sight of this pathetic scene.

What had your father observed? Was it this that his son meant by never upgiving his fight? Sitting in a locked, blue-colored, previous pet studio and fantasizing forth a revolution? Had his son questioned his will to fight in order to himself spend his time in the false world of fantasy?

Your father thought: "My son has lost his mental balance. He is crazy. He has been captured in the fog of role-playing." He remained sitting in the storeroom, with an accelerating desperation and a growing need to pee. Out there you played pumping hip-hop music and howled your shouts where you constantly named each other "ey bro" or "ey *blatte*" as though they were delicious compliments. Then the music was stopped. It turned into noises of bags and your voice, which again, for the third time, compared your father's existence with that of an "Uncle Tom."

Then your father experienced a rage that he had not known since his youth. It was a fury that collectioned all the years of degradation, all the years of invisible striving and struggling and providing for his family that was now flushed into the drain by a crazy son who hallucinated forth invisible forms that he called "his army" and cyclically shouted:

"Let's jet, bros! It'll be a *blatte* revolution with no mercy! Maximum fat caps up their asses."

And I remember that night because the sky is cinematically starry clear and we've puffed zut and sipped near beer and as usual I was the evening's game master, and as usual it was a wild success. We left Dungeons & Dragons a long time ago, now it's a new time new battles and instead of Miss Super Zulu and MC Mustachio everyone is themselves. Almost. With a little extra strength and increased courage and maximum talent for handling paintbrushes at night. We're ready for the next task, it's black sky and autumn night, cold wind in frozen-stiff gloves, paint cans in plastic bags, and just-bought wide brushes.

.   .   .

The door was locked, your shouts died away, the studio was left in silence. Your father crept out from his hiding place and emptied his bladder in the bathroom with relief. Then he left the dark of the premises and followed your four silhouettes toward the commuter train station. He had gotten an overdose of something. He was pushed over a line. Perhaps it was your repeated insultations that ached him. Perhaps those words turned on his innermost fear? (For certainly it is the truest insultations that ache us the most?)

From the footbridge, Abbas saw how you painted the nocturnally deserted train station with a multitude of light blue words. Quick as rats you wrote idiocies like BLATTE 4 LIFE and FUCK WAR on the platform floor and the glass panes of the waiting room. Your father thought satirically: "Wow, this will no doubt have a broad political effect." At the same moment, he noticed his dangling camera around his neck. This was no planned intention. It was just hanging there. And without knowing why he exposed the lens and began to shoot.

Your father followed your steps all night. He saw how you painted your idiotic letters on the white triangles of Sergels Torg, random electrical boxes, the chess squares at Kungsträdgården. He saw how you sullied the statue of Charles XII with light blue color and how Patrik wrote BLATTE POWER on some nearby steps. He saw how you spelled on the bridge that leads over to Gamla Stan. He saw how you were seconds from being discovered at the palace, how you painted your letters on the antique palace wall, hid the brushes, and half-ran whistling to Slussen when the patrol guard came stamping. Your father's camera documented everything.

That night we stamp the city with our words. Melinda, Imran, Patrik, and I. We cover everything in our colors, we leave our mark. I remember the excitement that pounds in my chest, my mouth steamed by the autumn air, the hoodie's neck warmth, the smell of paint, paint-sticky brushes, my worn-out right arm, steam breath in the face-shielding scarf.

After a few hours we're almost done and the paint starts to run out. There's just one attack point left, absolutely the most risky one. But what do you say, maybe this is enough? Melinda adjusts the comb in her hair and stares at us. She has a little drop of blue paint on her chin, and at that moment she's the most beautiful in the world because she's standing there in the yellow streetlight and yelling: If you want to give up, fine, do it, I'm going to keep going.

Of course we keep going. All in a quartet down toward the skinheads' helicopter platform. The giggling is long gone. Imran's Adam's apple goes up and down, Patrik checks over his shoulder, the cans clang, and taxis are watching. Melinda goes first, the bag paint-flecked with light blue, her furiously hopping comb that glitters in the cold tunnel light.

Then keep watch in the dark on the other side and there's the starry sky and there's the lapping water and there's the rocking helicopter platform and traces of the skinheads. Empty beer cans, fluttering Systembolaget bags, racist graffiti. The silhouette of Riddarholmen towers to the right and you can hear music from a distant party. But we are alone. No one there. Melinda's hissing cry: Go! and with the clumsiest glove fingers pry open dented paint lids; Patrik and I start while Melinda and Imran keep watch in different directions. The water laps and sweat dampens my upper lip when I dip the brush in the soon-empty can and start crossing out all the Nazi signs. Then painting letters that run tearlike over the concrete wall, words that shine sharply and they will sit there for always and they're written like in a trance and I barely remember what I write, just words upon words upon words and at this point all the fear disappears because it's just me and the paint and the eternal feeling of being permanent. And obviously it would be cooler to claim that I was used to doing real tags and didn't write in a style that Melinda and Imran laughed at and called old lady writing. And obviously it would be cooler if we had fat caps and real spray cans and stood under a starry clear Compton sky and sprayed multicolored graffiti with starry shine and perfect shadowing on our lowriders. But there's also something beautiful in dirtying the skinheads' favorite place with big brushes and Grandma's leftover light blue garage paint.

Soon we change position, a nighttime commuter train passes, electric cables spark. Patrik watches the tunnel, I watch the dock, all clear: Go! I listen for boot stomps and *heil* shouts, I listen for that jumpy sequence of tones that comes from police walkie-talkies and that always makes me think of R2-D2 in *Star Wars*. But I don't hear anything more than the lapping of the water and distant bass lines from the party. Melinda's letters shine more clearly than mine, SCREW KSS! and Imran writes, FUCK WAR'S MOTHER! and then the not really equally badass BERT = DIRT!

Then suddenly you hear steps. Were they steps? I try to squint myself through the compact darkness. Is it a lost dog owner or a drunk or maybe ten or twelve skinheads who've been lying in ambush? Then suddenly I'm blinded by a flash. What the hell was that? yells Melinda and Imran drops the brush and Patrik yells: It's the train! But everyone realizes that the tracks are

lying silently deserted and Melinda starts to get paranoid, looks toward the dock: Is there someone there
or what? And I crouch down, am about to say no when
there's another flash, one flash, two, three: There's
someone taking pictures! and we tear down into the
tunnel and we pull our scarves over our faces way too
late as an army of hard-soled skinheads pant at our
necks and shout racist slogans behind our backs.

We have just come out of the tunnel when the car
motor growls itself up behind us. We slow down our
steps and try to walk calmly, no one hurries until the
world suddenly turns blue and someone's called the
cops and in one second we cut into the alleys of Gamla
Stan and it's forced breaths and shifted motor, walkie-
talkie sounds and loudspeaker voices, blinking blue
lights and Melinda who shouts: Drop the cans! even
though they're still sitting over at the helicopter platform. We rush through alleys, past a café, cobblestones,
into a backyard, catch our breath, watching from the
shelter of a rainspout. Waiting them out. Are you with
me? Right when we think we've made it, in the middle
of that laugh that's always at its biggest when you've
been close to being caught but succeeded in tricking the
pigs at the last second, they're there again and now
there are two cars and we run as a quartet, Imran just a
few steps after, hunted by sirens and accelerating
sounds, steps echoing between the narrow houses, clat-
tering up until we're caught in a dead end and it's a
cinematic ending, the loudspeaker voice in the shadows
that shouts STOP! and we stop, out of breath we stand
there caught with blinding blue light in our faces.

.   .   .

Write me . . . How did you dare, three thin teenagers (and one gigantically fat), to positionate yourselves at the helicopter platform? Did you not realize the risk? Your father chose to use his flash with intention. To teach you a lesson. And he enjoyed the view of your bodies which suddenly became trembling hares that rushed back into the tunnel of Gamla Stan.

But you must believe me about one thing. It was not your father who called the police. That he corresponded his photographs to the police is another matter. He did it in a haze of revenge. He did it in a betrayed temperament. He did it for YOUR future care. He was very careful not to include the photos where you were documented with brushes. Only Patrik, Melinda, and Imran were exposed. And these are three people who are not worth your escort anyway. These are three who should know better than to encourage my son's confused imagination! If they try to cultivate seeds of outsiderness in my son's head, this is the price one must pay! (These were your father's words.)

And this is the last fall we have left together, because Patrik, Imran, and Melinda's sentences come down in the spring, and they're harsher than expected. Maybe because we tried to run. Maybe because they discovered our tracks all the way from the helicopter platform to the palace to the statue to the studio. Maybe because we refused to confess to the very end (despite the paint flecks on shoes, hands, and jacket arms). Maybe because of the series of photos that someone gave to the police— the photos that documented everything from the train platform to the helicopter platform in blurry photos as though from a crying lens. Presumably it was the photo series, because photographs don't lie, as a judge says and smacks his mouth and fixes his eyes on Melinda, who's sitting thin-shouldered on an adult chair and she looks at her sniffling mom and her bodyguarding sisters and her Afro is combed down neatly and her green gold chain is hanging hidden under her Singapore shirt and her hand has an almost-washed-off BFL tattoo and her voice almost disappears in the courtroom when she takes the blame for all my letters without blinking and says: Of course I'm the one who wrote that all racists can fuck their mothers of course I'm the one who wrote FUCK THE FIVE-O and of course I'm the one who wrote that weird stuff on the far side that one with the kind of strange writing that I can't even explain what it means.

Dads stand strong.

I barely remember the final scene. I think it's blurry Moms who unscrew the padlock on Dads' *mémoire,* Dads who have returned to Sweden, Dads who are back to being a gate guard, notice has been given on the studio, and Dads are sleeping on the sofa while waiting for the divorce to go through. What else do I remember? Moms' gasping sounds? Moms' short moans?

Moms are standing there with the envelope, and it's overstuffed with negatives and out falls proof of things Dads have stubbornly denied. Do you believe it yourself? That I was unfaithful? Or that I would follow my own son and then try to get his friends arrested? Never!

But the negatives are lying there, and some of them depict faceless bodies and others depict an opposite world of nighttime colors where my blue panther back is painting a train platform. Melinda and Imran are painting Sergels Torg, Patrik writes BLATTE POWER on some steps, and all four silhouettes are standing in a row and coloring the wall of the Swedish palace.

Moms display their perpetual uprightness. Moms don't let in the tiniest compromise. Little brothers are sent down to the cellar to get Dads' suitcases, Moms get the orange kitchen scissors and start packing.

When Dads come home from SL that night, the bags are ready in the halls, filled with ties, socks, underwear, shirts, pants, and T-shirts—all carefully punctured with at least one or two scissor holes.

And I remember how Dads just stand there in the hall in his SL jacket with the evening paper in his right hand and his beret at an angle. Dads looks at Moms and looks at sons and at first he seems to think it's all a joke because he laughs nervously. You can't be this angry about a little white lie and some mistakes? Who hasn't done things they regret? Dads untie shoes and Moms roar with a mirror-cracking voice and little brothers start to cry and Dads try to explain, try to find excuses, try to say I did it for the good of our son and those women were a long time ago and meant nothing. But Moms' tears are as heavy as surprise rain on picnics on sand dunes and her cheeks as tight as when she saw Bert Karlsson give the victory sign and Dads try to say sorry in a bunch of different languages and layer French declarations of love on Arabic nicknames on Swedish forgive me's but Moms won't let herself be calmed in any language and when Dads try to touch Moms' cheek she steps to the side and shoves him toward the door and her cheeks are so red that her forehead shines white and Dads suddenly change voices and say: I refuse. You don't refuse at all. Dads look at me and I at him, our eyes meet, we stare at each other's pupils but I don't give up, not this time, because nothing ever comes between Moms and sons.

Finally Dads tie his shoes, pick up the suitcases, and walk toward the balcony walkway. Little brothers are crying even louder and Velcroing themselves to Dads' legs and Dads are biting lower lip and Moms are crouching with her hands like pitchforks in her hair. I wave Dads' farewell with words that I will never forget and that I want to but can't include in the book.

Oh? You may certainly exclude things, but your father may not? Here shall be injected exactly what you said because this is a vital phrase for your long silence. You yelled your father's adieu with the words:

.   .   .

When your father returned from Sweden I barely recognized his exterior. His hair was silvered and in certain places his hairstyle resembled a cue ball. His eye bags were swollen and he was limping from a foot sprain he happened to get in the airport bar of the layover in Frankfurt.

"Well, how did your reunion with your family happen?" I wondered with concern.

"Oh, it happened well. My wife was sorry and wanted to have me back as a spouse. And my son and I are the best of friends."

"So . . . what are you doing here again?"

Your father compressed his lips.

"Aren't you going to tell me?"

"Yes."

"But another time?"

"Another time."

"And now?"

"I don't know."

Your father settled himself permanently in Tabarka. He took over Achraf's old atelier, modernized it, and offered tourists the chance to be photographed with their heads stuck into Arabic milieu scenery. There was the desert scene where one became a dromedary driver, the harem scene where one became a fat sultan, the Kaaba scene where one became a Muslim on a pilgrimage.

Abbas bore a constant longing for his family, for the delicious tap water of Sweden, for bridges' views in sun layings, for the summery odor of lilacs. But to live isolated in that country where he gave his all was to him impossible. He had transformed his name, he had curved his tongue to perfection the Swedish language. He had even named his son Jonas instead of Younes! What more could be expected? For all that, Sweden was the country where he was still seen as a constant outsider.

I must admit that during the following years he still considered your betrayal the most devastating. Late at night when we shared our company over a whiskey he would say this about you:

"What right does that snake have to say that I have betrayed my roots? What does that confused damn idiot know about roots? What does he know about fighting? He spends his constant time in the phase of confusion. Because what else could one call a person who is born in Sweden of a Swedish mother and still spends his time in the company of idiotic immigrants, eagerly proclaiming the fight against racists as his goal? What else can one call a person who, with intention, has an accent in the language he himself was raised with? My son is a sad figure who lacks culture. He is not Swedish, he is not Tunisian, he is NOTHING. He is a constant cavity who varies himself by his context like a full-fledged chameleon."

(Excuse me, Jonas, but I must write you your father's true words.) I responsed:

"But . . . aren't you too?"

"Yes! But for me it is a proud prestige. I am a free cosmopolitan! But for my son this is a shame."

During the following years I did my diplomat. I tried to convince your entirely too proud father not to stifle his relation with his sons. Call them! Correspond them your begun but never terminated letter! Your father only refused my propositions. His pride blockaded him. And so you know: I was the one who indicated to your father that he should send those postcards to your little brothers in the fall of 1997. It was my fault. Sorry! I thought it might be good if your father let out a bit of furious steam and therefore we formulated the text of the cards in an alcoholic intoxication. Your father already regretted this the next day. But as usual his prestige blockaded him from telephoning you with an apology.

And you remember that day because soon it's double little brothers' birthdays and you've started high school and you come home from school at lunch and it's you and your school friend Homan who are going to watch last night's *Yo! MTV Raps* and your home is his so you kick off your shoes in the hall and Homan rewinds the video while you look through the mail. The absolute worst is your second-long joy when you see the postcards and the motifs from Tabarka and the Tunisian stamps, the joy of seeing Dads' classically beautiful handwriting with the specially bent numerals in the zip code. And although you have the feeling you're going to regret it, you read the text on the two postcards that have been sent to your two little brothers and although you know it's going to leave traces that will never be rubbed out you read the phrases, which are exactly identical on both postcards:

Everyone in the entire world has betrayed me. Except you two.

And you remember that Dads even specify "you

two," and you don't crumple the postcards into balls and you don't swear out loud but Homan notices and he understands without questions because his dad is a betrayer too because his dad has started hitting his wife in fear of her new colleagues and in frustration about never getting to go on job interviews and now he's working as a popcorn seller at the Röda Kvarn theater and Homan understands exactly why sometimes you can get tear eyes and back shivers just from seeing other dads with their sons in the subway or why you always get goose-bump skin when Treach in Naughty by Nature raps: I was one who never had and always mad, never knew my dad muthafuck the fag. Homan gets the rage that you can feel for a country that's stolen your dad.

The years passed, the tourism expanded, your father lived very isolated with his business and his Sweden memories. In 1998 we made the relation of an American tourist by the name of Alex Baldwin (that was actually his name, almost like the famous Hollywood actor). Together we partook the majority of drinks in hotel bars before Alex said that he had many relations in the erotic branch in the U.S.A. He said that pornography was always looking for new markets and the only thing not represented was the Arab world.

"Do you want to assist me in the creation of local Arab erotic photos? It would collect you serious finances."

Alex paused to see how your father received his idea.

"Or perhaps you have religious protests against—"

"No worries," I interrupted. "No traditional backpacks weight our backs. Right, Abbas? But you must be able to find Arab women in the U.S.A. who are ready to eroticize themselves before the camera? Why not just use props and actors and photograph women in veils in Los Angeles or Beverly Hills? Why take the roundabout way in doing it here?"

Alex smiled my naïveté.

"Of course we can use actors, of course we can maximize our attempts to falsify an Arab atmosphere in a studio in L.A. And even now there are many such photo series. But our customers are not the crowd of routine. Our customers are the creamy crops, very particular with a great hunger for authenticity. Our customer will detect a false fez or an American studio immediately. But this, things like this can't be simulated!"

Alex aimed his index finger at the cracked plastic globe of the button that controlled the hotel bar's ceiling light.

"Do you understand? Besides, erotica is a branch that sways in rhythm with politics. Soon after the Gulf War we noticed how the demand for Arab pornography grew among our customers. The future looks very positive."

"Just one thing," said your father. "It is very important to me that our photos do not violate anyone. I only want to photograph erotically and not pornographically. I still have a broad talent that must not be abused. We must carry on the torch from photographers like Weston, Kertész, and Bill Brandt!"

"Of course," responded Alex. "Who are these three?"

"This trio made the naked photograph respectable."

"Trust me," Alex calmed, and delegated us his business card.

I must admit that Abbas collaborated with Alex for a few following years. I assisted him. Together we contracted Tunisian student-ettes and prostitutes, who, in exchange for expanded finances, sexualized themselves before the camera. Initially he photographed only solitary sexy women who, clad in veils, widened their legs, pouted their lips, and tempted the camera with hints of the delight. But in connection with the expansion of the global world net I convinced your father to expand into photographing women who also sexualized themselves with men in front of the camera.

I had an obvious motive: The conflicts between the Western world and the Arab world increased the demand for our photos exponentially. Every oil conflict, terror attack, or Gulf invasion fed the hunger for photos where veiled women were sexualized. Your father finally gave in and the public success was total. Our first success was the humoristically erotic *Aladdin and His Magic Tramp*. Then *Lawrence of Hoe-rabia* and *Casablanca the xxx Version* arrived. A very popular series, particularly in France, presented principals who had their one-eyes sucked to ecstasy by veiled students who wanted to levitate their grades (*Principal's Office, Fail in Veil, Parts 1–6*). Another combined the soldier format with Muslim food erotica (*Dessert Storm—Feeding the Soldiers*).

Our photos found a well-built success in both the U.S.A. and Europe. Almost all of our series found their specific customers and only a few made fiascos (the unfortunately named photo series *Saddam and Gonorrhea*, for example, only had a very limited distribution, except in an extremely selective circle of customers). Soon we created our own photo heroes who returned in repeated series. Our first female heroine was called Miss Honey Milk Sheik—the female nympho. She was a Muslim oil-well proprietress who happily let herself be bound and sexualized in triangular holes at the same time by white men she found at abandoned gas stations. The American success became rocketish and the woman we collaborated with was soon invited to Miami for solo scenes with erotic giants like Peter North. We replaced her with a male hero where we borrowed the format from the comic Rowan Atkinson. Instead of Mr. Bean we created Mr. Bedouin, a very humoristic man who constantly happens to localize himself in hilariously sexual situations. He rents a hotel room and is welcomed extra generously by the proprietress's twin daughters (*Too Cool for School*). He gets lost and is welcomed extra generously in an oasis by seven sex-starved Saudi aerobics instructors (*1,000 and One Tights*).

Soon we noticed that particularly popular were the photo series where we let men penetrate veiled women in an acted situation of coercion. The man was preferably as white as possible. The woman was preferably forced to sexualization, the veil preferably ripped in two, and the penetration preferably happened according to the pattern: orally, vaginally, anally, and then back to orally. The man could, for example, play a soldier who invaded an erotically steam-ing hamam or a business director who called in a veiled employee to his office room. The scenario did not seem central; the vital thing was that the woman's veil would be ripped off, that her hair would be exposed, and that the white portion of the man would be planted in the woman's face.

I was responsible for all the practicalities while your father pho-tographed our series with that sort of creeping indifference that had colored him since his Sweden move. His finances flowered, but still he was so far from happy. It was NOT the ambiguity of mor-als that disturbed him. Memorize that all women who acted in our photos chose this entirely solitarily. For every slurped spunk and penetrated anus they were compensated very generously. And what does one have for legitimacy to question a woman's right to her own body? Your father is an enlightened Western man who would never fall into the trap of naïveté-declaring those models with whom he collaborated.

Consequently it was not morals that darkened his humor. Instead it was his bizarre position. His whole life he had fought to get an excess of economy to delight his family. He had washed dishes and picked up dog poop and driven metros and photo-graphed pets. And now when his economy had finally flowered, he had no family to portion it with. He regretted much in his life and soon started to be disgusted with wasting his photographic talent on unessential things.

In the year 2000 came the magic day when your father could repay me my loan with expanded interest. Even though he was now free, his humor seemed far from sunshine. I said:

"Praise my congratulations, now we are finally square! What will you do now?"

"I do not know. But I am going to stop photographing erotica. I have economy enough."

While I prepared the final dedication of my own hotel, your father wanted to collection his memories into a summarizing biography. Just like his idols Capa and Frank, Cartier-Bresson and Avedon, your father longed to have his life and work documented. In the book, his favorite photos were to be blended with texts that explained his actions to his lost family. For frequent hours he sat in his room with the pencil frenetically bitten to splinters between his teeth.

"How is your biography going?" I sometimes interpellated.

"Very badly," responded your father. "It is very difficult to bring order to my life. All of my memories are mixed helter-skelter and I cannot even sense how I should initiate my history."

"Perhaps we can help each other? Perhaps you can tell your life to me in order to cure your writer's cramp?"

And your father began to tell. And he told and told and told. The words filled the morning office and the afternoon *casse-croûte* stand and the beach walk at dusk. He talked and talked with an open-heartedness that I had NEVER seen in your father either before or after. In the company of the night we transported our bodies up on my brand-new hotel roof. Just as in our youth we shared the enjoyment of hashish, we stared the starry sky's pulsating nearness while your father distributed word cascades. Words about his Algerian home village, chestnuts, the TV star Magnus Härenstam, and the sunshine in the Stockholm archipelago were blended in bizarre disorder. His words never wanted to stop; they followed me into my bedroom despite my demonstrative yawns, they followed me through the bathroom door when I brushed my teeth, they could even be heard when I turned off the lamp for falling asleep. It was as though everything your father had not told to anyone finally must be emptied out.

The next day at breakfast he continued to repeat about his disappeared father blah blah blah and his kind mother blah blah blah and the art of photography blah blah blah. Monstrously full of his constant, self-centered word waves, I cut him off.

"Just one thing . . . How can you know that your mother was telling the truth about that Moussa? Couldn't she have made it up?"

Your father was frustrated:

"That is the most idiotic thing I have ever heard, why would she . . ."

"Perhaps because she . . . had happened to sexualize herself with someone else? Someone improper? Like for example a neighbor farmer?"

"What do you mean . . . That Rachid would have . . . But he would probably have said when we met in . . ."

Your father opened his mouth, again and again, but just like when he was little no sound was heard. He disappeared and returned a few minutes later with the photograph where he had captured Rachid's exterior.

"Express honestly—certainly our likeness does not bear likeness?"

Your father held Rachid's photo before him. And I must admit. The likeness was not large. It was identical. It was the same person holding a turkey in the photo from the souk of 1984 in Jendouba who sat across from me in the year 2000 in Tabarka. The same heavy eye bags, the same sorrowful gaze, the same silvery hair with a blank patch, each hidden by an accouterment. Your father with a beret. Your grandfather with a keffiyeh. It was as though the common experience of losing a relationship with one's son for political motives had left exactly equivalent marks in their faces.

"Wow," I said.

"Wow," said your father. "But then who is that Moussa?"

"Perhaps a result of your mother's imagination?"

Your father nervously rubbed his forehead and found no response. Later that same night he knocked my door. As usual, I sat connected to the global world net, searching for new comedy series.

"This is going to sound like a bad joke, Kadir. But I need to borrow a little economy. I promise that you will get it back soon. I must take my last chance to not make the same mistake as my father. I will NOT LET FEAR OF POLITICAL CONSEQUENCES SEPARATE ME FROM MY SON!!!"

I smiled him and delegated him my economy. The next day he had disappeared. Again. His tradition true, he had made his leaving into a surprise. He had collected his photo equipment, closed his studio, and left Tunisia.

Can you guess where your father traveled? In the autumn of his age, he journeyed out in the world to dedicate his life to the defense of the weak. Since that day he has not squandered a single frame to pets, touristic humor motifs, or veil-inspired erotica. Instead, his constantly changing aliases present photos of American war crimes in Afghanistan, African war tragedies, and negative environment effects of multinational companies. Under the name Paul Vreeker he has photographed Iranian asylum seekers who sewed up their mouths with needle and thread in protest against Holland's strict immigrant rules. In Hong Kong he has photographed South Vietnamese child prisoners, in the U.S.A. he has photographed steel barriers that have been erected to shut out Mexican immigrants. He has also documented Chinese slave factories and Palestinian children's scars from "rubber bullets" (constructed from pointy steel).

Via the global world net I have followed your father's goldish success. When he is not photographing, he is establishing close relations to political intellectuals all over the world. He drinks righteously pressed juice with Sting, he brunches with writers like Arundhati Roy, and once a month he plays traditional Scrabble with Noam Chomsky. And do you know that song by Bono and U2 called "Even Better Than the Real Thing"? Guess to whom it is dedicated! It is a song of homage to your father! (Verify the CD's interior in the American version yourself.)

But despite all this, he is a very solitary man. He always misses his family. He mourns his nonexistent relation to his sons. But he does not know how he should seek their excuse. On the other hand, he knows with magnificent certainty that he will NEVER let himself be trampled upon again. Never again will your father let himself be duped into integrating. Never again will you see him compromise himself in the hunt for finances. It is not worth it. And perhaps this is a discovery your father made too late in his life . . .

Do you want to know how the book should be terminated? With a magnificent final scene where the now-published author (= you) reencounters his disappeared father as the result of chance.

Let us first show how you leave your apartment on a nightly walk. You wander your sorrowful steps around Stockholm, you are tired after yet another night of fruitlessly writing, you are taxed by the gazes of passersby, you hope no one recognizes you, you regret all the words you have ever written. You miss your father. Stuff the scene with severe depression, tragic strings, dark rain clouds, stormy winds, bending rain forests, shot-down small birds. Everything is sorrowful like in Otis Redding's "Fa-Fa-Fa-Fa-Fa (Sad Song)."

Then . . . as you cross the bridge from Gamla Stan in toward Kungsträdgården, your eyes are captured by the gigantically large chestnut tree that stretches its embrace toward heaven. You stop, you look at the tree, you squeeze the old chestnut that your father gave you without you remembering why. You are just about to wander on when you discover another person standing at exactly the same angle on the other side of the park. He has a newly transplanted virile ponytail, his shoes are Gucci, his exterior signals a very rich and successful man. You reflect each other's eyes and you suddenly realize that it is your sunburned father!

Without thoughts of historic conflicts you both roar your happiness, rush your steps toward each other, hug each other's bodies, sprinkle phrases of greeting in French, Arabic, Swedish. Change the scene to euphoric happiness! Let the sun begin to wake in the east, let taxicabs make cheering honkings, let the paperboys, the homeless, and nocturnal fishermen start a gradually growing American film applause, one by one, with tear-filled cheeks, they start to applaud a son's and a father's rediscovered relation. Everything is jubilation like in Otis Redding's "Dum-Dum-Dum (Happy Song)." Chestnuts rain from the tree, your eyes smile, and with exactly mirror-image mouths you both say the phrase:

"All I have wanted in my entire life is for your pride in me to be as eternal and universal as my pride in you."

Then you stop short, sharing first surprised looks and then laughs of relief.

Then let the reader see how you and your father, in the accompaniment of happiness, wander away toward Gamla Stan, you nostalgize the Dynamic Duo, you point at some light blue traces of paint, laughing. The last thing the reader hears is your father, who says:

"My isolation from my family became too severe. I was depressed so heavily that I was ready to do anything to rediscover my relation to my family. I was even ready to let an antique friend correspond you e-letters that perhaps exaggerated the success of my current status. All so that you would understand the choices I have made in life."

The reader sees how you smile at your father and promise him your eternal friendship and forgiveness. Your silhouettes disappear in a carefully awaking haze of heat while the reader remains standing teary-eyed under the chestnut tree. The reader bends to the ground, transports a chestnut into their pocket, and then wanders toward home in time with the waking sun. The reader smiles and thinks: This was truly a brilliant book about a brilliant man!

EPILOGUE

FURIOUSEST GREETINGS!!!

Your document has been delivered me. I have read it. Carefully. Every phrase. Let me try to control my burning fingers in an attempt to find at least ONE positive surprise about your text.

Pff.

Calm . . .

Calm.

The idea of initiating the book with my prologue and my authentic e-letter to you is not so stupid, not to say rather intelligent. My phrases become the first tones in what will become your father's symphony. Unfortunately it will soon turn out that the symphony is sooner a total FIASCO! Let me dissect your flat-fall point by point.

My premier disappointment was the title of the book. Why have you named the book *Montecore—The Silence of the Tiger* despite my opposition? Google indicates that Montecore was a white tiger that was trained by the celebrated tamer duo Siegfried & Roy in Las Vegas. But where is the reference between this tiger and your father? Why not a more adequate title like *My Father: The Man, the Myth, the Legend*? Or *My Father: The World-Internationally Celebrated Photographer*? Or a Proustish name in order to butter up the critics: *In Pursuit of the Dad (and the Time) That Was Lost*? Even if you persist in guarding your ridiculous title, you still MUST suppress all the scenes in the book with Siegfried & Roy. Why do you let their white-draped sequin bodies escort your father from Algeria to Jendouba to Stockholm to New York? Why do they whip in the air, why do they speak German-Swedish about their notorious tiger control, and why, write me why, is poor Roy covered in blood with his stomach half scooped out in the final scene of the book? Is this in order to motivate the title of the book? Suppress ALL of this!

My secondary disappointment was that you have cracked in the ambition of capturing both your father's and my linguistic tone. The text you present as Kadir's if anything makes repeated humor at the expense of Kadir. Is this really the way a person who learned Swedish with your idiotic Swedish rules would write? NO! You exaggerate my grammatical glides. You increase the volume on my linguistic idiosyncrasies. You sprinkle my text with embarrassing metaphors. Why must I constantly refer to deserts and sand dunes? Why do you let me write things like "steaming hot like a hamam" or "she was long-necked and humpy like a camel"? When have I said that Cherifa's backside was "wide as the Sahara desert"? My metaphors are different and considerably more quality-filled; cultivate these instead. I also find numberous inconsequences in your linguistic attempts. Sometimes you let me say "ask," sometimes the more advanced "interpellate." Sometimes "walk," sometimes "march." Sometimes "feeling," sometimes "emotion." Which are my true words? You who seem to claim that you know?

My triangular disappointment was that your text is sprinkled with repeated factual errors. You spell village names wrong, you are sloppy with numbering the years, you fantasize forth things that never existed (like for example that Emir's cookie factory had automatic tray turners in the Jendouba of the sixties. HA HA! Very comical. This was first introduced in the seventies.)

You also ascribe bizarrely uncommon names to people. I soon realized, however, that this was more intention than sloppiness. Do you believe I can be duped so easily? Do you think I do not see what is spelled if you read all the letters of the personal names in order? Do you think I will not discover the code that is visualized if one links the introductory letters of your chapters? These fatal attempts at smuggled politics must be suppressed! For the sake of both your future and mine.

My quadratic disappointment was that your text seems amorously enamored with creating comedy that completely lacks humor. Why? Certainly farting camels are a little funny. Once. Or maybe twice. But it is NOT humor to let a farting camel enter your father's mythic story six times. Suppress all farting camels!

My pentagonal disappointment was that you STILL, despite your father's warnings, seem to find it very difficult to separate truth from fiction. As usual, fantasies are mixed with realities into a disgustingly stinking porridge. Phenomena that are correct (such as your father's photographic talent) are mixed with sheer falsifications (such as that your father would be a notoriously unfaithful beach flirter). Why do you call your father's late photos pornography when they were more erotic? Why do you maximize the volume of both the chestnut theme and your father's late success to such a level that the reader could begin to doubt their correctness? Why do you choose to inject real friends' names into the meeting in the studio when these were imaginary characters? Why do you let your father repeat the phrase "Like Soyinka said. A tiger does not broadcast its tigership"?

Your text is far from the versions of both truth and compromise, and only in glimpses do you manage to capture your father's real story. My only explication: You lack adequate talent. You are a miserable make-believe author. You are a PARASITE who has exploited your father in order to shape a FALSE story. You are a disappointment. You are everything your father has ever accused you of!

My sex-... No, do not even try, I KNOW it is called "sixth." My sixth disappointment was all the unmotivated passages in the book. Why the analysis text about Luke Skywalker and Darth Vader? Why the sudden personal portrait of Félix Bonfils? And why devote a central spread to what you call "My personal hate list." Who are all these people who are insulted? They are completely unknown to your father! Why menace a competent female journalist from Norway with the phrase "watch your back, my next book is going to be called *The Book Counterfeiter of Cable TV* and it will be about YOU!" And who is the poor male critic at *Svenska Dagbladet* who is first saluted as "the king of autobiographical readings" and then portrayed in repeated erotic scenes, first with an orange and then with a wire-haired dachshund? Suppress this childishness!

BUT the ABSOLUTE worst thing in the book, what is unforgivable and which renders publication of your text IMPOSSIBLE, is the terminating epilogue where you write that in preparation for *Montecore* you returned to Tunisia, spent six months in Jendouba, and interviewed your father's old childhood friends.

You write: "Everyone maintains that Kadir was not only Dad's best friend from his time at the orphanage. He was also an alcoholic gambling addict who disappeared without a trace one day in the beginning of the nineties. According to the rumors, he hanged himself after a huge poker loss. Is this really true? How did this affect my father? Was it actually this tragic incident that made him go into the deep . . ."

This is NOT TRUE! KADIR LIVES! KADIR HAS EXCELLENT VIGOR! Otherwise, who would be writing these letters? It is NOT your father who has started a little hotel in Tabarka, it is NOT your father who surfs the world net and downloads comedy series. It is NOT your father who has started an e-mail address in his former friend's name with the ambition of rediscovering his relation to his son. It is me, Kadir, who is writing you this. UNDERSTOOD?

Here is my prescription in order to save this bookly project from its fatal fiasco: Follow my above indications. Replace ALL your falseness with my authentic text. Correct any spelling errors. Renovate my grammar. Replace all my *aao* with correct *åäö*. Replace your epilogue with this e-letter.

I do not want any part of your bookly finances. I do not want my name on the cover of the book. All I ask is that you present a tolerably true version of your father's life.

This will be my farewell.

Your lost friend
Kadir

ABOUT THE AUTHOR

Jonas Hassen Khemiri, born in Sweden in 1978, is the author of
two novels and one collection of plays and short stories. His first
novel, *One Eye Red*, received the Borås Tidning Award for best
literary debut. His second novel, *Montecore: The Silence of the
Tiger*, won several literary awards including the Swedish Radio
Award for best novel of the year. Khemiri has also received the
PO Enquist Literary Prize for the most promising young European writer. He currently divides his time between Stockholm
and Berlin.

A NOTE ON THE TYPE

This book was set in Scala, a typeface designed by the Dutch designer Martin Majoor (b. 1960) in 1988 and released by the FontFont foundry in 1990. While designed as a fully modern family of fonts containing both a serif and a sans serif alphabet, Scala retains many refinements normally associated with traditional fonts.

Composed by Creative Graphics, Allentown, Pennsylvania

Printed and bound by Berryville Graphics, Berryville, Virginia

Designed by Maggie Hinders